Spur Of The Moment

Deena Nehring

This is a work of fiction. Names, characters, places and incidents are either the product of the author's imagination or are used fictitiously, and any resemblance to actual persons, living or dead, business establishments, events or locales is entirely coincidental.

No part of this book may be reproduced in any manner whatsoever without written permission from the author.

Cover art by Ashley Grosskruger.
Background photo by Jennifer Carr.

Copyright © 2013 Deena Nehring

PinkRibbonPress
All rights reserved.

ISBN-10: 0615822940
ISBN-13: 978-0615822945

DEDICATION

For hopeless romantics everywhere.
And for my favorite Texan, Bobby.

Spur Of The Moment

ACKNOWLEDGMENTS

My fiancé, James: Thank you for believing in me, for inspiring me and for always nudging me to excel, for understanding my artistic temperament, not minding when I stay up late to make deadlines, and last but not least for never once complaining when I talk incessantly about my characters, plots and story ideas. I love you.

My favorite cop, retired chief of police and dear friend, Walt: Thank you for always having fresh coffee at the ready (even though we now have to share a cup by phone), for not minding whenever I call at odd hours just to 'talk cop', and as always thank you for being my sounding board and allowing me to run all of my questions and ideas by you.

My beta-readers: The editing process is long and tedious so I thank each and every one of you for your eyes, time, and assistance. To my cousin Terry, I extend a special thank you for not only your time and eyes, but also for all of your insightful input throughout the entire editing process.

My talented and gifted daughter, Ashley: Thank You!! Once again you've designed an amazing cover! As always, you rock!

My friends and all of my fans: I thank each and every one of you for your encouragement and continued support.

Spur Of The Moment

Prologue

"*Elaine!*" erupted from the depths of Mark Bowman's lungs. Torso catapulted upright, his body lurched, arms thrashing, legs trapped and immobile. Desperate, his frantic fingers labored fumbling with an intangible release lever and a nonexistent nozzle as a cacophonous explosion echoed against his eardrums.

Horrified, he stared at his hands as the fire extinguisher shape-shifted into a plump feather pillow. Squeezing he eyes tight he worked to regulate his breathing. His senses continued to battle; perception teeter-tottering amid harsh reality and an inescapable dream realm. Growling, Mark strangled the pillow until his knuckles blanched and then focused his rage on the glowing digits of the alarm clock.

Three minutes to three…

Suppressing the gut wrenching sob, he lashed out, assaulting the clock. Under duress, the nightstand itself teetered and pitched, causing everything atop it to topple and crash. Swearing under his breath, Mark squeezed his eyes shut. Untangling his legs from the sheets he abandoned the idea of sleep all together. Scrubbing his face with his palms, he once again focused on the upturned alarm clock…heart heavy, mind restless.

…two minutes to three and counting…

Six years…What took you so long, Cowboy?

Pushing himself up, Mark stumbled to the window blinking away the fragments of a life that once was. But it was useless, everything was a constant reminder. Bracing his palms on the sill, he searched the outlying landscape cloaked within the murkiness of predawn. Scanning the shadowy pasture, he spied No Limits…once a tiny colt matured into a majestic stallion; yet another relentless reminder of that ill-fated dawn.

A feral beast which he allowed to daunt and control him.

Six years....one minute to three and counting....

"No more," he promised the horse on a low dangerous whisper. Slate gray orbs narrowing on his own reflection, Mark declared, "It's time."

Squatting, he yanked the plug of the alarm clock from its socket causing the glowing digits to blink out. Snagging his Levi's as he straightened, he jerked them on, and then rammed his bare feet inside of his worn boots. Grabbing a shirt he headed out.

It was time. Time that he take back that control. Time for him to forgive; learn how to once again live. It was time that he break-and-ride No Limits.

CHAPTER 1

Beyond late, Hannah Bryans groaned at the idea of yet another delay after spying the rapidly approaching squad car in the rearview mirror. Tapping the brakes, she slowed and piloted her sleek Beemer onto the gravel shoulder, grumbling, "Just my luck," as the squad car slowed to pull in and park a few feet behind her.

Begrudgingly she threw the gear shift in park. Then, and in somewhat of a panic, struggled with the seatbelt hoping to somehow inconspicuously clip the thing in place; before the deputy could notice. The sharp rap of knuckles upon the driver side window cued her to the fact that it was too late. Rolling her eyes, Hannah resigned and assembled her best game face—an acquired skill of circumvention. For this particular occasion: a flirtatious grin. Her mission: to sidetrack this hunky deputy with enough guile and charm to weasel her way out of a citation.

Sending down the window she chimed in manufactured innocence, "Morning, officer. What seems to be—"

"License and registration, please," the curt request interrupted her premeditated salutation.

First attempt thwarted, Hannah took note of the twang,

as rich as royal velvet, alerting her to the trivial detail that this man could not be an Iowa native. Excellent. Something to work with. He had to be a transplant, just like her. "Hey, you're not from around here," she cooed, batting her eyelashes.

"Not originally," was all he supplied. "I'll need to see proof of your current auto insurance as well, ma'am."

"Sure is hot out," Hannah observed, taking another stab at pleasantries while producing her driver's license. "It's got to be at least ninety, already. Wouldn't you say?"

Confiscating her ID without comment, the insipid no-nonsense twitch of his lips was a clear indication that this man was in no mood for idle chitchat. "Do you know why I pulled you over, ma'am?"

"Well that's sort of a no brainer," Hannah quipped deadpan, inspired by this man's own crankiness.

A quick nudge of his sunglasses revealed pulse-staggering slate gray eyes; pitiless spheres barbed with an acute glint of censure. "Clocked you at seventy-nine, Miss—" pausing, he searched the ID for a surname, "Bryans." Examining her driver's license more in depth, his mask of indifference toggled between what looked to be ironic incredulity and that of sheer curiosity. "Ah…are you aware your driver's license is expired, ma'am?"

Oh, for the love of Mike. Mr. Hunky-By-The-Book would just have to notice that. Hannah's eyelids slid shut, mind racing to formulate a credible defense. Nothing came to mind. Truth was, she'd been meaning to find time to renew it, yet had forgotten all about it.

Collecting her poise, Hannah glanced up at the deputy; savvy enough on the laws of human nature to bet those once again concealed stunning slate gray orbs were probably right now on the hem of her skirt. A hem which had managed to crawl up her thighs. Having survived six years at Haden Milly Law Firm as an overused, underappreciated, junior defense attorney, she was well versed when it came to dealing with males. So how was this any different? Besides, showing a little leg might help get her out of this unforeseen predicament.

Considering it, Hannah inwardly cringed. It wasn't beneath her...however she'd packed up those tactics with the resolve to never unpack them after relocating to Iowa in the first place. She'd moved with the sole intention of making a fresh start. Life in what she'd dubbed Hicksville USA was supposed to be boring, simple and uncomplicated. And she was going to keep it that way.

"Wouldn't surprise me. You wouldn't believe the past few months I've had..." she began; determined to stick with the simple truth.

~ ~ ~

Mark appraised the sluggish thunderheads gathering along the horizon, not a bit phased by this woman's mile-a-minute explanation. In his line of work this was typical. No one liked being pulled over, let alone, issued a citation. Nine times out of ten, the people he happened to stop always had themselves a bagful of excuses; this classy dame included.

While she prolonged the inevitable, somehow trying to now justify why she was driving on an invalid DL, his attention was snagged by a miniature D-bit, a charm of a trotting foal, a riding crop and assorted tack, all dangling from her slender wrist. Well-manicured mulberry fingernails drummed the steering wheel, as she rambled, setting the tiny sterling silver charms in motion. Staring at the charms themselves evoked a barrage of images and emotion; memories which threatened to sabotage his focus.

Tugging off his Ray-Bans, Mark pinched the bridge of his nose. Parting his lips to speak, the ingrained courtesy to never interrupt a lady prevailed. He blamed that degree of politeness on his Texan pedigree, coupled with a stricter upbringing. Both of which, he'd concluded a long time ago, were nothing but a professional liability.

"...spent half the night switching out fuses—in the

dark, no less—just to then realize the stupid utilities had been shut off. Have you ever tried to apply make-up? Blow-dry your hair even, without the simple benefit of electricity?"

"Ah...?" Mark finger combed his overgrown crew cut rendering it a rowdy spike of black onyx. Preoccupied by the very nature of the question at hand, he examined this woman's angelic features. Her natural beauty was so pronounced, he could not imagine why she'd even need make-up. Easing his eyes off a rather succulent pout, he tackled a beguiling duet of bottomless fawn brown wells. "Can't rightly say that I have, ma'am," he heard himself state aloud.

"Well, let me tell you, it's a feat to just..."

As she once again rambled on at the speed-of-light, Mark kicked himself for having had missed the opportunity to take command.

"...and I swear, I'll take care of this today. You have my word," she at last promised.

Subject to those eyes, that pout, his pulse staggered, trotting off in a two-left-foot jig. In much need of a distraction, Mark searched the horizon as he contemplated the situation at hand. Seatbelt and speeding violations notwithstanding, this woman was operating a motor vehicle with an invalid driver's license. Worse, it was an expired, out of state—Wisconsin—driver's license. Which, in the state of Iowa was...well, it was complicated. Wisconsin did not participate in the Interstate Driver License Compact, which basically required him to seize her plates, impound her vehicle and collect a mandatory bond—an amount that equaled one and a half times the fine itself. This woman simply had no clue.

Mark grimaced feeling a pang of empathy. This, of course, furthered his discomfort and only served to tick him off. He was not one to let a pretty face dissuade him. He was a deputy sheriff; duty-bound to uphold the law. But why did it have to be such a stunning creature now breaking that law?

Shunning those imploring eyes and that succulent pout, Mark pinned his gaze on the outlying cornfields and mustered indifference. "I still need to see that proof of insurance, ma'am."

∽ ∽ ∽

Presenting her proof of insurance card, Hannah then cut the rearview mirror a nasty look as the deputy strolled back to his squad car. She then scolded herself for ever gawking at the man who would be writing her…well, Lord only knew how many citations?

Great. She glanced at her watch and scowled. 8:01 AM. She was officially tardy and all because she had to cross paths with Mr. Hunky-By-The-Book-Deputy-Unfriendly. Because of him, she was right now losing prep-time to prepare for her first consultation, and she still needed to familiarize herself with that client's case before she represented that client in court today.

Hannah snagged her cell phone. Flipping it open, she snapped it shut. Why alert the seniors she'd be a little late getting to the office? She'd be there in person soon enough. Glancing backwards at the cruiser, she then sent the window up. Annoyed, she jabbed a finger at the AC controls. It was now 8:04 AM. Welcome to Altoona, Iowa a.k.a. Hillbilly Hell. Mid-July, and it was already ninety plus degrees outside. Nudging the AC to full blast, she made the mental note to contact the utility company and demand they turn the electricity back on and do it today, or else. She then rifled through her purse in search of lipstick, and then abandoned the very idea. Why bother? It was apparent this deputy was hell bent on up-holding the law. Which, as a legal representative of that law, she had to respect. Just not when she was on the receiving end of it.

The mere notion cued her left eyelid to twitch; a sure bet that by noon she'd be battling a mind-numbing migraine. And gee, wasn't this ever going to make a grand impression. After three short months at Brecker Haley & Merit she was going to walk in brandishing a speeding ticket as well as a fine for having an expired DL as her only justification for why she was late. How lame. She would probably be fired on the spot for using those same tickets as her only excuse for why she'd missed out on their usual Monday morning interoffice powwow.

Crap...Double whammy. Hanging her head at the mere thought, Hannah expelled a wretched groan.

CHAPTER 2

"Ma'am, I'm letting you off—" Halted by a victorious grin, Mark cleared his throat and, taking it at face value, soberly clarified, "On the seatbelt violation. However, I am citing you for speeding, as well as for operating a motor vehicle on an expired DL…and that being so, I'm afraid I'm required to retain you and impound your vehicle, until you can—"

"Wh—what? But...but I—" the argument began.

Not wanting to be further delayed, Mark raised his tone a notch over her high pitched whine and continued, "Please shut off the engine and step out of your vehicle. I am placing you under arrest…"

Debate stymied by his remark, she gasped, "You've got to be joking."

"Ah…no ma'am. Afraid not." Mark winced at his own callousness. Marshaling indifference, he cleared his throat and tried to explain the situation yet again, "Due to the fact your license is an expired out-of-state—"

"Yeah, heard you the first time. Are you always this by the book—?" she cut with an incredulous scowl. "What? You don't have anything better to do?"

Not commenting, Mark ground his molars. The snotty

malevolence was something he could do without. "Miss Bryans, please shut off the engine and step out of your vehicle. I'm placing you under arrest for operating a motor vehicle on an invalid Wisconsin driver license in the state of Iowa. You have the right to remain silent—"

"Oh, I know all about my rights. Trust me *you* do not have to inform *me* of *my rights*."

Mark arched a questionable eyebrow and, without skipping a beat, continued to recite her those rights as she now proceeded to call him every name in the book. Apparently she wasn't going to observe the right to remain silent. Losing his own cool however, he surmised, would only add more fuel to her...well at the moment, that rather unflattering and rabid disposition of hers. Once he finished reciting her those rights, he waited, and then groaned inwardly as she continued to rant, making no attempt whatsoever to turn off the Beemer's engine.

"Please shut off the engine and step out of the vehicle, ma'am."

"Fine!" Killing the engine she slammed both palms against the steering wheel, nicking the horn in the process, producing a curt prissy *YELP*. "This is ridiculous. It's not like I'm putting anybody in danger—I simply just forgot to renew my stupid driver's license. How on earth is that— "

"Please step out of the vehicle, ma'am. Now," he ordered and then edged back; right hand instinctively resting on the grip of his holstered Glock when she twisted and those fidgety hands disappeared from his full view. Ignoring her verbal dressing-down, he tracked her erratic gestures as she now began collecting her things. "Reckon you oughta send that window up. Smells like rain," he suggested as she continued to dilly-dally.

Catching a heated glare his patience waned. He watched as she twisted the keys in the ignition to send the window up. The door then swung open, and with such force it wound up slamming shut. Mark choked on a grunt. This classy dame was indeed a spit-fire. Wonderful.

He hadn't requested back-up. Maybe he should have? Eight years in law enforcement was long enough to know a situation could turn sour in flash. Regardless of gender, a subject could become volatile at the spur-of-the-moment. Subduing an irate subject, who wasn't eager to be taken in to custody, could be a challenge for any deputy. He knew that first hand.

Mark waited, a million scenarios pumping spurts of adrenaline through his veins as she now took the time to untangle what looked to be her purse straps with that of a briefcase. He now had the distinct feeling she was stalling. When she twisted to reopen the door, he had to suppress the urge to step forward and open it for her; knowing himself that any gentlemanly gestures on his part might be taken in the wrong context. Which, in this case, all odds were on: it would just make matters worse.

"You'll want to be sure and lock your car as well, ma'am. It could be awhile before the tow truck can—" he began to advise her, that was until a glossy sling-back stiletto hit the gravel and completely zapped him of his train of thought.

Enraptured, his gaze shifted to a graceful ankle; lingered on a well-defined calf; loitered on a supple thigh straining against a taut hem as his subject exited the vehicle. That inspection ended once his subject abruptly twisted to duck back inside of the car. Establishing that she was indeed simply retrieving what looked to be a business jacket draped over the passenger seat, his eyes took it upon themselves to zero in on the liberal slit cut in her snug fitting charcoal colored skirt.

Slamming the door shut she whirled around, facing him, matching bolero jacket dangling off one finger. "There. See?" Not skipping a beat, she made it a major production of rattling the handle and then tugging on the door itself; just to prove that the Beemer was indeed secure. "It's all locked up. Are you happy now?"

Mark unconsciously nodded, professional demeanor

polluted by a newly found appreciation for sling-back stilettos and snug fitting business skirts.

"Well. What are you waiting for? Let's go."

Beleaguered by her caustic command, Mark snapped to attention and cleared his throat. "Do...do you have—?" he began yet, gaining an eyeful of cleavage as she shimmied in to that bolero styled jacket, found himself tripping over his own tongue. Frame of mind sullied, for the life of him, he could not recall what it was he'd intended to ask this female.

Crossing her arms, that female cocked one hip and now tapped her toe. "Do I have...what?" she prompted, impatient.

Easing his eyes to a more appropriate altitude, Mark swallowed hard struggling to rearrange his train of thought. "Ah...any weapons or drugs on you, that I should know about before—" Mark abruptly coughed then attempted to clear his throat. His confident tone, for some reason, was sounding more like that of a teenager suffering from off kilter hormones. He grimaced at the idea, with a sneaky suspicion that was all due to the very nature of the question he was still trying to spit out.

Why even ask? It was obvious she didn't. Who could conceal anything under that sausage skin of a skirt? Let alone, hide anything in such a form-fitting jacket? Mark already knew for himself that there was nothing under that but a voluptuously filled silk camisole styled tank-top. But, it was procedure that he ask.

"Ah...before I search you, ma'am?" he at last finished, and to his surprise having successfully regained a somewhat dignified and stable tone.

"Excuse me?"

"Procedure, prior to placing you in my vehicle," he began to explain. Mark knew himself he was in deep jeopardy the instant they made eye contact. Reading her skeptical glare only served to make him feel that much more inept. "It's a simple, quick frisk, ma'am. Nothing to get excited about," he reassured her.

"You have got to be kidding," she snorted, tossing her hands up, palms out, as if doing so might fend off the very idea.

Mark scanned the heat hazed horizon and spelled out the outcome if she opted on being problematic, "I really don't want to have to cite you for resisting arrest, as well, ma'am."

Re-crossing her arms she narrowed her eyes, toe once again tapping. An outward display that she was not about to cooperate, let alone appease him.

That defiance grated on his nerves. "It's simple. You turn around and place your hands on the hood. I quickly pat you down." *...and as apathetically as humanly possible.*

"For what? It's not like I'm hiding an AKA assault rifle up my skirt." The tetchy expression toggled to one of extreme distrust. "Besides, shouldn't you call for back-up? If you haven't noticed, I am a *feeee*—male."

"Ma'am..." Mark bit his tongue, trying like hell to disguise his rancor. She was right, on both counts. But he did not need this particular female pointing that last tidbit out. He—right along with all those parts nonessential to performing his job, this very task—was well aware of that simple detail. "If you'd like, I'll request dispatch to notify the PD; send out their only female officer. She is, however, on maternity leave. So, reckon it might be awhile." For effect, he glanced at his watch. "Your call, ma'am."

"Oh, for crying out loud. Just get on with it, already."

"Fine," Mark managed somewhat civilly through clenched enamel while tossing a vague gesture toward the hood of the car.

"Fine," she shot right back then, spinning on her heels, slapped both palms against the Beemer's glossy hood with an indignant huff.

The performance itself set his blood to a low rolling boil and staring at her backside, Mark attributed his reluctance to actually search this female to that of sheer disgust. Funny thing, disgust had never once launched his hormones to a nosebleed altitude... Nor had that particular emotion ever been capable of rendering him cross-eyed, tongue-tied, or anxious.

Maybe he should request that back-up? Maternity leave...jeez.

Pinching the bridge of his nose, Mark squeezed his eyes shut and tried mentally coaching himself. This was routine protocol; required prior to placing anyone inside of his squad car. It was a simple frisk. Something he'd done a million times. Nothing to get excited about. So why the heck were his pores now squeezing out bullets?

An exaggerated sigh broke the silence and cued Mark to the minor detail that he was the one now procrastinating.

"Could we please just get this over with already?" she whined tartly while craning her neck to see for herself what the holdup was. "I don't know about you, but I've got better things to do than to stand around while you gawk at my butt, Stud."

Stud? Mark cocked an eyebrow, lips parting to refute her allegation. Truth was he had been gawking. Busted, he tackled that laser sharp stare just to find the intensity of those bottomless fawn brown eyes way more entrancing than the cut of that skimpy hemline of hers. Slightly abashed, he gestured for her to face forward then rested his palms on what had to be two inch thick shoulder pads, while simultaneously nudging the toe of his boot against the instep of her stiletto—an ingrained reflex; one which wasn't necessary considering she was sporting that skirt.

Taking a deep breath, to somehow calm his nerves, didn't help. Ultra-rich notes of warm vanilla, yummy cocoa, and a dash of woodsy nutmeg tickled his nostrils engulfing his senses and leaving him a little lightheaded. Threatened, his eyelids slid shut and his train of thought ran amuck as he grappled to finish the simple task at hand;

doing so rather chaotically and while now feeling like a complete moron.

"You getting your jollies yet, Stud?"

"Trust me, lady—" Mark stepped backwards, putting himself in harms-way by retreating half onto the highway; now wishing he could put a cornfield between him and that sinfully provocative body. "Takes a hell of a lot more than some—" Pinching the bridge of his nose, he cut himself short then bit off a muddled oath.

Unfinished or not, that remark had to have sounded crass. What angered him more was this woman might just have a legitimate complaint against him. That had to be the most unsystematic—if not slapdash—frisk he'd ever executed in his entire eight years as a deputy sheriff.

"Gee, you were right. That was quick and unexciting," she taunted while twirling around to now face him.

Mark opened his mouth, tempted to counter her blatant innuendo. Knowing better, he defused the rather uncouth retort snarling his lips with a simple, "Let's go."

"What, no cuffs?" she dug, offering up both wrists to him.

Unable to contain his frustration, Mark fished out his Ray-Bans and rammed them on his face then jabbed a finger in the general direction of his cruiser without comment.

"Well thank God for small favors,' she cut, turning to head for the squad car.

Scowling, Mark lagged behind needing a moment to recoup. Subjected to a rather voluptuous sway didn't help much. He was powerless not to notice the sinuous sashay of her gait. Looking skyward, he jerked the microphone of his portable radio off his shoulder and growled into it, "Altoona six to dispatch."

"Go ahead Altoona six," chirped through the static of the radio.

"I'll be—" He paused, mid-stride, cutting his transmission short when his subject stopped to now face him. When she didn't say anything, he nudged his sunglasses to the tip of his nose granting her a most inhospitable what-now expression.

"I…um…well, I forgot my purse," she half laughed on a rather nervous note.

Mark stared at her over the rim of his Ray-Bans, none amused. "I'll get it for you, after you're secured. That is, if you'll be kind enough to give me your keys, ma'am."

Narrowing her eyes she snubbed his proposal with snarky tongue-in-cheek smirk. "They're in my purse. The purse which is still in my car. The same car you had me lock."

Ripping off his Ray-Bans Mark ground his molars, straining to keep his temper in check.

"Altoona six, did you have traffic?" the dispatcher's pleasant query belched forth.

Disregarding the query, Mark rammed his sunglasses back on his face and, taking a hold of her elbow, steered his subject toward the squad car. Opening the backdoor, it took everything he had to retain a civil tone, "Get in. Watch your head. And fasten your seatbelt. Please."

"But, I, I need my purse," she argued while settling herself within the backseat. "How else am I supposed to pay your stupid—"

"Fine." Mark drew a calming breath then heard himself ask, "Would you like for me to get you anything else while I'm at it, ma'am?"

"Just my briefcase. Oh, and grab my cappuccino also," she had the audacity to instruct him with an almost too sweet and satisfied smile. "If I don't get some caffeine in me, and soon, I'm liable to get a major migraine."

Mark stared at her incredulous and then, trying like hell not to slam it, shut the door.

Jerking off his sunglasses, he once again pinched the bridge of his nose. Eyelids sealing shut he expelled a soft grunt of resigned irritation. His morning had started off on a sour note and was only getting worse. No Limits had bucked him more times than he cared to admit or count. By five fifteen, his hired ranch hand hadn't shown up. Trying to locate the man while finishing what chores he could himself, before 6:00A.M., he'd lost just about everything that even resembled a hint of composure prior to cleaning up and heading in for patrol. A mere two hours into what would now be a tedious twelve hour shift, and his professional poise had just been sullied. He'd been blindsided; all thanks going to this gorgeous as sin speed-demon who'd succeeded to rattle his cage in less than twenty minutes.

Depressing his shoulder mike, Mark growled, "Dispatch, Altoona six is ten-eight. Please be advised I'll be in route—" Hesitating, he glanced between the BMW and his squad car. Because they could no longer provide the simple service of unlocking cars doors these days (due to some asinine liability clause), he was now going to catch hell for having to request a locksmith Swearing under his breath, he grimaced. Forget politeness. He now questioned his principles regarding chivalry, especially when it pertained to appeasing unreasonable women.

"Altoona six?"

"With one female," he croaked.

"Ten-four. Please advise your ETA."

Not responding, Mark backtracked. The driver side door may be locked—how could he have forgotten such a display?—but he was optimistic the passenger side wasn't. Discovering that side secured as well, he snarled, a pang of guilt fusing with frustration to sever his last ragged nerve. Eyeing the ragtop he entertained the idea of just jimmying the lock himself, and then ditched the notion all together with a deranged snort.

"Altoona six? Your ETA?"

"As soon as you send me a locksmith," Mark barked, then immediately apologized.

Requesting she switch to a secure channel, he gave the dispatcher the particulars as well as the necessary details of his location. Contemplating the sleek Beemer, Mark figured at least the tow truck driver could also unlock the door once he arrived. With that thought, he then toyed with the notion of just staying put right here on the broiling blacktop until that tow truck arrived. The heat index suggested otherwise. Ambivalent, Mark squinted at the blazing sun then glanced in the general direction of his air conditioned squad car. Digging in his shirt pocket he pulled out a toothpick, popped it between his teeth and began to gnaw as he debated: Stay put and roast on the blacktop? Or retreat and wait it out with the tetchy yet sinfully beautiful creature now sitting in the backseat of his squad car?

Mark grunted at his options; at least the latter included air-conditioning. Wagging his head at the prospect, he muttered, "Way to go, *Stud*," as he backtracked to wait it out inside his squad car.

CHAPTER 3

"Girl, are you late!" Monique Bernard exclaimed.

"Yes, I realize that…" Hannah stopped short to tug on her skirt then glowered at the marathon sized run spanning the length of her nylons. She wasn't even sure how, where, or when, that had occurred. Great.

"Is there anything else you need since I'm here?" Monique quizzed while zigzagging her way through the inner hallways of the courthouse.

Hannah eyed Monique's suitcase sized Coach handbag and debated on inquiring if she happened to have a spare pair of *L'eegs Sheer Energy*. She heaved a sigh. She was due in court in ten minutes. Even if her secretary had a spare pair, there was not enough time to stop and swap pantyhose and also consult Mr….Mr….? Well whatever her client's name was. Flustered, she glanced over her surroundings in hopes of centering herself. The building itself was majestic with its high ceilings and polished marble floors. And although her left eye now twitched with the vigor of disco light, she took in the detailed craftsmanship with admiration. Here was where she belonged; at home within the halls of justice.

Hannah swept a handful of strawberry blond corkscrews off her face. Untangling the straps of her briefcase and purse, she lugged them along and picked up her pace to catch up with her squat fireplug of secretary's brisk trot. Heels clapping against polished marble, she chased Monique through the inner matrix of the Altoona County courthouse.

Once she caught up with her, Hannah whispered, "Thank you for coming down, and, well, I mean, for bailing me out. I owe you big time and I'll pay you back as soon as—"

"That's the least of your worries." Monique gave her a skeptical glance then gestured to a door marked Interview Room One-A.

A rather bored looking deputy, lounging on the chair next to it, glanced up at them. Without comment, he stuck his nose back in the pages of a Field & Stream.

Monique lowered her voice and informed her, "You have less than ten minutes," and then gave her arm an encouraging little squeeze. "Good luck, girlfriend."

Hannah cut her secretary a brave smile, and then knocked on the pebbled glass window to announce her arrival before pushing through the door itself. She wasn't at all prepared to take on this case. Nor was she the least bit ready to represent the seditious faced kid, who more resembled a strung-out Howdy-Duty, who greeted her with a most disrespectful sneer.

According to the information Monique had given her, or what she had read of it, Mr.—well, whatever his name was—was a nineteen year old kid charged with vehicular homicide. She was going try her best to downgrade that charge to manslaughter. Either way it was a harsh consequence, considering this was his first arrest, let alone only recorded offense. Nonetheless, it was her job to represent this kid—correction, this young man.

Setting her briefcase down, she offered Howdy-Duty her hand. "Hi. I'm Hannah Bryans, your court appointed attorney. Before we discuss your situation, I want you to understand that anything we talk about is strictly between us, therefore don't be afraid to disclose—"

"You're late," he stated, interrupting her brief rendition of client confidentiality.

"Yes, I realize that." Hannah retracted her hand when he didn't accept her handshake and rifled through her briefcase. "And I'm real sorry about that, mister …?"

"Chaz." He gave her the slow once over, roaming eyes pausing on the run marring her nylons. "What happened to that other guy? Bender—Render—what's his name?"

"Mr. Kender? Oh, well, he…he had a family emergency," Hannah fudged.

She had no idea why Kender, one of their firm's own seniors, had abandoned the kid's case after the prelim setting. She wasn't even sure herself why it had then been dumped in her own lap at the last minute, no less; which hadn't allowed her the time or access to the necessary documents she needed to review the case over the weekend. At the idea she glanced around the room, slightly stressed. Three short months with Brecker Haley & Merit and she was now being baptized by fire? Not that she minded. She was more than happy to take it on. At least this case beat the molehill of humdrum minor offenses that she'd been stuck with representing within the past three months.

But my God, vehicular homicide? How on earth did they expect her to pull this one off; especially after the morning she'd just had?

"An emergency…right, and I'm a—"

"I believe it was a family illness. Anyway, I'll be representing you now, Mr. …?" Finding the correct document, Hannah smiled in relief. Mr. Charles Holm. She looked him over. The boy was in dire need of a haircut and was still dressed in his orange jail jumper. Great. Not the best impression for any court appearance. "You do understand this is your preliminary hearing...right, Mr. Holm?" *...one I'm not even prepared to deal with?* Hannah opted on not filling her client in on that minor tidbit. Why alarm the kid?

"Yeah, whatever. It's Chaz."

"Chaz. Right. Well, okay…" Frowning she gnawed on her bottom lip. "Could somebody—your mother, or a friend—possibly bring you a suit, perhaps a dress shirt and slacks…a tie?" *A new pair of L'eggs Sheer Energy for your down-on-her-luck attorney?*

Glancing questionably at her frazzled appearance, the kid outright snorted. "Look, lady, I don't need no suit. All the judge needs to know is I'm not guilty. So you're gonna get this bogus wrap dropped, dismissed, or whatever it is you people do. Right?"

"Well…." Contemplating his request, Hannah provided him with the standard explanation she gave all new clients. "At the moment, I'm not really worried about whether you're actually guilty or not—in fact, I don't even want to know. What matters, right now, is what evidence the prosecution has against you. You see, they have the burden of proving you are guilty. So, in order for me to help you, the first thing we need to do is to find out what evidence the prosecution actually—" Hesitating, Hannah grimaced at the kid's blank expression, at the idea that she probably sounded as if she were reading from cue cards.

Not the best way to establish the client-attorney trust, or for that matter present herself. But catching the case mid-stream, she'd missed out on the arraignment, the bail review, and more importantly the initial prelim setting. In reality, she had no clue. Which left her empty handed; with little to no bargaining leeway whatsoever.

"This is a class B felony," she told him, then explained, "Therefore, if the magistrate is satisfied with the prosecution's evidentiary showing, today…well, you'll be bound over, and a date for your arraignment for trial will be set."

When he didn't respond, Hannah searched his clueless expression and simplified, "Today the judge himself

30

decides if the evidence against you is solid enough for trial. Do you understand, Mr. Holm?"

"Chaz. All my friends call me Chaz." He grinned at her now. "So you can still get this dismissed, right?"

"Well..." Skimming the information Monique had provided her, Hannah hummed a discouraging note. It appeared the prosecution had filed a neat and tidy complaint against her client. The hub of their evidence was substantial. "I might be able to get the charges downgraded to—"

"Downgraded? But I wasn't even driving!"

Hannah glanced at her client and then read aloud from the document she held. "Upon arriving at the scene, Mr. Holm was found unconscious on the driver's side—?"

"Only because I was put there to make it look like I was driving," he insisted.

Hannah glanced at him, dubious. "Put there? Why—better yet, by who, how and when?"

"To make it look like I was the one driving after we crashed."

Hannah shook her head, as if that might make the boy's ludicrous claim better register. "By who?"

"By the same so-called friend who told me to take this wrap—" sticking his tongue out grotesquely, he cocked his head and pantomimed being lynched. "—or else."

Hannah stared at him a moment, not amused. "Are you suggesting your defense should be that...that I prove your innocence under the pretense that you were....well, that you were framed?"

"Did I stutter?"

"By who?" she again demanded, growing more annoyed than sympathetic.

"By the one that was driving."

Exasperated, Hannah narrowed her eyes, toe tapping. Right now was not the time for twenty-one questions. "And that would be?"

"Jake Bremer," the kid announced matter-of-fact.

Hannah's jaw dropped. She'd only been in Altoona for three months, but knew the name well. It was as common a household name as Clorox, and was also about as corrosive.

Although the kid's claim was preposterous, she heard herself ask, "Jake Bremer. As in Jake Bremer the county attorney's son?"

The kid sat back and laced his fingers behind his head, wearing a smug grin, obviously enjoying her befuddlement. "That'd be the one. So you gonna get this whole thing dismissed or what?"

Hannah stared at him dumbfounded. He actually wanted her to believe such a ridiculous allegation? Whether she believed him or not was irrelevant. It wasn't that simple. Apparently Mr. Holm did not understand, nor did he appreciate the complexity of the legal system or courtroom procedures. Yet still, he expected her to appear before a Judge, in a court of law, and request a motion for dismissal? Not only wanted her to do so off-the-cuff, but on the grounds of some outlandish claim: that Jake Bremer, the county attorney's own son, had somehow magically swapped seats with him after they'd crashed?

My God...she'd be laughed right out of the courthouse; the county itself.

Not knocking, the deputy on guard poked his head inside the door and barked, "You're up, kid. Let's go."

As the deputy escorted the kid out into the hallway, Hannah stood a moment to collect her thoughts. Bloating her cheeks, she blew out a long silent breath then, snagging up her briefcase and purse, assembled her game face and headed out to catch up with her newest client.

~ ~ ~

"Monique, where's those medical records and witness statements?" Hannah pushed away from her desk and glanced over the heap of documents cluttering it. Standing, she smoothed her skirt, then in afterthought hiked it up, kicked off her heels and peeled off her nylons.

Balling them in a wad she tossed them in the trash. "And I could use any newspaper clippings covering Mr. Holm's arrest. Oh, and I need you to file those motions for—"

"Already filed," Monique reported, breezing into her office. Hugging a box to her vibrant African print bosom, she sauntered up the desk, bangles a-jangle. Plunking down the container, an empathetic smile displaced her chunky caramel colored features. "Anything else?"

Hannah gave her secretary a feeble smile, then snorted, "A handful of water to chase down a glassful of aspirin?"

"Girl, what you need is to call it a day. If you haven't noticed, it's after five. Go home, get yourself gussied up and join us for double bubble and—"

"I don't have time for double bubble. I have fifteen days before trial arraignment. And since it's illegal to break into the judge's chamber and change the docket, I'm stuck figuring out a plausible defense for this kid." Hannah frowned and sifted through the pile of files, then glanced over the box. "Thanks. Oh, hey, and thanks again, well, for this morning."

"Always happy to come bail me friends out." Monique winked. "Let's just not make it a habit. The seniors might begin to talk."

"What *did* you tell them?" Hannah asked. Despite relocating, she was once again a mere no-name tadpole treading water in a whirlpool of ruthless sharks who called themselves The Seniors.

"That you smarted off to some deputy and got yourself arrested."

Hannah stared at her, eyes as wide as Betty Boop and gape mouthed. However shocking that may have now sounded, it really wasn't that far off from the truth.

"I told them nothing of the sort," Monique assured her. "I merely told them you would be late due to a personal predicament, of which, you needed my expertise assistance."

Hannah cocked a brow, uncertain which sounded

worse. The actual truth or Monique's sugar coated version? Not that it mattered. Once it hit the gossip mill, everybody would know exactly what her so-called personal predicament entailed. With that idea, she sighed, "Well, that at least explains the strange, almost sympathetic, looks I kept getting today."

"You're welcome. And if you no longer need my expertise, I'm off."

"Wait…" Hannah reached for her purse. "At least let me write you a check. Repay you for—"

"Call it a night yourself, that's how you repay me. Go out, girlfriend. Have some fun. Go find yourself a handsome hunk to keep you warm this winter. Be coming soon enough."

"I'm just fine by myself, thank you very much. I don't need a man. And I don't want one either."

"Is that so," Monique jabbed an astute, well-manicured, fingertip at her. "What you need girlfriend, is some *body* like that good looking deputy sheriff who—"

"*Paah—leeeez*," Hannah scoffed, throwing her hands in a peremptory gesture, an acquired skill of circumvention which at the present moment was annulled by the scarlet blush searing her cheeks. "Not even remotely interested."

"Uh-huh…try telling that one to the judge, girlfriend."

"I'd take the fifth," Hannah blurted, further incriminating herself.

"Afraid you'd perjure yourself, mmm-hmmm, I see." Clucking her tongue, Monique moseyed out. "Did I mention, he was eyeing you as well?"

"So." Hannah scowled and called out after her, "Wait, he was?" thinking about it, she rolled her eyes and snorted, "Doesn't matter. I'm a criminal defense attorney—Cop repellent. Speaking of, call first thing tomorrow and see if you can't schedule a meet and greet with the arresting officer. Oh, and the paramedics, first responders and whomever else you can think of."

Exhausted, Hannah sank into the plump leather

cushion of her comfy chair. Scooping up a handful of files, she took a moment to regroup, and then rearranged a mountain of paperwork. Peeking inside the box, she grimaced. How on earth was she going to pull this off? Get this kid acquitted of vehicular homicide under the hypothesis that he was framed? And do so without losing her credibility as an attorney? What credibility? She had yet to establish herself—correction, reestablish herself....well, in this town anyway.

On a mission, she rummaged through the information the prosecutor's office had supplied then set off in search of the police reports. The first thing to do was simple. Familiarize herself with the prosecution's case against her client, as well as acquaint herself with the arresting officer. Retrieving the correct file, she hunkered down to thoroughly go over the report. Eyes coming to dead stop on the first signature found, Hannah sat at attention, did a double take and then groaned out loud, "Should've just called in dead this morning," while chucking the report aside.

Discouraged, she buried her face within her hands.

"What's that?"

"Nevermind." Hannah expelled a wretched breath, and then sighed, "Just the usual. Murphy's Law is once again working overtime."

"This Murphy..." Monique's soft laugh trickled back into her office, followed by the jangle of bangles and beads. "If he hands you lemons, you make lemonade....yes?"

Hannah peeked through her fingers, suspicious and not amused as Monique waddled herself belly-up to her desk with a scheming smirk. She knew better, but agreed, "Sure. Why not."

"So...if this Murphy hands you an incredibly handsome, arresting deputy—" Monique launched a conspiratorial wink and produced a rolodex card with happy flourish, keeping it just out of reach. "—why wait for a formal deposition to make sparks?"

Hannah snatched the card from out of her grasp and glanced it over. The information printed upon it was that of Deputy Mark Bowman's home address and phone number; the same deputy who'd hauled her in this morning. "And what do you propose I do with this?"

"You need details...and fraternizing with the enemy is the best way of picking its mind, girlfriend."

Considering it, Hannah frowned. The idea was tempting. But she had vowed to resign such tactics. "I don't know, Monique. It's...well, it's unscrupulous for one, and—"

"You're an intelligent, beautiful and clever lawyer—who's single, I might add. Is there a bylaw somewhere saying you can't use your assets to your own advantage?" Monique quizzed.

Hannah rolled her eyes then, glancing over the card yet again, snorted, "If I didn't know any better, Monique, I'd think you were in cahoots with Murphy, Fate, and Cupid."

CHAPTER 4

Body calmed by his horse's lazy gate, eyes trained on the fence, Mark patrolled the highest crest of his property. He snapped out of his brooding stupor detecting, not another gaping breach in the fence, but the distinct and urgent whine of a transmission conflicting with the remote but peaceful echo of a freight train's whistle as it rambled over the outlying tracks neighboring his land.

Squinting, he pulled hard on the reins halting Hop-Scotch with a bamboozled, "What the——?" spying the silver streak, kicking up a dust storm in its wake, racing along his gravel lane.

The idiot had to be going seventy-five, if not eighty. Upon identification, disapproval collided with surprise then bottomed out in sheer exasperation. That silver streak belonged to a pretty as sin criminal defense lawyer who had the attitude the size of his hometown stomping grounds of Texas. He grimaced as his slap-dash frisk job and their exchange of words tumbled throughout his recollection; a queasy sensation of dread clutched deep within his gut, conjuring images of inflated complaints and lawsuits. And, he somehow figured, this particular lawyer would be gutsy enough to bypass the departmental channels themselves just for the opportunity of serving him with such a complaint herself.

Jerking off his leather work gloves, Mark swore. Casper, his faithful companion, rushed up alongside his horse, yapping to now alert him of such a rare phenomenon—a visitor.

"Oh, you're on the ball. Stay put," Mark growled as soon as Casper sprang forward. The order itself confined the Border Collie to an impatient pace, tail wagging in anticipation of a new face to slobber.

Annoyed, Mark squinted skyward toward the squall line of still dormant thunderheads. Chucking his tool belt and gloves, he coaxed his horse in to a dead-heat canter, racing at full gallop across the grazing pasture. Hop-Scotch took the enclosure gate with the grace and expertise of a steeplechase show horse. Mark slowed Hop-Scotch to an easy trot as they rounded the barn; just as the silver streak screeched to a halt alongside his Silverado, parking mere inches from kissing the rear bumper of his squad car.

Eyeing his truck, then his prowler, Mark had half a mind to cuss her out. His resolve stalled out once a wild mane of strawberry blond corkscrews emerged from the pricey sports car. The zesty spaghetti-strap halter and those snug-fitting Daisy Duke shorts, tipped his hormones south of all logic and had his heart now pumping triple time in order to recover.

Oblivious of her poor parking skills, or for that matter his presence, she made a bee-line for the house and as if on a mission. Mark groaned. Just what he needed to end his evening with, the same problem that he'd started off his morning shift with; an ill-tempered, tetchy, pretty as sin criminal defense attorney. An unwanted visitor who, at present, was cupping her hands with the audacity of pressing her nose to one his front windows.

He raised an eyebrow and watched her Peeping Tom routine a few seconds more; somewhat amused. He then nudged Hop-Scotch toward the steps of the veranda, deliberately blocking her only escape route.

"Sure hope you got that driver's license of yours renewed, Miss Bryans."

⁓ ⁓ ⁓

Lurching at the sound of his voice, Hannah cursed silently then spun around. "I...?" All logic escaped her upon encountering a half dressed male seated atop of an extremely large horse.

Perplexed, she studied the worn toe of a rawhide boot just south of a kneecap playing peek-a-boo through a frayed rupture of threadbare denim. Fascinated, she openly gawked; first at a sweat glossed slab of sun-kissed flesh then chiseled pecs, a pair of powerful shoulders anchored to a duo of labor toned arms flaunting ample biceps. "I..." ...*aye—yii-yii! Hunky-By-The-Book-Deputy Unfriendly by day...unapproachable-Calendar-Pin-Up-Cowpoke, minus the classic Stetson, come sunset?*

Swallowing hard, she focused on the baseball cap pitched backwards sitting snug atop of his head. A rebellious tuft of onyx poked through the adjustment band, proposing a rather reckless and silly boyish charm. Not so silly however was the toothpick jutting cockeyed from his carnal lips; a mouth which was unfavorably set in an inhospitable hyphen of discord.

"Deputy Bowman. I...well, I..." she attempted to explain herself yet again.

Brooding poker-face notwithstanding, once their eyes touched, her heart did a one-handed cartwheel to hurtle out of orbit. At a complete loss she contemplated the masculine silhouette mounted bareback on that rather large steed of his; half-dressed, bronzed skin bathed by the fading sunlight. Maybe this wasn't such a good idea...? As if telepathic, the tall buckskin colored horse snorted, bobbing its head in what seemed to be a decisive nod of accord.

It cued her to talk, and fast. "I called first. But got your machine. And well, I needed to talk to you, so I decided to, well to just drive out. I hope you don't mind."

When he didn't respond, Hannah inched down the first step, just to realize she was trapped. For a distraction, she caressed the horse's velvet muzzle. She needed a few seconds to regroup, to recall the very reason of why she needed to speak to this man in person.

"I was hoping to speak with you," she stated, more so to the animal itself.

The horse starched its ears and whinnied in response. The man atop it remained taciturn. Those sober slate gray orbs now analyzing her every move, cued her gut to ball and clench.

"About a man—er—well, I mean a case. A vehicular homicide case, actually."

"Reckon you'd be referring to Mr. Holm."

Hannah nodded, relieved to hear him speak she clarified, "Yes. He's my client. I was hoping to speak to you about the musc—er—the details. Manly—er—ah…um…." Taking a calming breath she eased her eyes off of that slab of sun-kissed flesh. *My God, she must sound like some babbling nitwit.* Summoning her professional poise, she reiterated, "Mainly the details concerning my client's arrest." *…and preferably after you put on a shirt.*

"Ah, yes. Mr. Holm's arrest." Displeasure crimped his lips, hitching one cheek as if utterance of the subject itself left a sour aftertaste. He extracted the toothpick and studied it, expression dour yet reflective. After a moment he surmised, "That there would be a waste of taxpayer's good money." Dismissing the topic with the simple flick of that toothpick, his expression grew dogmatic—a fair warning to not challenge his opinion. "And of your time, Miss Bryans."

"I beg to differ," Hannah countered. "Everyone has the right to counsel, Deputy Bowman. Innocent until proven guilty. Correct?"

"Might be right so, ma'am. But Mr. Holm was—" Hesitating, he squinted at her, mouth twitching, as if gnawing on the ideal sentiment. "—if I dare say, caught with his britches down."

Hannah ignored the air of ridicule and pressed on. "My client..." Trailing off as the steed nuzzled the crook of her shoulder and neck, she found herself once again sidetracked. Smiling, she combed her fingers through the animal's dark chocolate forelock. As the horse inched forward sizing her up, Hannah wound one arm around its thick neck in a semi-hug, while stroking its mane and half whispered, "Well, now, aren't you just a little interested."

The spicy masculine scent of hard labor invaded her nostrils as Deputy Bowman leaned forward caressing the animal himself. Their fingertips collided, drawing her full attention back to him. Dodging his gaze was impossible, and she was now unable to flee the unexpected invasion of her own personal space, as his seductively velvet murmur concluded, "Feelings mutual," a little too matter-of-fact.

Catching the glint of awareness in those stationary slate gray orbs, Hannah snatched her hand back and, after giving herself a good mental shake, gave the horse's neck a good slap. The buckskin colored stallion whinnied and pranced, setting its rider straight.

On edge, she blundered blindly backwards up the steps, putting the safe distance of a few feet between them. "Deputy Bowman, I came out here to discuss my client's case. Not—"

"Easy—?" His biting gunmetal eyes narrowed on hers. The steed itself snorted and whinnied, flipping its tail; rightly affronted.

Hannah crossed her arms and silently challenged him. She was the first to forfeit. Looking away, she searched the horizon. Despite the soft melody of songbirds overhead, the inflexible silence pressed in against her eardrums. Her left eyelid began to twitch. Macho jerks she could deal with. But this man—his deputy, was a drop-dead-gorgeous know-it-all, intolerant, Spartan.

"Yup. Smells like rain," he at last proclaimed, concluding their agonizing stalemate.

Half thinking he was as telepathic as that horse of his, Hannah studied his impassive poker-face as he too now scanned the horizon. She felt the desperate need to say something, make small talk, but for the life of her couldn't think of a single thing to say.

"Horses, they can sense a kindred soul." Once their eyes touched, he further clarified, "And all I meant was it appears that Hop-Scotch here is as smitten with you as you are with him, Miss Bryans."

Hannah hugged herself; insides a-wobble, a blush tip-toed across her cheeks. Glancing away she felt utterly moronic for having mistaken his earlier comment for anything more. And by the looks of it, if she was going get any information from this man, she had a feeling she had better make amends herself and fast.

"Oh, um...yeah, I know. I mean that thing about horses. I grew up around them. My parents, they breed them." A spontaneous laugh bubbled disarming the air of animosity and lessened the clutch of anxiety twisting her gut inside-out. "Guess you could say I was born with a ridding crop in a one hand and a manure shovel in the other. Been tromped on and bitten more times than I care to count."

"Then you won't mind giving me a hand." He tossed a nod toward the distant barn, the paddock teeming with horses. "I'll give you lift. Can discuss Mr. Holm while I finish up chores."

"Oh, that's okay. Really," Hannah blurted, shaking her head no, caught off guard by the easy display of those awesome dimples. More so, that this half-naked man was right now offering her his hand; expected her to just hop up on that huge horse with him and ride off into the...well, she didn't want think about that. "I...well, I haven't ridden in years...and, well, you're riding bareback...and...um, well, I can just walk."

"It's a ways for you to walk, ma'am."

Hannah eyed him, indecisive. The concentration of his drawl was an intriguing infrequency which paralleled his unreliable bouts of genuine hospitality. A degree of politeness that when displayed—coupled with that smooth velvet twang—insinuated strong roots from somewhere within the Deep-South.

She calculated the distance to the barn. "I'll be fine, walking that is."

"Liable to find yourself stepping in apples." He nodded at her leather sandals with indisputable respect. "Ranch hand went AWOL on me this morning, ma'am."

Hannah surveyed the outlying stables, the dirt trail littered with those apples—globs of horse manure—then glanced at her sandals. She then eyed the massive stallion and its handsome mount, the generous hand which was still stretched out. Meeting his easygoing expression, her heart did a funny little dip then thumped hard against her ribs. Forget about butterflies, what felt like a flock of condors took flight within her gut.

"That's okay. I, I mean, it's not that far," she insisted. She felt caged as he piloted the steed in a semi-circle and parked it flush with the steps, again blocking her only escape route—and as if that would somehow change her mind and get her to hop up on that huge horse with him. Gnawing on her bottom lip, she glanced over her shoulder and tossed a vague gesture at the vacant and rather inviting porch swing. "Or...I could wait, um, there...until you're done...?"

"It could be awhile." Retracting his hand, he squinted at the growing umber sky. "Got a fence to finish mending, ma'am."

Hannah followed his gaze to an inert squall line of hostile looking thunderheads that held the potential of becoming vindictive. She searched the rolling meadow of lush grass dotted by clumps of gnarled oaks and tall elms.

Dusk was beginning to stretch across the outlying fields, where a sunflower crop and the level rows of corn stalks blended into the horizon, rambling far beyond the naked eye's comprehension.

Surveying this man's private sanctuary, his eye-catching yet somewhat imposing dimensions, Hannah was hit with an alarming sense of total isolation. Having been arrested by him this morning notwithstanding, deputy or not, she was not at all acquainted with this man. "You know what, I'll just have my secretary—"

"Hate to think you drove all the way out here for nothing, Miss Bryans."

"Oh, it's not that big of a deal," she fudged.

"Reckon it must be, ma'am." He squinted at her; as if examining a foreign specimen that he wasn't quite so sure of himself yet. "Beings how you drove out—unannounced—to discuss your client's arrest, after hours."

Catching the subtle trace of censure in his voice, holding that concrete gaze of his, Hannah's nerves jangling with the vigor of wind chimes caught up in a tornado's vortex. Why had she even let Monique talk her into this? *Fraternizing…Ha.* Who needed sparks in this heat? "Yes, you're right. I shouldn't have bothered you at home. I mean, it's not like we know each other intimately," she croaked, immediately kicking herself mentally for having used such a term.

"Innocent until proven guilty. Correct, Miss Bryans?"

That sexy eyebrow gave her the distinct impression he was in no way referring to courtroom legalities. Self-conscious, she glanced away and tucked a wayward strand behind her ear. In spite of the stifling humidity, the sweltering heat, a shiver prickled just below the surface of her skin. She could feel those gunmetal pools still upon her, and now as palpable as a melting ice-cube being drawn across her hot sticky flesh.

Ambivalent, she scanned the horizon. She needed details, and this man was the only person who had those specifics. Specifics she'd rather discuss when he was in full uniform and they were both seated in the tame comfort zone of an office. Out of her depth, Hannah dodged his analytical stare. She now wasn't even sure what exactly she hoped to accomplish by driving out here.

"Um, that's okay. I mean, it sounds like you have a lot of work to do and I…well, I'd just be in the way."

"Hop-Scotch doesn't mind the company." He extended his hand again obliging and patient, the gesture itself drawing her own eyes back to his. "And to be honest, neither do I, Miss Bryans."

Hannah told herself that last disclosure should not have excited her as she eyed the large, tall, horse and the half-naked deputy atop of it. There should have been a million reasons racing through her head of why she should refuse his invitation. At present, she could not think of a single one of them.

"It…?" She nodded at the horse, stalling, still searching for a reason to reject this entire idea. "It won't buck, or bite?" was all she could come up with.

"Reckon I'd be liar if I promised he wouldn't. Gets him a wild hair now and then—if provoked. But, never known Hop-Scotch to buck or bite a lady, ma'am." Hesitating, the vague nuance of an innuendo hung in the air as the inkling of a grin twitched the corners of his sensual mouth. "And neither have I, Miss Bryans."

Hannah brought up both hands to decline, then flat-lined the instant his fingers enclosed around her forearm. Before she could even think to argue he'd pulled her to him, had secured her under the armpits in a semi-hug and was hoisting her up off the porch. She had no choice now. Stubble snagged her hair as his masculine scent assailed her nostrils. His very touch set her skin ablaze, leaving every nerve fiber a-tingle and her mind in an utter daze. Her limbs automatically responded, legs negotiating the animal as he helped her on to the rear of the horse.

Just as quickly, however, he'd released her and had

faced forward. She instinctively slipped her arms around his stable trunk, fingers lacing together at a junction of taut flesh and the tattered waistband of wash-worn denim. A pair of button-fly Levi's, of which, she realized the top button was either missing or had just been carelessly left unfastened...

Jerking her hands away Hannah abruptly scooted back then panicked as the large horse shifted beneath them. Balance jeopardized, her chest collided into Hunky Cowpoke's back. The impact pitched them both forward. Her forehead careened off the bill of his cockeyed baseball cap. Launched skyward the thing soared then plummeted, nicking the horse's ear before toppling to the earth. Spooked, the animal sprang ahead a foot, then tip-toed in a hoof-scootin'-boogie, stomping the life right out of the ball cap; desecrating it's neatly embroidered *Altoona County Sheriff's Department* insignia.

"*Easy*—?!"

"Sorry." Unnerved, Hannah wiggled back then yelped hemming her fingers around the deputy's neck as the horse did a side-to-side two step tap. Glancing at the earth below, she squeezed her eyes shut. Her heart lodged betwixt nonexistent tonsils. Had she neglected to mention to this man, the only horse she'd ever been able to stay on was of the steel-poled carousal variety...?

"Um, this probably isn't the best time to tell you this. But—"

"If-rrr-ittish-ill-e-ittish," burst forth a garbled incoherent half-cough-half-croak.

"I'm not skittish. Why would I be skittish?" she argued, working to regain her composure. "I grew up around horses..."

"Eck—et—oh—of –iii—eck...pleeeez!"

"Why this is..." Frazzled, Hannah quickly retracted her hands. Wriggling farther back just sent the horse prancing, throwing her off balance and once again flush against Cowpoke's back. "...as simple as..."

Knees scaling his thighs to flank his narrow hips, her nails anchored into flesh. The Stud lurched with a hard curse; the horse reared. Frozen with fear, Hannah clamped her arms tight around his neck and now recalled the very reason of why her being on a horse in the first place was just plain ludicrous: it was hazardous to her well-being.

"Settle down, will you." Grumbling a volatile streak of muddled oaths, he regained control of the horse; effortlessly doing so, she thought, considering that she was clinging to his back with the spinelessness of a terrified chimp. "...liable to get us both bucked!"

Hannah pried open one eye after the horse stalled. She had to admit she was most impressed. They were both still seated atop of it. *It* rattled its entire body with a loud shuddering neigh, of which she interpreted as extreme disgust that they were still seated atop it. Or rather, he was while she was herself still affixed, and now almost piggy-back, to this man's back.

"...riding a bike. Right?" she squeaked in conclusion once she rearranged her heart and larynx and located...well, what was left of her courage.

There was a brief moment of silence. A less than discrete grunt then buttonholed her eardrum to inspire insecurity, which adhered to a clumsier bout of anxiety only to be ensued by absolute mortification. But, only after she realized the rhythmic breathing bathing her eardrum, belonged to this half-naked deputy. And that grunt had to have come from those sensually carnal lips...lips that were at present glancing the shell of her ear.

"If you don't get off my back and let up on that chokehold—right soon, ma'am—I can guarantee you this'll be about as smooth as riding a dirt bike with square tires," he enlightened; on rather calm note considering the circumstances, she thought.

Hannah tipped her face askew to tackle the slate gray eyes that were, much like his mouth, up close and real personal. She detected flecks of thunderbolt, shards of liquid mercury, slivers of sea storm and specks of pewter, swimming in those endless gray pools. Breathtaking halos, emphasized by piercing black pupils, which were right now transfixed on hers in astute question.

"Oh, um...right." Abashed, Hannah untied her elbows and, sitting back, eased her cheek away from his. "Sorry," she squeaked, glancing at the desecrated ball cap. "Maybe this isn't such a good idea...?"

"Riding crop in hand, huh?"

"Yes. Um, well, about that." Fidgety, Hannah struggled down a tremor of giggles. "I should've probably told you that even though I grew up—"

"Keep all that squirming up, ma'am..." Eyeing the baseball cap himself, he wagged his head. Unable to tamp down his mounting annoyance, he shot a heated look over his shoulder. "And it's a sure bet we'll both be bucked, bitten and trampled."

"I'm sorry. It's just, well, if you'd let me finish, I was going to explain that I—" she began to argue.

"Relax!"

"Okay, okay. Relaxing." Hannah figured there was now no turning back. She took a deep breath then, after a moment of bumbling, apprehensively rested her hands on his hips. "Um, I'm ready now," she announced, then quickly added, "And I'm real sorry about your ball cap, Deputy Bowman."

"Not as sorry as I am, ma'am," Hannah swore she heard him mumble half under his breath.

Narrowing her eyes, a scathing reprimand formed across her lips. They lurched forward. Her intended reproof, as well as any and all argument, lodged in her throat. Knocked off balance, heart racing, she lost every scrap of inhibition and wrapped her arms tight around Hunky Cowpoke's stable midsection.

"Just like riding a bike. Wouldn't you say, Miss Bryans?"

"Yeah, well, bicycles don't go this bumpy or fast, nor do they buck you off, deputy Bowman." Vision joggled, a bouncing barn neared then blurred past. Confused, beset by the sensation of her body pressed snug to his, Hannah swallowed hard at the precarious situation she'd just gotten herself in. "I...um? I thought we were just going to the barn?"

"Told you, I got a fence to finish mending, first, ma'am."

He pulled on the reins, redirecting the buckskin colored horse with its pretty chocolate mane toward a fenced in meadow. Hannah released a silent breath and loosened her hold a smidgen. They'd have to stop first to open the enclosure gate. Therefore she could get off this dangerous vehicle and go home, where it was safe. Their means of transport, however, did not show any signs of slowing. In all shocking truth, it was accelerating.

"Reckon you'd best hold on right tight. Ah, now would be good, Miss Bryans."

"Wh—what?" Distrustful, yet alarmed by the urgent nature of his suggestion, Hannah cinched her arms secure, inadvertently molding her body to his yet again. She was almost afraid to ask, "Why?"

"Hop-Scotch, he thinks he's a world class steeplechaser. Ready? Here we go—just hold tight and follow my lead."

Ready? "Deputy Bowman, I, I…"

Hannah swore she detected the earthquake of a repressed chuckle resonate deep within his chest. She opened her mouth to further dispute this entire idea, then clamped it shut while squeezing her eyes tight as they flew over the enclosure gate with the clack of hoofs nicking metal. The horse hit the earth in a dead-heat sprint to race across the pasture—amazingly enough, with them still atop of it, and now at the alarming velocity of a Kawasaki crotch-rocket.

CHAPTER 5

"About my client's arrest—"

"Hand me those nippers, can you?" Mark asked, rerouting the conversation for the umpteenth time. Stretching his free arm backwards, gloved fingers a wiggle, he waited. Blinking away the sting of perspiration he cranked his neck to see what was holding her up—beside the obvious: that he'd been dodging her attempts to discuss Mr. Holm's arrest—to be greeted by a clueless expression. "Those needle nose pliers? The ones with…aw, you know what, just toss me the tool-belt instead."

Mark straightened turning just in time to snag it mid-air, mere inches from hitting his chest. Or maybe she'd aimed for his head and had miscalculated? He stared at her a moment then, and without comment, returned his undivided attention to the fence. Squatting, he reexamined the scrap of wire mesh which he'd curtailed in order to repair the existing panel.

Admiring his own handy-work, he deduced this patch-up would hold for at least a couple of weeks. Making the mental note to look into electrical fencing, he rummaged for his pliers and went back to work. Sensing the absence of her once vigilant gaze—that laser-sharp glare no longer boring a hole in his back—Mark glanced over his shoulder to see that Miss Bryans had abandoned her post all together. The post—a tree stump—which he'd deposited her on in order to recoup, after their little roundabout jaunt through the pasture.

Wagging his head at the thought, he frowned. It had been downright mean. But, he figured, it was comparable to her dropping that little bomb of her being a lawyer on him this morning.

That lawyer was now humming while wandering about picking a variety of weeds that masked themselves as wildflowers. Mark watched her for a couple seconds, and then went back to work. Or, at least he tried to. Glancing over his shoulder, a reluctant smile twitched his mouth as she tucked a blossom behind her ear. It appeared Miss Bryans was lost within her own world.

Twisting around, Mark watched his guest sashay up to Hop-Scotch, then grimaced when she adorned the horse's bridle with her gathered bouquet of wildflowers. Casper, of course, chased after her, dancing about her feet, vying for her full attention. A giggle escaped her when she stooped to greet the dog and Casper took it upon himself to slobber up her cheek.

Chucking the tool belt, Mark sat and stretched his legs out. Lounging against the fencepost he took a sip from his canteen while contemplating the sunrays streaming through the trees. It created a fleeting kaleidoscope of colors to compete with the onset of dusk. Remnants of castaway dandelions floated lazily, magically suspended in the touch-and-go breeze. He told himself he was only taking a breather, then would get right back to work although that quick break spanned to minutes as he became captivated by his visitor's graceful beauty.

For a criminal defense attorney, she looked more like a naive pixie wandering about an enchanted forest than being that of a possible threat or enemy. As Hop-Scotch grazed on the tall grass ingeniously edging his way toward that fairy, Mark sat forward brow knitting. An incredulous grin spread once his horse raised its muzzle and nuzzled the back of Miss Bryans' knee; earning himself a sharp startled gasp released on the soft sigh of sheer rapture.

Sly stallion...Mark mused, as Hop-Scotch nibbled on the thin straps of her halter. "So you grew up around them?" he heard himself ask while watching her retie the strap.
"Huh?" She turned toward him, startled, a scarlet map of self-conscious embarrassment coloring her cheeks.

Caught loafing, as well as gawking, Mark jerked his eyes away and scrambled to his knees feeling the immediate heat crawl up his own cheeks. Reaching for his tool belt, he watched via the corner of his eye as she squatted to once again bestow her full attention on Casper. *Lucky dog.* "Horses...you said your parents breed them...?"

"Oh, yeah. Mostly Appaloosa, but we had a few Paint, couple of French Trotters."

"You don't ride much," he stated and then immediately kicked himself.

"Guess that's sort of obvious, huh," she snorted.

Glancing away, he pretended to study his pliers. "Reckoned with you growing up around them and all, you'd be the barrel-racing-show-riding type."

"My sisters are—well, were. I, however, couldn't stay on a horse to save my life."

Mark half shrugged, half nodded, somewhat uncertain of how to respond. Casper saved him, flopping on his back and sprawling with no shame as Miss Bryans granted the Border Collie a good belly scratch. Hop-Scotch himself continued his own courtship, bumping his muzzle about her shoulder looking for his own fair share of attention. Watching the duo's dedicated contest to win her sole affection, Mark shook his head then turned his full attention on repairing the fence.

"My mom, she couldn't understand that one, herself,"

she explained. "Swore I wasn't a Bryans. Somehow switched at a birth. Out of four girls, I was the only Bryans who'd rather climb trees and play in the mud than ride. God...I dreaded riding school."

"Riding school?"

"I ditched a lot. Hid out with the ranch hands; learned how to wield a mean manure shovel. Mommy would have rather I wore those stupid little britches and blazer that went along with that dorky velvet bowler and riding crop. Because I refused, I became the only Bryans dubbed the tomboy klutz."

Mark shot her a look. Turbulent start-offs notwithstanding, Miss Bryans did not appear to be in any way a klutz, nor was that dainty voluptuous frame of hers tomboyish.

"Your family, they breed Appaloosa in Wisconsin?" he snooped. Not that he wanted the details of this woman's life, just anything was better than discussing a drunk driver.

"Oh, no. Virginia. Shenandoah Valley actually. My mom, she was born and raised here in Iowa, but still professes Shenandoah's her real home. As the eldest, I was expected to stay-on, help with the family business. My mom planned on me becoming a vet—*if you can't ride might as well learn how to treat them.* I, however, had different plans. A Harvard law degree for one. Practiced in Boston a while, but then relocated to Milwaukee when I met..."

Mark glanced over his shoulder when she clammed up, somewhat curious. "So who—er—how'd you land in Altoona?" he asked, revising his original question of wanting to know whom she'd followed to Milwaukee. He wondered if that same person had followed her here to Iowa as well. And that, right there, was none of his damn business.

"Altoona?" she chirped, looking a bit surprised that he'd even ask. "Oh...guess you could blame that on chance."

"Chance huh?"

"I..." She drew long breath dwelling upon the question. Or rather, Mark thought, deciding whether to supply the answer itself.

Staring at the fencepost, Mark could feel the current of indecisive consideration zinging around them. It didn't take a rocket scientist to recognize she was herself debating on how much information to share with him. Personal information, which was none of his damn business. Just as well. The less he knew about Miss Bryans' personal affairs, the better.

"I...well, I guess you could say I was unfortunate enough to inherit my grandmother's estate."

Mark cringed at the very idea that she had opted to share. He then heard himself ask, "That's a misfortune?"

"In a way. I was notified of Grams' death after the funeral, via a fax mind you, that I was the sole beneficiary of her estate."

Via a fax? Mark grimaced at the gaping hole in the fence. So far they now had at least two things in common. Family and the distance they had themselves put between those blood relatives.

He twisted, giving her his full attention. "I'm real sorry to hear that, ma'am." He wasn't seeking a lengthy explanation, rather simply offering condolences as it was the proper thing to do.

"Oh, no. Don't be." As quickly as she'd said it, she then made a face; as if knowing herself how bad that must have sounded. "I mean, we weren't close. Visited her as a child, yes. But...after her and mom...it's just...well, I guess Grams wanted to get one last dig in." Glancing toward the heavens, she sighed, "Way to go, Grams. Really showed her, huh."

Mark studied her a moment, perplexed. "Ma'am?"

"Oh, um...Grams and mom, they...well, they didn't view things quite the same." Frowning, she absent-mindedly toyed with her charm bracelet. "They stopped speaking when I was young."

"Irreconcilable differences," he surmised aloud, then grimaced, considering how his assumption might have added fresh salt to old family wounds. "I'm sorry. I didn't mean to—"

"No, don't be. I mean, it's not a big deal. Really," she assured him with an obligatory smile, then glanced away; now looking outwardly uncomfortable for ever having allowed herself to expose such personal family turmoil.

Mark felt a strange twinge tighten across his chest as his beautiful visitor gnawed on her bottom lip doing everything possible to avoid his gaze. However intriguing, he went back to work; told himself he didn't need to know the specifics or the reasons. He could do without that kind of a connection, especially with this woman.

"After probate court, paying off back taxes to Uncle Sam, there wasn't much left afterwards but the house. So, here I am," she at last summed up, breaking the uncomfortable silence. Then to his surprise, outright snickered, "I do have a sneaky suspicion the house itself was supposed to have been condemned, but somehow that never got mentioned during the reading of Grams' will."

To hear her laugh over such a loss, let alone such a tale of bad luck, was a weird yet wonderful upshot. Mark couldn't remember the last time he'd relished in the basic gratification of hearing a woman laugh. Listening to her ramble on, an involuntary smile tugged his lips. She was once again talking at the speed of light, but at least she now sounded optimistic.

As her infectious giggles threatened his own sober mindset, he couldn't help but to ask, "Condemned?"

"I swear," she roared, "it's a two story money pit stuck in the middle of the sticks."

Mark laughed with her, although wasn't himself sure if the house was actually a laughing matter. "Could've just sold it," he mused as he went back to work, trying to unite the patch of uncooperative wire fencing with a unaccommodating stationary post.

"Believe me, it's crossed my mind more than once."

When she heaved a sigh, Mark glanced over his shoulder. She'd plopped herself back down on the stump. Greeted by playful doe brown eyes and her tantalizing grin he glanced away, not even wanting to acknowledge the byproduct that duo had ignited.

"And what about you, Deputy Bowman?"

Mark cringed. That otherwise pointless get-to-know-each-other chat that he had hoped to himself avoid, was already in full swing.

"I mean, you can't possibly be from Iowa. Well, not originally anyway."

Busy working, he shrugged. "What makes you say that?"

"Your accent, um, well it sort of gives it away," she snickered.

Turning toward her, Mark summoned his thickest Southern drawl, "Us Texans don't rightly take kind to being made fun of, ma'am." The dramatic eyebrow, arched to display bogus offense, only instigated more giggles.

"Texas? Wow."

The proud grin and nod were both unconscious and automatic. "Yes ma'am."

"Why'd you—I mean, how'd you wind up..." she shook her head in disbelief, tossing her arms out in an elaborate gesture embracing the landscape. "...here, of all places?"

Reflectively, Mark squinted toward the hazy sunset. Dropping his gaze he stared at his gloved hands battling the memories, the reason, which threatened to spill forth. Exasperated, he granted his visitor a rather aloof flick of a back-off glance. That information, those details, were private and none of her business. "Chance, I reckon," was all he said.

The awkward silence was back.

"Yeah, chance," she parroted in a somewhat

disappointed whisper.

Mark glanced backwards as she propped her feet and rested her chin in her hands. Not paying him any attention, she too now gazed out across the horizon lost in thought. Eyes straying, he took note of the fine spray of freckles splashed across her delicate features, admired how the dying sunset accentuated her fiery locks. His lips parted, then in afterthought he shrugged whatever it was that he was now feeling off and turned toward the fence. A fence that he'd come out here to fix. A fence he hadn't done much to or with yet.

Picking up the pliers, Mark scowled. The seconds spanned to several minutes as he sat waiting for her to pipe up once again in an attempt to make small-talk. Maybe a part of him wanted to know; wanted to make that connection? Those forgotten about parts which ached to tell-all and craved the comforts of a woman. When she didn't say anything more, he reassured himself that it was better this way; reminded himself that this female was off-limits.

He was then half relieved when she chirped, "Anyway, I'm stuck here. Especially since that cutthroat construction crew supposedly repaired—or as they put it, completely revamped—the roof, the windows and renovated the dry rot. Three months it took them. You should have seen the mess..."

Snatching up his canteen, Mark twisted off the cap, half listening while indulging in a healthy swig of water as she told him about the repairs to her house.

"...and now expect me to—Ooooh, whatever that is, I hope you're planning on sharing it."

Twisting around, Mark felt a jolt the strength of a thousand volts sear his nerves confronted by that Cupid's bow at mock pout. Dropping his gaze to his hands, he leaned forward and offered her the canteen. Then gawked, enraptured with the view—the exposed flat tummy adorned by a navel jewel—as she used the hem of her halter to wipe off and decontaminate the spout. He about choked on his own spit when she leaned back, tossing her head while simultaneously bringing the spout to her lips to take a long greedy swig. His eyes transfixed on, then chased each glistening rivulet of water which dribbled off her chin. Wiping the back of his glove across his own, Mark was unable to tear his gaze off the droplets snaking their way along the sensual arc of her throat, slipping over the delicate contour of her collar bone, disappearing within the valley of exposed cleavage.

"Thanks. God, with this scorching heat a person's just parched."

Mind-a-jumble, Mark fumbled the canteen after she bent forward handing it back to him. Retrieving it—before it totally emptied out in the dirt—he eased his eyes off the generous view that her halter provided. Turning away without comment, he drained what water was left; unable to quench a now insatiable thirst. Chucking the canteen aside, he stared at the fence; could feel that laser sharp gaze now tracking his every movement once he went back to work. Ignoring the ego boost it gave him, Mark curled his fingers within the wire mesh just to realize the strength in his hands, in his own damn arms, had been zapped.

Scowling, he gave the fencing a good yank, manhandling it until he was able to manipulate the cumbersome material around the post. Holding it in place, he groped for his pliers then began pinching the jagged metal prongs together. The heaviness of her watchful silence crackled against his eardrums. His usually agile fingers had for some reason gone weak and were now inept. He blamed that on the heat; the thickness of his leather work gloves.

Mark snarled. Why the hell was he on edge, feeling so damn jittery? He eyed the horizon and assured himself it was the sweltering July heat prickling across his flesh, depleting his energy and leaving him lightheaded. Heat exhaustion, probably. Exhaustion due to insomnia. Had to be. He convinced himself of that while watching the sun surrender its reign, veiling everything in a tranquil semi-opaque gauze. A steadier breeze kicked-up cooling his fevered skin. Mentally and physically exhausted, his eyelids slid shut as he fought to regain his wits.

"It's so peaceful out here."

"Yup." Mark snapped to. Staring at the fencepost, he grimaced. Peacefulness...an atmosphere which always surrounded him, yet always seemed to somehow elude him. And at present, peacefulness wasn't quite the right description for what was now plaguing him.

On that note, he went back to work, wanting to finish the repairs before the pitch of night swallowed them whole and before that squall line itself decided to become active. As the rhythmic call of crickets engulfed them, he felt...well, obligated to say something. He needed to detour the vortex of emotions overriding his ability to concentrate; wanted to vanquish the uproar he felt just knowing this beautiful creature was watching him...and now like a predator who was stalking its prey.

"Reckon a person could sell it—the house—use the proceeds to pay off the construction crew?" he offered.

"Yeah, guess I could." She heaved a disconsolate breath. "After this morning, who knows, I'll probably have to. Be lucky if I have a job once the seniors' hear about my arrest."

Hands stilling, Mark stared at the fencepost. He could hear the wake of that message loud and clear. She wanted him to feel bad...worse, feel sorry for her. Not acknowledging her recent comment, he mutilated each prong with unnecessary vigor then sat back on his haunches to survey the slapdash repair job. He squinted skyward and scrutinized the now brewing squall line illuminated silver by the climbing moon

"Well...I may not be proficient at riding horses," she declared, then acknowledged on a paradoxical laugh, "But like mamma always said, I can sure tickle my tonsils with my toes."

Grunting, Mark flicked a you-nailed-that-one-on-the-head glance over his shoulder then once again reexamined the mess he'd made of the fence. He pressed his lips together determined not to comment, or for that matter not let it bother him—her arrest.

"Since we're on the subject...I wanted to ask you few questions regarding my client's arrest. I...well, I think I found some discrepancies regarding the night of the accident, Deputy Bowman."

Correction: Predator snagging its prey within her razor sharp claws; all while sounding and looking like a harmless little minnow...

Cursing under his breath, Mark gazed out past the shadowy field, not even listening as she proceeded to explain the so-called flaws that she thought she had found pertaining to her client's arrest. And all while now feeling a cramp of guilt bayonet his chest. What irked him wasn't her discrediting his report. It was the impulsive desire to apologize to this beautiful creature for having had arrested her this morning.

But why should he? She was a criminal defense attorney for crying out loud; a Harvard-schooled barracuda at that. She should have known, should have had enough common sense to have remembered to renew her damn driver's license. And why should he even care what happened? It wasn't his fault she'd forgotten to renew it, or apply for an Iowa license. It's supposedly now all his fault she might lose her job over it because he had hauled her in? For crying out loud, he'd just been doing his job; which brought him full circle.

That revelation whacked him with the enthusiasm of two-by-four upside the temple. Miss Bryans was here, right now, hoping to undo what he as a deputy sheriff was duty-bound to do; had done. She was doing her job, and doing a damn fine job at it as well as on him, in that zesty halter and those snug-fitting Daisy Duke's.

Mark figured it all boiled down to one basic ingredient. Human nature. All she wanted—needed from him—were details. Leave it to a siren of a defense lawyer to employ this type of tactic. Violate his downtime, while doing her utmost to exploit him with her feminine wiles. Or, if that didn't work, lay a guilt-trip on him. All in all she was trying to manipulate him to gain information. Information that if retrieved, she would—and in any way possibly—twist around and use against him in court in order to exonerate her own client.

He wouldn't even be sitting here right now feeling like a complete heel, if this woman hadn't barged in on him to do so. And what about that? Maybe he was the one lacking in good sense for thinking integrity was ever a factor regarding her surprise visit.

"And I also had some concerns with—"

"Storm front's moving in," Mark announced cutting her off. Jumping to his feet he jammed the pliers back inside the tool belt, and then draped it over his shoulder. Staring out across the field he felt duped and about as dense as the dumb fencepost in front of him. "We'd best be heading back, ma'am—before it lets loose."

CHAPTER 6

"It's breathtaking. I, I don't think I've ever seen so many at one time."

Mark snapped out his brooding stupor. It had been a good fifteen minutes since they'd left. Fifteen minutes of sheer silence after leaving her discrepancies at a fence that he knew he'd have to come back to sooner or later to contend with.

"What's that, ma'am?"

"Fireflies. My God, there has to be a gazillion of them."

Oblivious of the night, Mark was more attuned to the feminine softness which had managed to talk him straight out of completely shunning this woman. Glancing skyward he scowled. It had to be the full moon. He'd pulled enough graveyards to know it made people act and think crazy.

"Is—" Pausing she twisted, and as if oblivious of the fact that they were seated atop Hop-Scotch, to somehow face him as she spoke. Instinctively his arms roped tight around her midsection, pulling her in snug, just to safeguard their combined balance atop of his horse. "—Is it always like this?"

Staring at the outline of her mouth as she leaned further back, now resting her head on his shoulder in order to look up at him, Mark assured himself he was only holding Miss Bryans so close to prevent them from both falling off Hop-Scotch. Wispy corkscrews of spun silk tickled his nose, his jaw, calling his bluff. Tackling a set of bottomless fawn brown wells, Mark realized he had no clue what this beautiful creature was even talking about. The body language, on the other hand, was loud and clear. Letting his gaze slip back to those succulent lips, it cost him every bit of control he had not to take that mouth of hers hostage.

Dragging his own eyes back to hers, Mark stared at her perplexed. "Ma'am?"

"All these fireflies," she said, her whisper waning to downright breathless, "It's just so…so, surreal."

Grunting a muddled response, Mark fixed his sights on the outlying ridge grateful that she'd faced forward. Something other than surreal was whittling away at his strength-of-will. Something he could not discount, or deny. But he wasn't quite willing to fess-up to, give in to, or outwardly acknowledge; no matter how wonderful this beautiful creature felt against him. That prejudice sent the blood squeezing through his veins as their bodies bobbed and rocked in perfect unison; all due to Hop-Scotch's torpid gait. Annoyed, Mark dug his boots into his stupid horse for the umpteenth time to no prevail. His eyelids slid shut, pulse jumpy, way too reactive to the alluring body still swaying against his.

Surreal. Ironical, he mused; because in all truth he did have to admit that this was a little romantic, if not outright seductive. If the circumstances were different, it would have been the perfect setting for… He banished that thought with ruthless precision, while inconspicuously scooting himself back another half-an-inch. Nudging his boots against Hop-Scotch, yet again, he attributed the maddening electrical current humming along his nerve endings on the looming squall line, other than that of primal attraction. Just because they happened to be under the serenade of the rhythmic call of crickets, making their way across a moonlit field surrounded by a never-ending wall of flickering fireflies, all while Mother Nature provided an elaborate display of silent lightning along the horizon, did not mean a damn thing. It was simply a fluke. A freak of nature….sheer happenstance.

It was unfounded to think otherwise. They had nothing in common. He was down-to-earth, simple, no-frills. She, by what he'd so far gathered, was extravagant, pushy—not to mention more than likely very high-maintenance. He upheld the law. She did everything in her power to nullify it. And it wasn't as if he'd planned for this to happen. It was a mere safety precaution on his part to have Miss Bryans seated in front of him during the ride back. Plain and simple.

Mark tried convincing himself of that while staring at the strawberry blond corkscrews cascading over her bare shoulders...and down that back. He groaned inwardly as she drew her fingers through her hair, bunching it up within her small hands; as if conjuring the sudden downdraft herself in order to cool her lovely neck. Mark knew it was just the onset of the storm approaching. But by her doing so—and however innocent—heat spiked his groin contemplating the fine spray of freckles splashed across the silky soft flesh at the base of her neck. The same ultra-rich notes of yummy cocoa, woodsy nutmeg and warm vanilla enticed his nostrils, and he pondered which of those scents that masterpiece of her neck might taste like.

"Hell of a storm moving in," Mark grumbled while averting his attention to assess a now menacing night sky.

"Good. Maybe it'll cool off for a spell? I feel as wilted as my poor petunias."

Mark opened his mouth in agreement then snapped it shut. Squeezing his eyes shut, he grimaced. Wilted definitely was not the correct term to depict what he felt, what was now flowering to an uncomfortable full bloom within his Levi's.

They rode in silence. She holding up her hair; he playing connect-the-dots with his eyes amongst the freckles dotting her back.

Tearing his gaze off her shoulders, Mark fixed his sights on the outline of the barn once the halogen flood lights came into view. Although it was only but a few minutes ride, that last quarter of a mile seemed to take his dumb, yet sly, horse forever and a day to get through.

Parking Hop-Scotch, Mark slid off and, depositing the canteen and tool belt, rescued his discarded shirt from the fence. He jammed his arms inside the ratty holes where the sleeves had once been then gave up on trying to button it all together to instead swing the gate open and force his boots to move his body toward the barn. He needed to finish chores before this storm hit; wanted to create some distance between him and his unsolicited seductress.

"Um...Deputy Bowman? How do I steer it back to the gate?"

Mark wheeled around then swore under his breath. In his hast to vacate, he'd forgotten to tie off the reins. They now dragged against the ground as Hop-Scotch made tracks for the watering trough. Berating himself he took off after them.

"Real sorry about that, ma'am," he apologized taking a hold of the horse's bridle, half stooping while jogging alongside of them; nearly getting himself trampled while trying to retrieve and untangle the reins.

Giving the bridle a good tug stopped the horse a few feet from reaching the trough. Mark was reprimanded by Hop-Scotch's hard neigh, and then was greeted by bottomless fawn brown spheres set in a pale white orb of fright. He stared up at her in disbelief. For someone who claimed they grew up around horses, this woman sure the hell didn't know the first thing about them.

Mark relinquished the bridle then tossed the reins when she made no attempt to dismount. Reaching for her, his instruction was clipped, native to agitated, "Swing your leg over and slide off, like before. I'll catch—"

Silencing his instructions, thunder rumbled with vengeance as lightning sizzled, nailing the crotch of a distant oak with ruthless precision. Spooked, Hop-Scotch bolted, spilling Miss Bryans square against his chest and entangled within his arms. Swearing, Mark scrambled to maintain his own balance while also attempting to somehow manage hers; all while she contradicted his efforts to keep them both afoot. Floundering, she stomped on the toes of his boots, hands groping, unable to re-establish her own balance. Liquid fire tore through his veins the instant her fingertips glanced his navel, clipping the waist of his jeans then, urgently backpedaling and pressing firm into his lower abdomen in an effort to find an anchor and push him away.

"Easy. I've got you," Mark asserted, and he'd meant to assure her of that on a constructive note, yet an overt huskiness had sabotaged his confidence. Clearing his throat was futile. He was powerless to disguise it. "You okay?" he at last croaked.

Stilling, her startled eyes transfixed on his. A breathless, "I think so," leaked past her lips.

Commanding himself to release her was ineffectual. His hands were not receiving the signal. Apparently, his mind and body were no longer communicating on the same wavelength. He masked that delay by giving her a quick once over, eyes resting on her luscious mouth. He could not ignore the proximity, the sensation of her palms still pressed against his flesh. And however innocent, her simple touch sparked an electrical firestorm within him; incinerating the last bit of his self-control, and rendering him incapable of preventing the inescapable once she popped-up on her tippy-toes to thank him with a quick peck.

Just the feel of her lips scantily glancing his jack-knifed his self-restraint and had his own mouth settling a little too decisively against hers in order to properly reciprocate.

Mark assured himself this harmless little peck would absolve that nuisance of curiosity. Subjected to such sweetness, however, that notion proved fleeting as he tentatively skimmed the swell of her bottom lip with the tip of his tongue, politely requesting the privilege to explore. Granted liberal access, he established straight away that he'd grossly overestimated his strength of will. Knew he was in deep trouble the instant she surrendered, allowing him to become intimately acquainted with the satiny depths of her mouth.

Her fingers found the base of his neck, pulling him closer. The luxurious softness of her rayon halter teasingly grazed his chest. His last scrap of will staggered then trotted off to oblivion when she arched into him, as if persuading him to negotiate the loose hem of her halter. Susceptible, his fingertips set out, leisurely navigating ultra-soft skin, familiarizing themselves with the dips and contours of each and every lean rib. Stumbling upon the supple swell of naked flesh, the firm perkiness of a bare breast, a stifled oath welled deep within his chest. His pulse stopped, teetered momentarily, then plunged in a steep vertical free-fall to hammer relentlessly through his groin; heightening his arousal to a dangerously irreversible level, leaving him undeniably male against her more fragile and voluptuous frame.

His fingertips stilled once that prudent voice of annoying reason piped-up; suggesting that he'd best be putting a halt to this. He'd gathered enough to know this woman might be a wheel-barrel of trouble, considering she'd had no qualms about coming here unannounced— and whether premeditated, or not, in an outfit that would have led even the most prudent of saints astray—to dissect an arrest that he had himself executed. He wasn't too sure what she'd do to acquire those details off record. But he did not need a physics degree to recognize that his own body was now willing to wholeheartedly cooperate, that was, if this was indeed her last ditch strategy.

Recanting, Mark aborted their kiss, denying her, himself, of the very experience. "I got chores to finish," he snarled in gruff disapproval.

"You don't seem eager to get to them," she stated matter of fact. Her accusation nipped teasingly against his still loitering mouth. A sizeable misstep on his part.

Drawing back a scant inch, Mark felt gut punched fixing on her self-satisfied gaze. Pride dictated that he walk and just save-face. Yet self-discipline or his recent lack thereof, wasn't the sole issue here. No, his decision here would mark a distinction; would establish exactly who held the reins in what was now a rather complicated association. And this woman was smart enough to know he would not voluntarily walk, at least not on his own home turf. Not without him first laying down some ground rules. Which, in all truth, was irrelevant. Either way he'd already lost. She'd had him in the crosshairs all along, just waiting for that perfect opportunity to squeeze the trigger and had just bagged him like some trophy twelve-point buck.

Thunder grumbled overhead as the swollen canopy of blackened clouds ripped open unleashing a furious downpour. Eyes still transfixed on hers, having interpreted her audacious retort as a blatant challenge, his rationale snapped. Hauling her flush, undomesticated arousal bled with frustration and a low dangerous growl evaded his chest as his mouth once again took full custody of hers.

Now, Mark was well aware kissing her in such a manner was irrefutably unbecoming of any gentlemen. Acting like an innate savage wasn't proving anything; expect that maybe she'd gotten under his skin. As a rule, he treasured and adored women, treating them with the utmost respect. Yet, his faculties for right-and-proper—for reversing this flagrant error—were nowhere to be found. And those all too raring-to-go neglected male fancies of his did not much give a hoot to go hunt those well-mannered principles down.

So here he was, ravaging this woman's mouth like some unrefined hellcat out of sheer retaliation. Caving to utter lust; all while assuring himself that she was herself partly at fault. Why not? She'd brazenly tested his boundaries, had toyed with his sanity, his better judgment. She had *dared* him to kiss her. Be that as it may, he'd need to stop kissing her long enough to confront her about those issues. The problem was, he couldn't stop. She tasted so forbidden, just felt so damned luxurious and exotic against him, that Mark now had himself convinced that he could deal with those issues—to include any and all repercussions due to his own behavior—later...much later.

The more judicious side of his brain begged to differ. Deep-seated decency warned him to back-off. Integrity posed its own argument: Just what the hell do you think you're doing—? Whether painfully aroused, or not, he would never entertain the immoral notion of forcing himself upon any woman, for any reason. He was a gentleman. A deputy sheriff for Christ-sakes; sworn to uphold the law at all cost. But this woman, this shark of a Harvard-schooled criminal defense attorney, was steering him into believing that he could break every law and bend all the rules. And he wanted to do so, right now, and with way more than just her mouth.

With that inclination jarring his system, astute discretion slammed on the brakes. Mark took a firm grip on her shoulders and stood her back. Knowing himself, that if he hadn't, he'd have taken this a hell of lot farther than what either one of them had intended—real fast—and without the benefit of a roof or four walls to shield them from the torrential downpour they were caught out in.

That last bit of knowledge vaguely registered as he was more intent on interrogating his visitor. "Just what exactly are you out here after, Miss Bryans?" he grilled, the forcefulness of his query spewing the droplets of rain collecting across his lips.

He stared her down hard, ready for any argument she might come up with. When she gave none, he then perused her stunned expression. Although Miss Bryans appeared to be thoroughly kissed, his brow knitted noting mascara streaking her cheeks; the rain water dribbling in rapid staccato off the tip of her nose; beading across her lips and streaming off of her own chin. Lightning flashed, illuminating the dark auburn ringlets plastered across her forehead, glued to her neck and face.

Grabbing his full attention a more substantial bolt arced—a blinding white breach, which underscored a swirling canopy of raging hostility above them. It was pursued by a seismic shockwave of thunder that rattled the earth and vibrated his skull right down to the silver fillings wedged within his back molars. Mark swore once his brain defogged enough for him to appreciate the severity of the weather; that it was hail, not rain—the size of peas and growing in dimension—pelting their sopping wet crowns. Squinting toward the violent heaves, he berated himself. He was a spotter for cripes sake; should have had enough sense to recognize the forthcoming wrath of Mother Nature.

Pinning his full attention on his guest, his lips parted to speak. Instantaneously his muscles seized in an involuntary flinch as something more violent than that of just lightning zapped the outlying power-lines with a livid hissing *SNAP*, sending the finer hairs of his nape on end and his senses on high alert. Simultaneously, the halogen flood lamps blinked out leaving an impenetrable abyss of pitch blackness. The once sultry temperature drastically plummeted. Field derbies, leaves and twigs, became wayward projectiles carried along by a fierce comber of spiraling updrafts bulldozing the very pasture they were still standing in.

"Barn—Now!" Not explaining, Mark tucked a kiss-stunned, rather drenched and disorientated, Miss Bryans under his arm and snug against his chest. He herded her then, scooping her up after she lost her own footing against the slick wet earth, carried her; knowing himself she would never be able to keep up with his own urgent sprint.

He didn't need the benefit of a channel Nine weather alert, nor to even look back, to know that it was an imminent tornado now bearing down on them. He knew that sound all too well. It was a progressive echo, a sinister rumble similar to that of a phantom squadron of F-16 Vipers piercing the lower atmosphere. A force of nature spawned at the spur-of-the-moment if conditions were ripe. An unconquerable entity that could strike fear in the bravest of men; push two-by-fours through telephone poles with the accuracy of a master seamstress threading her needle with nimble hands. A force of nature that could rip apart brick buildings and splinter houses in seconds flat, leaving behind nothing but tranquil skies and mere rubble littered with plywood shards the size of toothpicks. And his only means of shelter to protect this uninvited seductress of a guest, would have to be the decrepit barn that he was now hauling-ass towards to get to, before it hit.

~ ~ ~

Dazed, Hannah clung to the masculine physique hustling her across the corral, mind still reeling, unable to recoup from the devastation produced by just his mouth. She squinted up at him to no prevail. Lightening had hit close, causing a complete blackout. The rain was now coming down in transverse horizontal sheets that turned to icy hail bombarding her exposed flesh like heat seeking missiles. She cringed with each deafening clap of thunder and buried her face against the howling roar of wind.

Abruptly, the elements battering her body then ceased, and a potpourri of vaguely familiar scents invaded her nostrils. The faint bouquet of worn leather. Sweat dampened wool. Hay. Straw. Raw earth eclipsed by the strong stench of manure. The distinguished aroma of horse.

"Stay put and keep that over your head!"

She cringed at his unyielding growl as he deposited her on a bed of what felt like straw bales, then tossed what felt like a thick doormat atop of her head. Sprawled, Hannah pushed the thing off and scrambled to collect her legs underneath herself. Groping for the mat she sat up on her knees and draped the thing over her dripping hair like a shawl; feeling a tad ridiculous for doing so once she realized it was a saddle pad.

It had to be. It reeked of horse.

Thunder shook the rafters. The structure around her bowed and flexed with an alarming ease, moaning with an even more disquieting wheeze. Rain and hail hammered the exterior of the building and drilled the tin roof, making one clamor of a racket and muddling the distressed whinnies and snorts of what had to be the horses. The proximity of their panicky hoofs pounding the wet earth intimidated her. It sounded too close, as if they were about to crash through the wall and trample her.

Squinting toward the noise, she couldn't see a thing. What lightening made its way in through the cracks and crevices was her only means of surveying her surroundings. What she could make out wasn't looking too promising.

The rain and hail let up; generating an eerie lull as the intense howl of the wind increased then mutated in to the unnerving clatter of what sounded to be a runway freight train magnified by twenty. Hannah crouched low pulling the thick fleece pad tight around her head. Numb dread skewered her gut with the realization of what that destructive high-pitched demonic drone was. Her entire body became riddled with tremors. She was shaking so violently she found she couldn't steady her own hands.

Not from the sudden drop in the temperature or the chill of being drenched, but from knowing herself what could happen if that twister chose to uproot the barn that she was now trying to hide in.

"Dep-dep-deputy Bowman?" she mustered around the terror clawing at her throat.

When he didn't answer her, Hannah peeked out from underneath the saddle pad, catching glimpses of him with each binding flash. Like an unwilling spectator of some horror flick, she shook her head no as he slid open the barn's massive side door. Under the strobe light of lightening, she spied him as he danced about slapping at the rears of his stock, scattering them from the paddock. The horses readily took off, charging the open gate, instinctively seeking safety in the pasture. Task completed, he then just stood dead center of the muddy pen, face tipped to the violent heavens above.

Hannah opened her mouth to shout at him but then lost her voice to sheer panic when an object smashed up against the exterior of the barn, jarring her stiff with a hard metallic thwack. She winced and, jumping to her feet, prepared to vacate. Deputy Bowman blocked her path detouring her escape. Backing her up and shouting at her to get down, his stern orders were barely audible over the howling roar of the wind.

Hannah obeyed without question. She was more afraid of him. His unyielding growl left her with the distinct impression that he was more upset with her, then for being caught out in this storm. And why shouldn't he be? It was her fault they were both here, now stuck in this barn. She was upset with herself; disappointed. Three short months in Altoona Iowa and she'd already succeeded in making a complete fool of herself. She sure had managed to accomplish that all in one day flat.

Tonight she'd really out done herself

Hannah closed her eyes and prayed the tornado would carry her off, just like it had Dorothy in The Wizard of Oz.

Maybe she could then go to the great Oz himself and beg him for some brains like the Scarecrow had—better yet, some tact. Maybe she'd be better off just living out her humiliation with those cute little munchkins? If she had little red slippers she'd be clicking the heels together, right now, just to get herself out of this mess and take her back home.

Home where? Shenandoah Valley? Harvard Square? Milwaukee? Who was she kidding? There was nowhere to go back to.

But wherever she happened to land, she had never been this….well, promiscuous. Flirted a little—okay a lot, but only when necessary. But, she had never outright thrown herself at any man, especially not a man like Deputy Bowman. And she had not intended on actually kissing him. Well, she'd thought about it, fantasized how it might feel to have that carnal mouth on hers. But that was all. It did not mean she was actually going to do it. Yet, the instant he'd caught her, he was looking and acting like he was going to kiss her himself. She had simply hurried things along by popping onto her tiptoes and pressing her own lips to his.

It was a natural mistake. Hannah frowned. Natural had nothing to do with. It was unprofessional. Not to mention, unethical. Not the best way for a woman in her position to gain credibility, let alone make a name for herself—well, not a good name anyway.

But then he was kissing her back, knocking her socks off with that wonderful mouth of his…yet then just as quickly had rescinded. The man was full of surprises all right. He was utterly confusing. One minute indisposed, the next semi-cordial, raring-to-go; then downright grumpy and yelling at her, no less. All of it done amid seducing her with those incredible lips.

That man was now squatting beside her. Uncomfortable Hannah edged away.

"Are you okay?"

"Just ducky," Hannah snapped, then closed her eyes. She felt sick. Ashamed, she tugged the saddle pad tighter to hide her face. "I'm sorry. I'm just..." *...what?...an impish moron with the relationship IQ of a male Betta? Don't worry about me, just put me back in my case, leave me be, and feed me three pellets a day to keep my fins pretty?*

She clamped her mouth shut. Her teeth were chattering and what else was there to say. Why had she even challenged his intent to walk away? It'd been unwise to have even goaded him. She was foolish for continually playing with fire; for always thinking that next guy might genuinely want to help and with no strings attached; losing her self-respect in the end because she happened to press her luck with all the wrong men.

And when it came right down to it, why would this man be any different? By now, he probably assumed she was some harlot, freely offering herself. And for what? The reward of a little information? Highly unlikely. She wasn't that reckless or stupid...then again, she was here. Guilty as charged; he didn't have to even say it. She'd seen it in those righteous steel gray eyes right after he'd pushed her away like she was some sort of infectious plague that might taint his honorable reputation.

"You're shaking."

"I'm—I'm j-just c-c-cold," Hannah insisted, cringing at the sound of what had to be splintering branches. Or worse, trees being ripped from the earth and tossed about with their roots intact.

Oh dear God. She was going to die in a smelly barn and with a man she didn't even know. A stranger who'd kissed her silly. Hannah shied away when he dropped to his own knees; flinched feeling his large hands capture her shoulders. She wanted to flee. He made her nervous, self-conscious and feeling a bit too vulnerable.

She wasn't so sure what to expect, what to do, or what to even now say to him. *I'm sorry—I didn't mean to give you the wrong impression?* What would be the use of even trying to explain herself, her actions? She already knew what was coming next. It was that same redundant scenario she repetitively found herself in. And why wouldn't he take the liberty? At least, if he did, his amazing mouth could dazzle her mind right off the idea of dying in this storm. And what a way to go! Sense of worth trashed, but at least she'd die content.

Hannah closed her eyes and now prayed that he would kiss her.

Deputy Bowman, however, did not do anything of the sort. He did something that no man had ever done before. He most reverentially gathered her within his powerful arms, gently but securely pulling her snug against his chest; selflessly, using his own body to shelter hers from harm.

Flustered, Hannah was awash with a sense of freefalling. While her body automatically responded to his touch, she understood that this man's sole intention was to now protect her. Relaxing, she was blindsided by an even headier rush. The sense that she was, for once in her life, in the right place. That unattainable desire of belonging, for the moment anyway, was being fulfilled; cradled safe within this stranger's protective embrace.

CHAPTER 7

"That was one hell of a ride," Mark murmured. Holding his breath, he lifted his head to see if there was indeed anything resembling a barn still standing around them.

The structure itself was in one piece—although its roof not so much, from what he could see of the clear night sky above them. Moonlight filtered in through the rupture where the roof itself had been torn back like a lid partially peeled off of a tin can. Rain water dripped from the saturated rafters, hitting the dirt floor in a rhythmic thud-thud-thump-thud.

For the most part the barn itself was still intact. More importantly they were intact.

His released his breath and eased himself off the quivering heap beneath him. Straightening, Mark sat back on his haunches and scanned the gossamer shadows feeling a little dazed, moreover amazed. He wasn't certain how much time had elapsed, most likely fifteen—twenty minutes, tops. Weathering it out, however, had felt more like a life-time; a hair-raising experience he'd rather not relive in this one.

Brushing bits of straw off his arms, he glanced over his visitor who had somehow managed to ball herself in...well, a fetal position beneath him.

"Miss Bryans?" Mark touched the trembling heap when she didn't reply, then tugged slightly on the saddle pad. It had to be smothering her. She gripped it with white-knuckled fists not letting him pull it off. "Miss Bryans, are you all right?"

When she didn't answer, Mark reached for it again but then hesitated seeing her stir.

"Depends," a teeny tiny voice rustled out from underneath the pad, muffled and sounding a bit abashed. "Am I in munchkin land? Or did I make it to Emerald City?"

Mark choked back an unexpected snort. "Ma'am?"

An angst-ridden groan escaped the blanket. "Nevermind."

Sitting up herself, she pulled the saddle pad off leaving her hair a disheveled mess of matted tangles with bits and pieces of straw poking out from every which direction. Despite the mascara streaks staining her cheeks and the disorientated expression she was breathtakingly beautiful bathed in the silvery moonlight.

"Ah...are you okay?"

She glanced herself over then gave him a miserable lopsided frown. "I'm fine, deputy Bowman." Crossing her eyes she studied the piece of straw adorning her nose. "A little drenched, feel and probably look more like a scarecrow, but I'm alive...I think?"

"Amen to that," Mark atoned, then pressed his lips together, shoulders violently boxing.

They were alive all right—both drenched to the marrow, mud spattered, and had straw and dirt clinging to every imaginable inch humanly possible between them. Giving her the once over, unable to now stifle his amusement those repressed snorts mutated into hysterical side-splitting-knee-slapping laughter.

"What's so funny," she demanded, flicking the straw off her nose.

Mark inhaled deep to somehow compose himself. It didn't much help. "Drenched would be an understatement, ma'am."

Glancing him over she pressed her fingers to her lips, trying to repress the beginnings of what suspiciously sounded like snickers. Shoring up her composure, however, her eyes narrowed. "Yeah, well, I may be a drenched scarecrow...but, at least, I'm not a water logged, mud spattered, rolled in the straw brute, Deputy Bowman."

Her remark, the less than understated censure in her voice sobered him. Although he should've taken this opportunity to get to the bottom of that little power play of hers, after surviving the wrath of what had to have been an F-2—if not an F-3—tornado, at present, none of that seem so terribly important to him.

"Ah...I'd say more of a straw covered, sopping wet, spattered with mud, major brute of a jerk. Who deserves to be tarred-n-feathered. But, I've been known to answer to just Mark." Perceptive of her puzzlement, he hesitated then shrugged. "Deputy Bowman sounds so...official. I thought since—" He grimaced, cut short by an aghast bug-eyed face of extreme discord.

"Deputy Bowman, just because," she began already up in arms.

Mark held out his palms cutting her short. "Look, all I meant—" He paused, and to now adjust his own riled tone. Why was it that this woman could rattle his cage, get under his skin, so darn fast? Clearing his throat he directed her attention toward the nonexistent roof above them. "—was, after surviving a near-death experience together, most people in general resort to a first name basis, ma'am. And if I acted like a major brute of a jerk, ah...early, in the pasture—"

"If—?"

He held up one finger stopping her before she could even get started. "My behavior was uncalled for and inappropriate. Please accept my apology, ma'am."

She jerked her eyes off his and fidgeted with the blanket, a scarlet map creeping across her cheeks. "In that case, it's Hannah. I mean, jeez, I feel like some sort of old spinster or something with you always calling me ma'am, or Miss Bryans all the time."

Surveying the barn, Mark wagged his head. "Never meant to imply that you were." Brow knitting, he recoiled slightly when she leaned toward him, then sniffed at the air himself after she did. "What?"

She sat back and burst out laughing.

"What?"

"Um—" Her face scrunched and she pressed her fingers to her mouth. "—that's not mud. I think it might be manure." Snickers leaked out as she flicked a finger at him then covered her mouth again, the snorts escaping her nose.

Mark wiped his jaw, examined the source of her amusement, sniffed it and then groaned. "I'm afraid it's a little of both."

"Um, you missed..." She gulped for air, her laughter ricocheting throughout the barn, a musical melody ensnaring his ears. "...on your chin...and you have..."

Just watching her make fun of him, Mark laughed himself as she now doubled over laughing hysterically while still trying to lift her hand to jab a finger at...well, either that was aimed at his chest, or...? He glanced himself over and gave up guessing. "What?"

"...straw stuck in...in your bellybutton, Mark."

Just hearing her speak his name sent a strange giddy wave of relief tumbling like stray bullet throughout him. As unpredictable as it was to have Miss Bryans here was as random as having had that twister scare the life right out of them both. And near-death experience notwithstanding, he couldn't recall the last time he'd ever felt so alive in the company of a woman.

Sobering, his laughter died out. The idea that he couldn't remember shocked him. He couldn't recall the last time he'd been privileged to have such a beautiful creature grace his domicile with her presence? Let alone, the last time he'd genuinely laughed, rip-snorting-let-loose laughed and had actually benefited from the sound of it; the experience?

Astounded, Mark glanced skyward. *Six years...* Six years was a hell of a long time for any man to detach himself from the simpler joys of life. He gazed at the calm night sky above, somewhat befuddled at the notion that that's exactly what he'd been doing. He'd been stuck in a downward spiral of self-torture; trapped in the limbo of bitter grief and anger. He'd exiled himself as undeserving and unworthy. He'd lost faith in himself, because he could not save the one woman that he would have died for.

With that eye-opening epiphany, he glanced about the quiet barn. It's a wonder he'd been granted this opportunity, to have this woman sitting Indian style across from him now.

Chance, Mark reckoned, watching her pluck straw from her own arms. He wondered what might be possible, if he had the courage to confront the flip side of that coin? Yet, and as surreal as it was, that better half was already working—had kept them both safe from harm, at least. Whether or not everything leading up to this point in time was coincidental, he still wasn't so sure himself.

Looking out past the jagged roof, the net of stars beyond it, Mark searched the heavens. The notion then struck him that maybe somebody up there was trying to tell him it was high-time he move on; while he still had the chance. Time he get on with actually living instead of just going through the motions; live that life to its fullest potential...no limits.

Fair enough...and typical. A faint smile tested his lips. Even in spirit, Elaine would have to resort to using the wrath of Mother Nature to rattle his cage in order to get her point across. On that thought-provoking concept, his gaze resettled on his visitor. Destiny, fate, chance—whatever it was—this beautiful creature seemed to have that same ability herself, and he'd just have to deal with it.

"Well, Hannah, this may not be the Emerald City. But if it's any consolation, I do have to admit...you make an adorably cute scarecrow." He chuckled at her flabbergasted expression and plucked a piece of straw from her hair. "Speaking of, the munchkins will be here bright and early. Reckon I'd best go see if there's a corral left for them to even play in."

"Wh—what?"

"The munchkins, weather permitting, will be here bright and early tomorrow morning."

Pushing himself to his feet, Mark examined a piece of straw. Popping it between his lips he surveyed the rafters, the roof. Despite the destruction, he laughed. He'd forgotten how good it felt to genuinely laugh; to be alive.

"Munchkins...?" she repeated incredulously.

"Yup." Mark glanced down at her then tossed a vague gesture in the general direction of the corral outside. "Can never keep all their names straight, so I just call 'em my munchkins."

"O—oh...you mean kids."

"Yeah. From Wylan Academy. They come out twice a week in the summer to ride the horses."

"Um, isn't that a...well, a juvenile detention center?"

"Yup, sure is. Promised them a rodeo to show off what they've learned at the end of the summer—coming out here gives them an opportunity to see not everything has to be about violence, gangs, or drugs." He shrugged. "Hopefully knowing there's folks still willing to give them a second chance...hell, who knows, it just might keep them on the straight and narrow."

He met her gaze then cleared his throat. "Ah...and it's good exercise for the horses," he made sure to add on a more apathetic note; as if the whole thing hadn't even been his brainchild. Nope, not even working. Busted. His cover was blown. He could tell that just by her more than interested expression.

"Uh...don't take this wrong way or anything, but you actually—"

"They're good kids, for the most part. Just got screwed up along the way, as well as caught," he interjected, then further explained, "If they exhibit good behavior during and also between visits, they're allowed to come out. It also gives me an opportunity to prove to them that not all of us in law enforcement are, well, what they consider to be 'the bad guys'."

Snorting, she stared at him as if what he'd just said was some sort of brainteaser, or worse a joke. And she was now looking unconvinced and more than just skeptical.

"What?"

"I just, well...you don't strike me as—um, nevermind."

Mark eyed her. "What? Mr. Hardnosed by the book can't have—" he hesitated. Aw hell, he'd already exposed his Achilles' heel. Might as well fess-up to it. "—a soft spot for kids?"

"Oh, uh..." Obviously humored, she was once again fighting to contain her giggles. "Um, well...I mean, I just didn't picture you as the type that'd—"

"Like kids?" he asked.

"Well, to be honest, yes."

"Shoot, love 'em to death. Scouts themselves come out every Halloween. Do have to crow, we do us up one righteous haunted house out of the barn you're sitting in right now." Mark laughed, then unthinkingly confessed, "Hell, want to have a dozen of 'em, myself."

A snicker squeaked out. "Now that'd be interesting medical achievement I'd love to witness, Mark."

And there she goes again, ribbing him. Maddened, he

held her now cynical gaze, and felt a snort threaten. He had to admit he was beginning to enjoy her razzing him.

"Ah, I meant I'll simply help rear them." Leaning over he offered his hand. "Don't you want kids?"

When she didn't readily reply or accept his hand, Mark arched a brow watching her dilly-dally; making it a great fuss to pluck the straw off of then fold the saddle pad all while now adamantly doing everything humanly possible to avoid him. Realizing he was the problem, he cleared his throat. Clamping his mouth shut, Mark plain gave up. Just watching her squirm was now making him as jumpy as spit on a hot skillet.

"Um, sure…I guess so…well, someday I mean," she mumbled.

The surge of a thousand volts traveled from his fingertips up his arms to spread throughout his entire body once she interlocked her own fingers with his. Pulling her to her feet they were again inches apart and now staring at each other in an almost too awkward silence.

"You need help with that?" he asked then kicked himself seeing her expression. He'd meant help with the saddle blanket that she'd tucked under her arm. He plain gave up once she jerked her hands out of his, stepped back and glanced about the barn.

"Well…It's getting late. I guess I…," she began.

Clearing his own throat, Mark shoved his hands inside his front pockets. "Yup, reckon," he commented as she herself finished, "should go," leaving a clumsy lull to zing between them.

"Um, I mean, you have chores to finish, and, well, I shouldn't have bothered…" Trailing off caused an even heavier silence of indecision to crackle between them.

Mark studied her, intrigued. She was gnawing on her bottom lip, dodging his gaze, and acting as skittish as a long-tailed tom cat in a roomful of rockers. And for some reason, he had the impression he was the sole rocker.

Maybe he'd pegged this criminal defense attorney all

wrong?

"Have you eaten yet, Hannah?" he surprised even himself by asking.

She looked at him both startled and confused that he'd even ask, then gave him a lopsided frowned. "I haven't even gotten as far as lunch today, deputy—er—Mark, to tell you the truth."

"Reckon you're about as famished as I am then, so might as well stay. It's the least I could do, after——" Mark hesitated, almost grateful for the distraction of the generator grumbling in protest. Kicking-over, a duo of globes flickered on casting the barn in a dim yellow safety glow. "You're more than welcome to come inside, dry off, clean up a bit, and have bite to eat with me," he finished.

"Oh, um—that's okay. I mean it's late and, um, uh, well…?"

Reading her illustrated distrust as she now grappled to make excuses, Mark held up his palms. "Strictly business." Watching her face cloud with question, he then added, "I believe we still have the business of your client, Mr. Holm, to discuss?"

"Oh…um, right. Okay, sure. Drying off would be good and…" Smile vanishing, she paused, sizing him up with that cynical air. "You do know how to cook…right, Mark?"

"Yup." Amused, Mark grinned and nodded. "Hope you like it hot."

Questionable was the profuse blush and the way she jerked her eyes away from his before vacating the barn, and like a bat-out-of-hell without comment. Puzzled, his smile wavered. He stood a moment slightly confused, and then groaned. *Hope you like hot?* Mark wagged his head and, chuckling, started out himself. In afterthought, he paused mid-step and, glancing up through rafters mouthed a silent, "Thank you," then caught a glimpse of a brilliant flash as a falling star streaked across the clear night sky right above him.

Cocking his head in bemused astonishment, Mark stood a moment longer staring up into the vast heavens, eyes searching beyond the net of twinkling diamonds. A faint smile then tipped his lips and closing his eyes he murmured, "Message acknowledged."

A gentle breeze eddied through the waterlogged rafters as if to caress his skin in response. And basking in the sensation, he recalled her smile, her laughter, the very scent of her…but he also knew himself that it was indeed time. Not to ever forget, but time for him to move on; to get on with his own life down here on earth. Time to once again live.

Sighing, Mark smoothed a palm over his crown and surveyed the mangled roof. The storm tossed barn in general. Taking stock of the damage—or lack thereof—he had a sneaky suspicion it was something greater than just chance…rather, someone other than Lady Fate herself, that had been watching over him and his guest tonight.

"Yup," he affirmed aloud. Plucking the shaft of straw out from between his teeth, Mark took one last sweeping glance about the barn, the stars overhead, then whispered, "message received loud and clear," as he headed outside himself.

Mark made his way down the muddy trail that lead to his house. Stopping short behind his guest, his recent carefree mood fluctuated as he too now surveyed the storm tossed landscape—moreover, the tree trunk the size of small tanker which had come to rest across his lane blocking the only exit.

CHAPTER 8

"Shoot...worthless generator. Must've—Ah, sit tight. I'll be right back."

Hannah held in a giggle and automatically nodded. Staying in the entryway, she hugged herself, peering about leaden shadows unable to make out her surroundings. She cringed when the clomp-thud of his boots came to an abrupt halt to be ensued by the attempt to tame a hard curse. Unsuccessful, it hissed past his lips; provoked by what had to have been Mark's kneecap colliding with something solid. His grumbles then waned as a quicker and heavier clomp-thud echoed throughout the vast darkness.

Hannah waited and listened, somewhat amused. Breaking the hushed tick-tock of a clock, a thick Southern drawl of indecipherable mumbles rose above the faint noise of kitchen cupboards opening and closing. Glass clinked. There was a brief delay then a muddled oath. A soft thud escalated in to what held the definite air of a frantic juggle. An outright string of curses ensued as something scattered—ranging in the hundreds—clattering across what sounded like ceramic tiles.

Hannah choked down a snicker. It almost sounded as if he'd dumped a bushel of pick-up-sticks across the floor.

She pressed her fingers to her lips, unable to mute her mounting laughter after hearing the distinct whoosh of a match being struck. Not looking too amused, Mark reappeared, his granite features bathed by the undulating halo of a hurricane lamp, a single red-tipped match jutting from a tight hyphen of displeasure.

"Go ahead. Laugh it up," he mumbled, sending the match bobbing between his lips.

He set the glowing hurricane lantern on a glass topped coffee table fashioned from an antique watering trough. Moving about, striking a handful of matches ablaze one by one via the sole of his boot, Mark bathed his rustic styled ranch house in the flickering glow of candlelight. Hannah took in the airy living room, the high vaulted ceiling. The place was huge but somehow captured the ambiance of a cozy backwoods cabin.

A signature which suited this mysterious Texan transplant well.

"Hang on a sec." Now on a mission, the heavy clomp-thud of his boots faded down a hallway, muffled by plush carpet. "...got a battery powered camp lantern, somewhere?"

Taken aback with the amount of candles he'd already set ablaze, Hannah glanced about. Spellbound, her gaze darted across the partially exposed rafters—support beams—which formed an eloquent arch above the hallway Mark had disappeared down. The craftsmanship of the balcony itself invoke an era of can-can dancers and high-noon showdowns. An intriguing atmosphere which carried her eyes to the shadowy cavity of the loft itself, which from what she could see, appeared to be the master bedroom.

Like the living room, the theme was masculine and rustic. Yet, and just as the rest of the house, it too was softened by a motif which embodied the subtle hint of a feminine presence. A charisma which emanated from every square inch—well of what she could see anyway—of his beautiful house.

Hannah re-evaluated the living room. Antique furnishings rambled together with the more modern design of distressed leather. Plump toss pillows and strategically placed tapestry throws accentuated the room's décor with picturesque wild horse landscapes. A handsome handcrafted wrought-iron-soap-stone wood burning stove squatted center stage. The stout wood-burner itself was flanked by weathered tarnished copper canisters. A few housed the normal fireplace utensils; the others sat atop the stove and about it, catering to thriving Spider plants, meandering Ivy, and Wandering Jews.

More hints of a woman's touch.

That spool of taut longing unraveled and knotted to a tangled ball of distrust. She'd never once considered if there was a significant other—well, not until now that was. A lump of anxiety formed upon recalling their torrid lip-lock. It brought to mind her own track record of getting mixed up with married, and, or, otherwise spoken for men.

Nosy, Hannah toed off her muddy sandals leaving them next to a cushion loaded down by a hoarded treasure trove worth of squeak toys and rawhide chews. Bare feet whispering over the hardwood floor she moved about the room hoping to dispel her recent hunch. Glancing over the unique furnishings seeking clues, she examined a knotty-pine display case built into one of the walls. Dedicated to various out-west-lawman paraphernalia, it was an all-male exhibit of cowboy spurs, sprinkled with an assortment of tarnished and rather authentic looking five pointed sheriff's stars, topped off by one pair of corrupted by age handcuffs. The focal piece itself was flagrantly good-ole-boy male. A glass-encased collector's piece Colt 45 pistol.

An even more pricey and ancient looking Winchester was mounted on the wall above the beautiful handcrafted curio cabinet, as if placed there to guard the assortment of priceless trinkets within it. Knick-knacks which further endorsed the hunch that a woman indeed dwelled within this house. Or had at one point...but had never returned to collect her personal belongings, or mementoes?

Highly unlikely...

Suspicious, Hannah scanned the assortment of porcelain figurines and bronze statues. Most were of horses. But all were clearly a woman's, who by the looks of it wasn't around enough or didn't bother to ever dust her collection of prized trinkets.

Stumped, Hannah searched the room for candid snapshots now needing to dismiss or validate her budding misgivings. She found a grove of stress-treated redwood plaques proclaiming various, and most humorous, Cowboy's Logic slogans. Scanning them she smiled at the simple wisdom each held, more at the idea that Mark Bowman probably lived by that very rationale.

Sighing she made a slow circle and scrutinized the room and was drawn to a far wall graced by large shiny belt-buckles, trophies, ribbons, and a parade of photos. She skimmed the hodgepodge of award buckles and ribbons and then the pictures themselves, a collection of photographs which depicted various rodeo events from bull-breaking to calf-roping. Intrigued, Hannah tipped her head askew and studied an eight by ten of a clump of rather goofy looking men standing together dressed like clowns.

"The guy in the middle there, that's me."

Hannah lurched as his velvet twang buttonholed her eardrum. Preoccupied, she hadn't heard his boots clomping against the varnished hardwood floor. Now however acutely aware of his proximity behind her, she forced herself to focus on the men within the picture itself and examined the dimple-riddled grin amongst the array of colorful smiles.

It couldn't be... "No way," slipped past her lips.

"Yup, 'fraid so," he chuckled.

Unconvinced she squinted at the painted-up face, and

scrutinized those rare but awesome dimples. That cheerful looking man in that funny looking make-up was indeed Deputy Mark Bowman.

"You moonlight as a rodeo clown?" she snorted.

"Ah...we prefer the term, barrel man. But yes, once upon a time, among other things."

"Other things?"

"Uh-huh."

Searching the frames when he didn't elaborate, she scrutinized an arresting eleven-by-thirteen of a bronco rider mid-buck. Fascinated, she studied the awry yet eloquent bend of his carriage, the fierce profile of determination setting his features granite. That was Mark alright on that wild bronco, bareback and in a cloud of dust, much younger and dressed to the nines in what she figured was standard rodeo gear; decked out in spurs and—mercy—rawhide leather chaps. Just staring at the image—the ease he conveyed manipulating that feral charger captured within the photo itself caused her heart to wallop against her ribs.

"Did you stay on?" she whispered in giddy astonishment.

"Yes ma'am. The whole eight seconds and then some," he testified, his rich velvet drawl teeming with immodest pride.

"No way—How?"

"Focus and—"

"Superglue?" she jeered, twirling around.

Confronted by that sexy bronco tamer in the flesh, her laughter snared in her lungs as her own balance teeter-tottered for a jeopardizing split second. Her pulse skidded off track as his strong hands captured her shoulders. Steadying herself, she stared at his carnal mouth, then met his own gaze and became acutely aware of his own indecisiveness after catching the tattletale of desire flicker within those penetrating slate gray orbs of his. She held her breath for a heart pounding few seconds, half thinking that he might actually kiss her; again.

"Superglue...huh. Now, there's a novel idea." Dropping his hands, he stepped back and nodded at the photo itself. "As for the rest of us, determination and a whole lot of faith go a long way. Although, it does help to just stay on and pray you always ride a good horse."

Hannah blinked, disenchanted. Maybe she had just imagined it? Clearing her throat, she crossed her arms. "Are you making fun of the fact that I can't stay on a horse?"

"No, ma'am. Just making a simple observation."

Hannah laughed as an incriminating grin snagged the corners of his mouth. "Is that what happens when you don't ride a good horse?"

"Ma'am?"

Unthinking, she brought her hand up, then stopped herself short and instead pointed a cautious finger at his jaw. "That scar. Is that what happens when you don't ride a good horse?"

Brow knitting, Mark ran his fingertips over his jaw. A bona fide smile then blossomed. "Shoot—This? Nah, this here's what happens when you have yourself a minor disagreement with one extremely p—ah, irritable bull."

When their eyes touched, she smiled charmed by his conscious effort to not outright cuss in front of her. It'd been a long time since a man had treated her like...well, like a lady. It was rather nice. "Um...that doesn't look like a minor disagreement."

"Shoot, this ain't nothing," he declared, now hyped with a dynamism she'd never before witnessed from him. The vibrancy sparkling in his eyes, beaming off his features, downgraded his normal authoritarian veneer as he bragged, "Think that's bad, you oughta see the scar I got when..."

Hannah listened, hypnotized by his Southern drawl. She, however, quickly averted her eyes as he tucked the lantern he'd retrieved under his arm. As he crowed about saving some poor bull rider's hide while barely getting away with his own, he was now working on unbuttoning the fly of his Levi's, and as if to back his story up with proof.

"Oh—um...that's okay. Really. I don't need to see it." Somewhat alarmed, Hannah took half a step back bumping up against the wall; trapped. Mark was either too caught up in telling his tale to hear her protest...or, he just had no stitch of modesty whatsoever when it came to showing who what. Watching him, she assumed it was the first.

Glancing away, she pinned her eyes on the ceiling. She was already aware of what this man had to show. That equipment was blatantly apparent due to those snug fitting rain-drenched Levi's. Just knowing herself that *that* equipment was also fully functional cued a searing blush. And now, out of some stronger sense of pride, he was going to peel off those Levi's to show her some trophy scar marring his hide?

Hannah sneaked another peek; grateful to see he'd paused mid-objective to elaborate on how wide the bull's horns were that'd clipped him in the butt. Oh Lord. She didn't need that tidbit of information. She'd been preoccupied with thinking about his backside for a good portion of the afternoon. Like the rest of him, the man had a mighty fine hinny.

Hannah tore her eyes away. Somewhat amused, she stared at the ceiling. This was the same man who'd arrested her this morning? The one who had yelled at her after kissing her silly in the pasture? The same man who had protected her with his own body; without groping hers?

She sneaked another peek. The man that she was now forced to spend the night with, due to the aftermath of the storm, was once again determined to unfasten those Levi's.

Typical. She had gotten herself in a real pickle. She and her Beemer may have been spared from that twister, but with a tree now blocking this man's gravel drive she had no way of leaving tonight. She wouldn't even be stuck here if Monique hadn't talked her into coming in the first place. Sparks...ha! Thinking about him actually peeling off those Levi's wasn't helping to discourage the fiery arousal smoldering to life inside of her.

"So…I'm starving. What's for dinner, Mark?" Hannah blurted hoping to derail him.

"...sixteen stitches and damn near had..."

"Um...Mark?"

"Huh?"

Hannah covertly watched him from the corner of her eye as he now follow her gaze to the ceiling. Feeling his eyes then rest on her in question, she kept her own pinned on the rafters while jerking her thumb just south of his mid-section.

"Oh...ah—Gotcha."

When he cleared his throat, Hannah chanced a peek, eyes lured by the ribbon of black onyx swirling around his naval enticing her eyes to wander south.

"So, need any help?" Meeting his gaze as he hastily finished refastening the metal buttons of his fly, Hannah squirmed under his tongue-in-cheek expression and clarified, "Um, with dinner…?"

"Actually, I was thinking more on the lines of getting you out of those clothes, first." As her eyes widened with alarm, his own face contorted with the realization that that hadn't quite came out the way he'd intended. "Ah...what I meant was, I was hoping to get you in the shower—aw heck—what I'm trying to say is…shoot." Hanging his head, a feeble snort leaked out. He pinched the bridge of his nose, now mumbling, "Never squat with your spurs on, and be sure to always taste your words before you spit them out."

Hannah pressed her lips together finding it humorous how his drawl thickened whenever he got excited or riled. And, if she didn't know any better, she'd have sworn Mark

Bowman was now blushing. Bringing her fingers to her lips, she strained to hold in her amusement watching him grapple for once. Imposing Mr. Hunky-By-the-Book was noticeably distracted by the gist of what his own comments had insinuated. Better yet, he was now trying to somehow recant it all, while struggling to just make his objective clear and without tagging on any more indecent connotations.

Heaving a sigh, he thrust the camp lantern in her general direction. Hannah took it, noting that he was the one now dodging her own tongue-in-cheek expression.

"Bathroom's down the hall. First door on your left. Towels are in the linen closet. I'll—" Hesitating, he cleared his throat and tossed a nod at the front door. "Ah…I'll just go check on the horses. Finish up chores. Might even take a go at that tree trunk? That should give you enough privacy to get showered and cleaned up."

"Sure, okay." Inspecting the ancient looking lantern, Hannah switched it on to find it indeed worked. She then bit her cheek to inhibit her giggles as he made tracks for the front door. "Uh, Mark? Do you intend for me to wear a bath towel all night?"

"Huh—?" Stopping mid-stride he wheeled toward her as if the question itself was a loaded weapon, then looked more visibly frazzled for having even paused to apparently consider the very suggestion. "Wh—What?"

Hannah crossed her arms, hugging the lantern, fighting to ignore those slate gray orbs now regarding her as if she was only wearing a bath towel. "You know, clothes?"

"Oh…gotcha." Shoving his hands in his front pockets, he inspected the toes of his boots and muttered almost to himself, "Yup…clothes would probably be good, I reckon."

Hannah smiled at his absentminded remark. Although she was thrilled, she was also wary of the powerful attraction zinging between them. How on earth were they supposed to spend an entire evening let alone the night together without… She put the idea out of her mind, and inquired, "So, do you have some clothes that I could borrow, Mark?"

~ ~ ~

Mark stayed outside even after finishing chores and checking on the horses. Which hadn't taken but about fifteen minutes, twenty tops. As the horses grazed peacefully in the shadows of the pasture, he had prowled the length of the veranda peeking inside of his own front windows every few seconds. Thirty-seven years of life experiences—most spent breaking broncos and clowning around with irate bulls, eight of those dedicated to perils of law enforcement—and he was wound up as tight as a charger before its first jaunt. No, he was as tense as the competitor atop that charger awaiting the opportunity to toss him off. Damn, he just as well admit it. He was as eager and as raring to go as a breeding stud right after sniffing out a broodmare. Plain and simple.

Jeez…what the hell was taking her so long? He would have thought by now she'd at least been out of the shower, dressed. Just the idea of her being undressed in his shower triggered images of her all suds up and glistening wet; cued heat to spear his groin, his heart rate to jump, and—despite the chilly breeze—manufactured a coat of perspiration that left him once again drenched.

Mark halted mid-pace and stared at her BMW. What the hell was wrong with him? He was a grown man for crying out loud. A grown man who hadn't been with a woman for…well, six years, now that he thought about it. That's what was wrong with him. And he didn't want to think about it. He had a feeling he was going to have himself a long night ahead just trying to not think about it, all while having this goddess spent the night with him. No, not with him—not even in that sense. She was a criminal defense attorney, and an uninvited guest, who had invaded his private sanctuary…a house now lit solely by candlelight.

How much more cozy and romantic could that get...?

Bracing his palms on the railing, Mark stared up at the heavens and grumbled, "You got me into this mess, so help me out here a little will ya?" Scowling, he resumed his pacing; right after peeking through one of the front windows.

Dinner and details—strictly business...Mark reminded himself. But that was way before he knew a tree would be blocking the lane, let alone that the main generator itself would pick this very night to malfunction. Coincidental happenstance...that he had himself a siren of a defense lawyer as an overnight guest.

He glanced at the Beemer. He'd just steer clear of his guest, and for the rest of the night. It was that simple.

Mark snarled at the stupidity of that idea and halted mid-stride to now stare at the trunk from hell, which he should have been able to remove with a tow chain and his Silverado. Of course, the thing refused to budge. Instead he'd wound up spinning his tires, digging a major rut. Chance... Chances were he'd need to call his neighbor and enlist his help to haul the damn thing off. Better yet, he could jump on Hop-Scotch right now and take a ride over to his neighbor's farm to ask for help. That way maybe he wouldn't be tempted to...

The front door creaking open broke his concentration. Mark pinched the bridge of his nose and tried pulling himself together.

"Um, Mark? I'm done. I mean, if you wanted to use the shower. Oh, but, you might want to wait awhile...I kind of used up all the hot water—sorry."

"Not a problem," he exhaled on lengthy sigh. At the rate his mind was cranking out indecent images and thoughts he'd be needing it cold.

"So...did you have any luck with that tree?"

"Nope," he croaked.

"Oh. Then...well, that's not a problem—I mean, we are both adults. Right?"

Facing her Mark choked on what would have been a reply as his eyes toured the feminine contours filling out his ancient—and now most cherished—Dallas Cowboys football jersey. Yup, they we're both adults all right. Consenting adults. Professionals even. No problems there. But at the present moment, he felt more like a drooling hoodlum in a candy shop casing out the prospective merchandise.

He stared at the faded official Starters patch affixed to the thin material. The thing should have been nonsexual, or so that's what he'd thought when he'd given it to her. But it never looked like that on him. Then again it wasn't about four sizes too big, nor did the V collar dip off his shoulder—*like that*—to expose silky soft flesh. The jersey itself—the one cueing his pulse to quicken and squeeze through his veins—never hung like a baby-doll on him. However, draped on her dainty frame it did, and the hem was just shy of covering those alluring kneecaps.

God bless those Dallas Cowboys...

Speechless, he openly gawked. Apparently she'd forgotten about the sweatpants that he'd also loaned her. Maybe he should've offered her his snowmobile overalls and goose-down parka instead? Powerless to stop himself his gaze swept to her feet, and just to confirm that the same mulberry polish on her fingernails was also on every one of her ten toes. His eyes backtracked, inch by torpid inch, to loiter on that official Starters patch, which was in the same vicinity of the jersey's hemline covering his guest's sensational thighs.

As if able to read his mind she tugged on the hem. The collar slipped off her opposite shoulder and hugging herself only hiked that Starters logo up those glamorous thighs. "Um, your sweatpants, they were too big. So, well, I hope this is okay...? I mean, at least all vital parts are covered. Right?"

Eyelids sliding shut, Mark gulped back an unsteady breath. All vital parts covered...uh-huh. Opening his eyes, she was still there, and he now toyed with idea of just sleeping in his neighbor's barn—with the rest of the animals. He could cozy up with the swine for allowing himself to openly stare.

What the hell had happened to those ingrained manners he so prided himself on?

Opening his mouth to say—something anything—he found his voice had also vanished; just like the blood that was now draining from his brain leaving him woozy and lightheaded. Probably on its way to rescue those missing manners. Manners which were lost down south, somewhere just short of rational logic and now being corrupted by those parts which had no use for logic let alone proper etiquette.

"So, well, it's not a big deal. I mean, it's only until my clothes dry," she added when he didn't respond. He couldn't, he was too busy untangling and reeling in his tongue. "And, well, it's kinda like wearing a...well, a dress—right? So, I don't mind...I mean, if you don't...?"

Mind? Averting his gaze, Mark grunted at the idea and stared helplessly at the fallen tree trunk still blocking his lane. Why should he mind if she doesn't?

"So...um...do you need any help cooking?"

Eyelids sealing shut Mark whimpered inwardly. A goddess was standing on his porch—wearing only a thin football jersey as a dress—asking him if he needed any help cooking. Where's the problem there? The only one he could think of was that he was already cooking—simmering hot—and he wasn't even anywhere near the damn kitchen yet. Opening his eyes once she came up beside him, Mark glanced at her, cautious. So much for that keeping his distance plan.

"Um...I mean, I'd like to help—that is, if you don't mind?" she probed, sounding hesitant due his sudden lack of communication skills, then on a more determined note decided, "No, I insist. It's the least I could do after..." trailing off, she then suddenly inquired, "Hey, when you said hot, does that mean you're gonna wow me with some spicy Tex-Mex dish?"

Correction: a half-naked goddess was insisting that she help him wow her with something spicy hot. Why should he mind that? Hell, what sane man would even object?

Eyelids sliding shut, Mark braced his palms on the railing—mainly for support. For some reason, his knees felt like they might buckle. Forget Tex-Mex, there would be nothing spicy on the menu tonight for them. She was doing a fine job stirring up his appetite for zesty hot dishes all by herself.

Taking a deep breath, Mark simply announced, "We'll be having steaks on the grill."

CHAPTER 9

"So, anyway, you can see why I wanted to discuss this with you in person."

Mark glanced up, mid-chew. Setting his fork and knife aside, he choked down a mouthful and stared at his flame-grilled, half-eaten, sirloin slathered with Tabasco sauce on his plate. For being famished—after digesting the major gist of the information she'd just shared with him—for some reason, he'd lost his appetite.

Mulling it over, he shook his head, incredulous. "You're saying you believe Holm's story? That he was framed? By Jake Bremer?" He barked out a humorless laugh. "The county attorney's own son?"

"After going over the reports, Mark, I feel there just might be some truth to his story. I mean, and no disrespect intended, Jake's own blood alcohol level was point two four, when Holm's was barely over point one."

Mark closed his eyes, nostrils flaring, trying to grasp the idea that in less than an hour this woman was once again grating on his nerves; now trying to discredit his report, questioning his ability to discern the details regarding an arrest he'd executed. Dallas Cowboys baby-doll, or not, she was becoming a major bur under his hospitality saddle.

"How could—" he paused taking a deep breath to adjust his agitated tone. "—an unconscious person get out of a mangled vehicle, let alone move his unconscious buddy to make it look like....Why would he even want to do that?"

"Well, I don't know that yet. That's what I need to investigate."

"Investigate huh?" Mark wagged his head, sat back and crossed his arms. He studied her a long moment. Investigate...*Ha*. "Tell you what I'll save you the trouble. I already did. You can find all the investigative facts and details you need, in my report."

"I'm just saying there may be some truth to his story. I asked around about Jake Bremer myself. And if he was driving, it wouldn't have been the first time he'd done so drunk. And, I'm sorry, but there are quite a few discrepancies concerning the night of the accident itself."

Sorry? She sure the hell didn't sound sorry. Mark stared at her—no, now more like glared at her. Pushing himself away from the table, his chair scraped hard across the floor. Not caring to argue this any farther, he grabbed his plate and went into the kitchen. Scraping the leftovers of his own meal in Casper's dish, he placed his plate in the sink, then went to the fridge and snagged a longneck of Budweiser. Pacing the length of counter he stopped and stared at the blackness of night via the patio's sliding glass door. Needing to create some distance between them, he yanked it open and stepped outside welcoming the coolness of the night breeze.

He needed to mellow out; before he blew a gasket.

Discrepancies... The only discrepancy he could see was that some drunk had gotten behind the wheel, and had done so with no regard to anyone else on the road. He closed his eyes and just to see a flaming Geo materialize with Elaine still trapped inside it. The onslaught of memories, the ghostly images of that ill-fated morning, swelled threatening to send him over the edge.

Twisting off the longneck's cap, Mark took a long healthy swig and flinched back a mouthful of foam. He then turned and, watching through the window, saw his guest fork a piece of grilled broccoli and pop it in her mouth. Like discussing this—no, finding fault in his aptitude to do his own job while implying that he was incompetent—it was no big deal. And why would it be to her? After all, she was only here to get as much information out of him that she could; just to turn it all around and use it against him in court.

"Discrepancies?" he finally asked wandering back inside.

She looked up mid-chew, hastily swallowed, nodded, and gestured with her fork. "Don't you find it strange that Jake wasn't driving himself? I mean, after all, it was his Porsche. If you owned a ride like that, would you even let a friend drive it?"

"Here's a thought—and I'm just tossing them out—maybe he had himself enough sense to know he was too impaired to drive, unlike...oh I don't know, Holm?"

"Come on, we're talking about college students. What frat boy is going to get loaded, and then think: Oh wait, you've had less to drink then me, you better drive dude...? Besides, Holm wasn't even intoxicated enough to be impaired to the point of--"

"Wasn't that intoxicated—? He was point one two—let alone under age. Zero tolerance, ring any bells for you?"

"I'm just saying what if."

"There are no what ifs. It don't matter how much he had. He was guilty the second he decided to get behind the wheel of a two-ton chunk of metal and... You know what, it doesn't even matter. You consciously drink-n'-drive, you're guilty of premeditated homicide in my book. Plain and simple."

"That sounds pretty black and white, even for a deputy,

Mark."

"Tell that to the victims—Their families," he spat before drowning his irritation with another gulp of Bud.

"But, my client's never been picked up for—well, for anything—before this, in his life. My God, he's only nineteen, Mark. He has his whole life ahead of him. I just can't see how you can judge—"

"Yeah, and so'd that young lady he plowed into. What about her life?"

"All I'm saying is none of it makes sense. Chaz's injuries don't even correspond with that of someone who was driving. Who knows? Might find something to run with once I go over the medical records, and—" Startled surprise washed over her face. Snapping her mouth shut, she looked away, and as if she hadn't meant to disclose those details.

So that was the backbone of her litigation? She was going to use medical records to try and get her client's case dismissed? What a crock.

Mark watched her push bits of food around her plate, feeling the resentment, the animosity, simmering just below the surface of his skin. Taking a long pull of Bud, he paused mid-swallow once their eyes locked. He was almost afraid to ask, "Medical records?"

She considered him a moment, then tossed her hands up and confessed, "It's a stretch, but I think the medical records themselves might shed some light on who was actually driving that night. Chaz said Jake's own face was all tore up due to the deployment of the airbag, and while he only suffered minor bumps and scrapes--most likely from his forehead hitting the windshield...? Neither of them were wearing seatbelts. And he said..."

Mark stared at her as she talked. Zoning out at the mention of the airbag, the very word had triggered a slow motion time warp of tangible images, memories. *What took you so long, Cowboy?*...snagged on a continuous loop within his mind and he was blindsided by the scent of the gas fumes, heard the snapping sizzle of sparks...saw the spider-webbed windshield, the Geo with its hood crunched beyond recognition...the flames meandering their way toward Elaine who was trapped...

The entire scene played out then hit automatic rerun to consume and haunt his vision. His fingers flexed, recalling how he'd franticly fought with the mangled door handle, then the faulty fire extinguisher itself. The sound of it deploying; of it quickly fizzling out. His muscles flinched involuntarily, cued by the phantom explosion. And isolated within that roaring inferno came the ungodly sound of her screams...

"Mark? Are you okay?"

Blinking, Mark focused on the voice, then the licking flames of the candles that he'd set on the table himself. Rattled, he honed in on the strawberry blond locks, the angelical features, and he saw a woman who was now staring at him in more than curious question.

"Huh? Yeah...I—" Clearing his throat, he pinched the bridge of his nose, and then rubbed the fragments of what use to be just night terrors from his eyes. Taking a long pull off his Bud, he realized his hand was trembling. He clenched the bottle white-knuckled hoping to make the tremors stop. "I'm fine."

"Are you sure? I mean, 'cause you—"

"I'm fine!" he growled, then immediately kicked himself.

Her lips formed a soft O of start and, reading her wounded expression, Mark grimaced. Closing his eyes he pinched the bridge of his nose and had to count to ten; powerless to neutralize the aggression buzzing like a disturbed swarm of hornets throughout him. The insistent tick of the kitchen clock echoed against the heavy stillness as the seconds slipped past. The sound grated on his nerves and was amplified by the dripping faucet.

Tick—dribble—tock-tick. Tick—dribble—tock-tick.

He glanced at the clock. *Six years...*

What took you so long, Cowboy?...chased throughout his mind a barely audible whisper. *Tick—dribble—tock*... His eyelids sealed shut but he was unable to block out the grizzly mirage. Sweat pebbled and trickled down his temple, his spine. Why was it so damn hot in here? Maybe that tick-dribble-tock wasn't the clock at all? Maybe it was his own internal fuse picking off the seconds before he hit total meltdown and blew? A sigh escaped at the last thought. If he did blow, maybe then the dark void of sorrow clutching his heart, his soul, would finally lessen.

"Um...are you sure you're okay, Mark? I mean 'cause you look a little—"

"It's been a long day, is all." He flicked a glance in her general direction to be confronted by an expression which looked a whole lot like valid concern.

The notion it was, threw him.

"So, would you agree then?"

Mark stared at her blankly, having no recollection of what they'd even been discussing. "Agree?" he asked carefully.

"That the discrepancies I've found, deserve a thorough investigation."

Her remark hit him square in the gut and defragged his stupor. Her persistence to pursue the issue, question his judgment—by doing so also ridicule his professional aptitude—snapped at his mentality like a bullwhip. The idea she wouldn't let it go, degraded his social skills and re-stoked his anger.

"Your client was driving under the influence. Hit her head on—Elaine never had a chance. I was there—I know what happened. End of discussion!" His wrath shattered the atmosphere and generated a more profound silence, leaving a queer ambiguity within its wake. Pinching the bridge of his nose a soft oath eluded him realizing why. Feeling the mounting tension, he felt that meltdown was beyond imminent.

"Um...are we talking about the same case, Mark?"

"Sure," he croaked. Eyelids sliding shut he increased the pressure on the bridge of his nose. *Jesus*...Mark grimaced and hoped to pass off his glaring slip-up with a blasé shrug. Once their eyes met he stared at her for a brief, but dangerously distressed second, and felt like a wounded animal trapped within its death crate. He cleared his throat and managed, "Yeah. Yeah we are."

Tick—tock—drip...tick—dribble—tock—tick...echoed through the silence as he stared at her trying to pretend there was nothing at all wrong with what he'd said. By the looks of it she wasn't buying any of it.

"No. You said, if I'm not mistaken, Elaine never had a chance...?"

He tossed a hand in disgusted resignation, mentality teetering in a steep free-fall as grief reared its ugly head, trying to claw and kick its way out from within him. "It's late. I suggest we call it a night and hit the sack."

"Excuse me?"

He stared at her hard, not appeasing her by correcting any misconstrued connotations. Maybe unconsciously he'd meant just that? Them, together, hitting the sack. Another minute passed, prickling with the frostiness of doubt.

"What about the time frame?" she persisted concluding the painful silence.

Mark snarled, jaw muscle flexing. "What time frame?"

"The time frame between the first responders, as well as you, arriving at the scene and the time the accident itself occurred. It's—" she began, her own voice rising with a growing hostility which was beginning to mimic his.

"What the hell would that matter? Some accidents go unreported for hours, days, weeks, before—"

"Who knows? Did anyone check the cell phone records?"

"Oh, this one's gotta be good," he howled on an unbalanced snort. "For what?"

"Maybe once Jake came to and realized what he'd

done, he called daddy?"

So there it was. She actually believed her client's own story? Why should that even surprise him? Why wouldn't a defense lawyer scheme up conspiracies to help get her client off? Possibly use it to launch her career? Destroy the pillars of their tight-knit community for juicy headlines that could gain her public attention; notoriety even. After all was said and done she'd probably take her win—if she won—and deport; transfer to some big inner city and land herself in some fancy law firm to rake in the big bucks. Sleep like a baby in some posh penthouse after an easy day at the office representing the riffraff who could afford to pay the high price it cost to weasel their way out of due justice.

The idea repulsed him, but he had to ask, "And daddy's gonna do what?"

"Rumor has it, coincidently, daddy's conveniently used his clout as county attorney, and more than a few times mind you, to get his son out of a whole lot less in the past. Why would this be any different?"

"You're making some pretty strong allegations there, Hannah," Mark warned.

"I've only been here—what, three short months?—and I already know who the kid is without ever being properly introduced. And you being a deputy sheriff, Mark, cannot stand there and tell me that Jake Bremer isn't a household name around here."

"What anyone says or even thinks around the water cooler, is hearsay. You go around spouting off in public like that, and you'd better bet you'll be brought up on slander charges."

"Well maybe it's about time somebody started asking questions. Did anyone interview him?"

"You lawyers never cease to amaze me," he snarled half under his breath then, tipping his longneck in an almost departing toast, cut, "Lady, with an attitude like that...might as well sell that misfortune of yours and flip that pretty little tail right back to wherever it is barracudas, like you, swim."

~ ~ ~

Hannah gaped at him, thrown by his callous tone, the cankerous expression, those piercing gunmetal eyes fierce with hatred and condemning her without justification. Tearing her gaze off his, she stared at her plate and told herself it did not matter what he thought. This man's opinion of her did not count in the scope of things. The only assessment she needed from him was concerning the night of her client's collision. Which, it was now evident Mark Bowman only held one viewpoint. His.

In all truth, it was the only reason she was even here. And she had to once again remind herself of that. She hadn't dropped by looking to make sparks—well okay, maybe hoping to while investigating her client's arrest. But she had not expected to be stuck here overnight with this man. A man who had knocked her senseless with just a kiss then protected her during that storm. A man who wasn't being so very generous or polite anymore. One, it also appeared, who didn't want to further discuss this. He'd made that crystal clear by exiting to the patio before she could even think to refute his cruel remarks.

Dropping her fork, Hannah stared at her steak. Maybe she should move back to Wisconsin? Why? To hook up with the good old gang, who'd laughed her right out the office? To contend with Mr. Cole Peyton himself? The man who'd wooed her then had turned on her like the true barracuda that he was?

All those years of hard work abandoned because of Cole Peyton. Which was just as well because, unlike Cole Peyton, she couldn't stomach representing the rich slime who swindled their way through the bylaws by purchasing favors and paying off judges just to protect their corrupt hides from real justice. She had chosen criminal law to defend the innocent, not the wealthy misfits. She'd made it a personal vow to represent the poor souls who'd out of happenstance had found themselves caught up in a legal snare. Those, however, were few and far between. Everyone had a story, claimed to be innocent. The majority of clients she'd thus far represented had been guilty.

But this case was different. She'd sensed that Chaz Holm was telling the truth. Now, all she had to do was come up with the proof. Tall order, when she couldn't even prove wrong Cole Peyton's own twisted allegations against her. Some defense lawyer she was.

Hannah picked herself up as well as her plate. Glancing around for a trashcan she then simply scraped it clean over the dog dish. Placing it, and the utensils, in the sink she then stared out the window. Hugging herself, she gnawed on her bottom lip and contemplating the man with his back half to her, face cloaked by the shadow of night.

Something had gotten him riled. But what? She had a hunch it had something to do with the woman he'd unintentionally mentioned. She wasn't too sure of the reasons, but she'd been left with the distinct impression that he hadn't been referring to her own client's case.

CHAPTER 10

After a couple of minutes, Hannah slid the door open and joined Mark outside, taking refuge on the opposite side of the patio; as restless as a feather weight boxer awaiting her next round with a heavy weight contender. When he didn't acknowledge her presence, she hugged herself and studied his profile bathed in the silvery moonlight. Jaw muscle flexing, ignoring her, he continued to gaze out across the shadowy outline of what looked to be another grazing pasture.

That same heady rush assailed her as her eyes swept down his masculine frame. How could she feel such a strong attraction towards this man? She'd only met him this morning when he'd hauled her in. She should've resented that. Yet for some odd reason she felt...well, that she could somewhat relate to him. As if his secluded lifestyle—which was equivalent to her pathetic existence— somehow linked them. And after that kiss, surviving that twister, not to mention having had him protect her, she couldn't help but to feel...well, a bond.

She knew it was foolish, but she wanted to know more about the real man behind that uncompromising veneer and those analytical, sometimes pitiless, always guarded slate gray eyes. The man who'd emerged from his bathroom looking comfortably at home barefoot, not bothering to button his shirt. The one who appeared approachable; at ease with himself. That was, until he remembered he had company.

At first glance he'd reverted back to that aloof, introverted Spartan. During the course of preparing their dinner he'd gradually relaxed. She'd even gotten him to crow more about his rodeo days. He'd become less guarded, had eased back into that, well, that friendlier person that she'd been introduced to in the barn. The one who'd impulsively plucked a piece of straw from her hair and had flattered her by saying she made an adorable scarecrow. The man who gave down-on-their-luck kids second chances; the one who had professed that he too someday wanted to have a dozen munchkins himself.

She liked that man. That's the Mark Bowman she wanted to learn more about.

Hannah wondered what had happened to that person as she studied the bottle of Budweiser dangling from in between his fingertips. At present, there was a volatile aura that emanated off his remote expression, reinforced his uncompromising features. It was an inflexible air which suggested this man did not care to be hassled.

She mulled over the idea of going back inside and doing the dishes, but instead focused on the outline of his mouth as he brought the longneck to his lips. That same heady rush once again destabilized her system.

Glancing away, Hannah stared at the grill beside her. The remnants of coals hissed and popped, as their glowing embers were sucked up by the cool breeze swirling in a fiery eddy of heat. The lingering warmth wafted her cheeks, her lips, and the earlier sensation of his torrid mouth loitering against hers hit replay within her head. She was blindsided by the recollection of how his fingers had fisted within her hair, how his palm had found a perfect fit at the small of her back, then ventured underneath the hem of her halter to set fire to her flesh.

Yet he'd recanted, denying her. Voicing his disapproval, he'd then contradicted himself by prolonging their kiss. That had however quickly turned to retaliation; much of her own doing. With just his mouth he'd wreaked havoc on her entire system. At the time, she'd been both frighten and thrilled; rendered speechless and left wanting even more of him.

She knew it was a mistake, their kiss, but couldn't help dwelling over it. That dangerous arousal she'd felt simmering just below the surface of his aggravation had been almost addictive. The instant that aggression had toggled to hazardous lust, he'd had her hooked. She pondered what might have happened if he had not have stopped. Even now, she couldn't seem to shake the sweet ache of longing, the residue of smoldering arousal, that misstep of hers had caused.

My God...one torrid kiss and she was already a junky.

Hannah closed her eyes and attempted to rid herself of the entire incident as she tried to collect her professional mindset. It was ludicrous to continually keep thinking about it. The man was a deputy sheriff, and was also a riddle. She was cop repellent; a competent attorney. She did not need another puzzle in her life. She'd come here, well, foremost in a professional capacity and had no intentions of letting herself get sidetracked by trivial emotions, desires or longings. She had her career, a client, to think about.

"Mark?"

No response. Not even a twitch of that wonderful mouth.

Annoyed, Hannah hugged herself tighter and waited for him to look at her, to at least say something. When he refused to even acknowledge her, she took a deep breath then let a few more seconds lapse. He may be a proud inflexible man, but she could be just as tenacious. She'd be damned if she would let him write her, or her client, off.

"Mark...all I'm saying is what if he—"

"I'm done having this conversation with you."

Hannah stared at him, chafed by his dismissive air. He hadn't even bothered to look at her. "And why is that, Mark?" she quizzed, tone oozing with contempt. "That pride of yours too grand to let you admit that I might be right, might be on to something?"

Still no respond, not even a flinch.

Not looking at her, he drained the longneck then set the bottle itself aside on the railing. Bracing his palms, his eyes searched the fence, the pasture. Hannah followed his gaze, curious. Scanning the shadows she caught sight of a majestic stallion shrouded by the slivery moonlight. Odd was that the stallion was isolated from the rest and—much as its owner—looked unapproachable and daunting.

Hannah eyed him. How dangerous could he be? He was a deputy. "Or, I know, maybe it's you're just too pigheaded to admit you might be wrong; made a mistake even," she plugged away, boldly stepping closer, adding more octane to an already volatile tension.

"Made plenty. Always take full responsibility of those I do make," a low unchecked grumble countered; an unmistakably clear warning that she'd best back-off.

Snubbed, Hannah shored up her courage and took a bolder step toward him, prepared to chisel her way through the iceberg he'd somehow manufactured between them. Her client's future was at stake and she wasn't about to let some high-on-himself deputy shelve the issue without a debate.

Sizing him up, she chose to exploit his code of politeness. "So that's it. You can't even extend the common decency to discuss this case with me?"

"Not unless it's at a formal deposition, ma'am."

So much for that leverage. She hugged herself tighter and needled away with pure spite. "Why bother with one? Sounds like you've already made up your mind, Mark."

"I did my job." Flicking a peremptory glance in her general direction, his gaze then returned to that lone stallion standing in the shadows of the pasture. "And I also recall telling you, I'm done having this conversation."

It wasn't the blow-off, it was his vinegary imperious air which fueled her anger and had her taking an aggressive step closer. "Oh, I get it now. In your all black-an'-white world there are no courts, juries, or the benefit of innocent until proven guilty. Mark Bowman has made his arrest, his investigation, and his ruling. So forget all about due process, rights or justice. Just lock 'em all up and—"

"Justice...*justice*—?" He wheeled on her, nostrils flared, a hard snarl splitting the hostility setting his features granite. Alarmed, Hannah blundered backwards as he advanced pinning her against the house. "Lady, it's people like you who get drunks like Mr. Graters off—just so he could go out, get all tanked up again, and kill my fiancée!" Feral eyes trapping hers, his heated growl eroded to a disquieting wheeze, "So you tell me where the goddamn justice is in that..."

Hannah stared at him, saucer-eyed, mouth a mute O. "It's, it's Holm...my, my client's name is Holm," she managed to croak out on a skimpy whisper, not knowing what else to say in reply.

Drawing back slightly, he cocked his head and squinted at her; almost perplexed. As the awareness of his actions washed over his features—calming the flash of rage, decelerating the abrasiveness of his physical aggression— his body relaxed, sandwiching her between his and the rough wood plank exterior of the house. Staring down at her, something else ignited eclipsing the dying fury within his eyes as they zeroed in on her mouth.

Hannah held her breath thinking he might actually kiss her. She toyed with the idea of just kissing him herself as his erratic breathing bathed her lips. She released the idea as well as the oxygen swelling her lungs and sagged once he backed-off, putting more than just a good few feet between them. Speechless, she watched as he pushed a trembling hand through his hair.

A soft curse slipped past his lips as he came to grips with his reaction. "I'm sorry," he then murmured before disappearing inside of the house.

Hannah slumped against the house. Baffled, she labored to stop the tremors gripping her limbs and fought to regulate her own rutted breath. She glanced at the open patio door trying to digest the brunt of his outburst; the significance of it. Closing her eyes she covered her mouth as his words replayed within her head. Battling a pang of nausea once the full weight of his words sank in, "Oh my dear god," slipped through her fingertips.

She stayed outside hoping the cool night breeze might deaden the trauma, then took a deep breath and cautiously crept through the kitchen. Scanning the overcast living room fluctuating with shimmering candlelight she found Mark seated on the edge of the massive leather couch. Elbows planted on his knees, his face was concealed, cradled within his hands.

"I...well, I...Jeez, Mark, if I'd..." *What? Known about, well that, I might not have pressed the issue?* Hannah closed her eyes to collect her composure, her thoughts. My God, this was way beyond open-mouth-insert-foot and tickle tonsils. "I'm sorry," she at last said. It was all she could say.

"It's not your fault," he murmured not looking up, "...it's mine."

Brow knitting, Hannah edged her way into the living room. "Why...? Why would it be your fault, Mark?" she asked carefully, her own voice as hushed as his.

Glancing up, he shook his head, a mournful laugh escaping him. "I was just passing through this dinky little town; working the rodeo circuit; just going from one event to another riding out my eight seconds, entertaining the crowds..."

As he spoke, his voice became a detached and distant whisper. Disclosing fragments, the bits and pieces of his life he looked a decade away. When he paused, Hannah took another few steps toward him curious to learn about his past, his own life experiences. Yet, considering what she now knew—what he was himself building up to, it left her a little uncomfortable and not wanting all the details.

"Mark, you don't need to—"

"Elaine, well, she was one of the vets that—See, when we came to town we had us an injured horse and she… Shoot, I was so smitten the first time I laid eyes on her, told her I'd trade it all if…" Trailing off a faint melancholy smile traced across his lips and he choked on a grief stricken laugh of recollection.

"She thought I was some sort of a crazy cuss, of course. Told me she didn't have time for full-of-themselves-sweet-talking cowboys. Said I'd just be wooing somebody else come the next stop, 'cause I'd never give up the thrill of the rodeo. And I actually reckoned she was right…'cause, it's sort of an adrenaline rush—once it grabs you, gets in your blood and doesn't let up. And just like she predicted, I was gone, had to finish out the circuit…"

A peculiar quietness settled when he glanced over his proud wall, silently reminiscing. "Once the dust settled and my crew headed back home to Texas, I found myself here."

Touched by such a hopelessly romantic tale, Hannah let her own gaze pass over the photos, the ribbons, the collection of belt-buckles and trophies. Achievements, a life's pursuit, all forfeited at the spur-of-the-moment on a chance encounter. A chance at the promise of love.

"So did she—?" Hannah began, and then cut herself short.

It was a stupid question. It was obvious the woman had. He'd chanced it all to prove his admiration and had given it all up to be with one woman. He was rewarded her love. That same fate had then dealt him a cruel hand; one which played out to a less than happy-ever-after ending.

Chance... She glanced at the grandfather clock nestled in the far corner, watched its lazy pendulum swinging off the seconds and wonder what it might be like to have a man give it all up for her. Risk chance just to be with her, win her heart over and to love her back.

"It was a little over six years ago, just after Thanksgiving," from out of nowhere his voice shattered the stillness, snapping her full attention back to him. "Shoot, guys razzed me the entire shift 'cause I couldn't concentrate on what the hell I was doing half the night...just couldn't wait to get home....was going to propose the minute I...

"But the weather, it was—and we just had so many damn cars in the ditch...then the call came over the radio—I was already off, half way home," his face pinched as if none of it made any logical sense to him. "A ten-eighty, four miles south of the truck stop—was north of it myself, but knew it'd take first responders too long to..."

"Mark, you really don't— " Cut off as he continued, Hannah stood silent now forced to listen as he recounted each and every detail of what sounded to be a horrific scene.

She wanted to stop him. But it was clear he needed to purge. And, for some reason, share this with her. As he spoke about the accident, she inched toward him then paused mid-step once he looked up. The lost expression, the torture of torment displacing his features unnerved her.

"You know the first thing she said to me was that she was sorry. *She* was sorry, 'cause the clinic had called, so she was on her way to deliver...she was so damn excited about that colt, she didn't even realize that..." Overcome by grief, he couldn't finish. Eyes wandering toward the kitchen, it was as if he was looking beyond the structure of the house itself. His voice then creaked out a mere whisper crackling with anguish, "I named him, her colt,

No Limits…'cause that's what she always—"

Watching the pain scroll across his face before he hung his head unable to finish, Hannah was compelled to…well, to do something. She couldn't take it—watching him beat himself up over something he'd had no control over. Skirting the coffee table, she knelt in front of him. "Mark, really, you don't have to explain. I understand how hard this must be—"

"I should have been able to—but couldn't, couldn't do a damn thing…not a goddamn thing."

As despair diluted his words to snarled mumbles, Hannah held her breath and took his hands within her own squeezing them gently to show her empathy, her support. "Mark, I don't need to know you to know you did everything humanly possible. You shouldn't—can't hold yourself responsible…it's not healthy."

Lifting his face level to hers his lips parted. A hoarse muddled croak leaked out. Hannah didn't need to hear the words to identify with the depths of this man's suffering. It was articulated by the single tear now tumbling down his cheek.

"Oh, Mark…if I would've—I didn't mean to—" Hannah bit her bottom lip once that solitary tear freefell and splashed onto their adjoined hands. "God—I am so so sorry. I should have never—"

Staring at her, his face knotted, a distraught, "Why?" seeped past his lips.

Hannah stared back, but remained silent. It wasn't a query toward her, nor one to be answered by her. Though his eyes were still fixed on hers, she could tell he was a million eons away reliving that one fatal intersection in time. Rehashing, trying to rework the events, searching the depths of his mind seeking the key that would unlock that why. A simple question. A question which had no logical explanation. An accidental chance of fate.

Still, it was unsettling to see this strong proud man reduced to nothing by a mere memory, cut to the core by one terrible moment from his life. Lord knew she had her own baggage, but nothing—*nothing*, could compare to what this man must have had gone through in those seconds of helpless horror not being able to save the one woman he'd devoted his own life to. A woman killed by a repeat offender; senselessly snatched away by a drunk driver.

Hannah felt helpless, her own eyes growing misty as he once again hung his head. She watched his broad shoulders box as he fought to compose himself and cringed with empathy as that first stifled sob eluded his chest. "Mark, I don't know what—Tell me what to do here—please," she pleaded, her own voice a shaky whisper of panic; both alarmed and distressed that she'd caused this.

When he lifted his face to hers, Hannah was devastated by the varnish of despair glossing his eyes; the kaleidoscope of raw emotion he was powerless to disguise. At the same time, he brought their joined hands to his chest and inconsolably implored, "Make it not hurt," in a meek whisper as rickety as rusted barbed wire while flattening her palm over his heart.

Hannah blinked back the onslaught tears confronted by such a poignant sentiment, sensing how hard voicing that had to have been for him. Just allowing her to see him like this—so vulnerable and broken—she knew was a rare privilege. Not knowing what to say to soothe his pain she did the only thing she could think of. She leaned forward and pressed her lips to his. His entire body lurched. Feeling somewhat foolish she retreated, then froze and held her breath once his trembling hands whispered up the sides of her neck, fingertips ever so delicately capturing her jaw and guiding her own mouth back to his.

Cautiously, he sampled her lips, taking his sweet time with each nibble and peck. Hannah shivered with anticipation as the tip of his tongue apprehensively skimmed the swell of her bottom lip and she willingly opened her mouth beneath his for what became a deliriously leisure experiment. More at ease, his fingertips slipped within her hair, knotting at the nape of her neck to gently angle her head as he shifted forward. His mouth settled, establishing dominance, his tongue now leading hers in a potent, slow seductive dance.

After an endless moment, that lazy waltz ebbed. Not wanting it to end, Hannah snagged his bottom lip playfully between her teeth; enticing him, inviting him to stay for an encore. He willingly obliged, his tongue once again tangling with hers. Her impulsive ploy to prolong that once leisurely kiss, however, had recklessly aroused a more urgent and fevered pitch. She realized that a little too late. Right after he'd effortlessly hoisted her up off the floor and had seated her securely straddling his lap. His agility to do so without once interrupting their blistering smooch scrambled her equilibrium and had her trying to now back-peddle. And before his ingenious tongue, right along with those roaming hands of his, could completely render her silly-senseless.

Teeth clinking against his, Hannah took the spilt-second opportunity and sidled back; awash with bombshell of lucid awareness and conflicting indecision. As seemingly inconsolable as this man had once been, at present, he was now raring to go and was being persuasively proactive about it.

"Mark...we really—"

"Shouldn't do this," he finished on a hoarse throaty sigh of resignation. Dropping his hands, he slouched into the couch and squeezed his eyes shut. "Sorry. I...ah, well it's just..." Lips crimping in embarrassment, a heavy breath escaped the depths his chest. "Shoot. In all honesty I reckon after six years, I'm a bit rusty...ah, with stuff of this nature."

Rusty? Hannah blinked in astonishment. Rusty was not the word that came to mind. She was more shocked at his confession. Six years? The idea touched a bittersweet cord within her and spoke volumes of this man's sense of fidelity, of his devotion. Longing stirred at the concept; at the very idea that he'd divulged such painfully private information to her. He'd exposed a piece of himself, his life, had bared to her his vulnerability. Wanting to share with him, offer him something in return—without thinking twice about it, Hannah pulled the jersey up over her head and free of her arms, then sat silently atop his lap, holding her breath.

Stock still, a soft oath eluded his lips as that sexy eyebrow arched in traumatized question. "If I were you, I'd put that jersey back on. Right about now, would be good, Miss Bryans," he advised on an unsteady and dangerously low breath.

Rebellious, Hannah leaned forward and sought out his mouth. Pausing mid-kiss, withdrawing a mere hair-breadth in order to gage her effectiveness, she smiled once he piped up, voice huskily suggesting, "You really need to stop doing that."

Selfish as it was, Hannah was thrilled to have such an influence on him. She didn't want to stop. She wanted to feel, to once again experience that dangerous desire she'd felt when he'd kissed her in the pasture; wanted to feel that sense of belonging she'd discovered within the barn afterward; wanted so badly to somehow understand for herself what it might be like to actually be with such a devoted man and what it might feel like to be loved by him…even if that was all only for pretend.

Defiant, she kissed him again and then challenged, "I at least get eight seconds, right? Think you can handle it?"

A throaty groan escaped as his mouth recaptured hers, hotly possessive and now with intense purpose. His hands formed to her breasts, thumbs grooming her nipples to achy ripe buds. She sucked at the air once his mouth departed and slid down her throat as he bowed her backwards within his arms. His lips roved, his teasing tongue explored, ravishing her flesh on an insatiable quest. Towed back up just as quickly, his teeth grazed her earlobe. A low throaty drawl buttonholed her eardrum, questioning her intent, her very proposal; now asking her if she thought *she* could handle it. Before she could form words to respond, his mouth was already on hers as his hands set out, fingertips skimming the flatness of her belly, then the flare of her hips and down between her thighs. Trailing along the hemline of her thong, he coaxed the barrier of damp satin aside, parting the seam of her silky soft flesh; cueing her to instantly climax.

Hannah sucked a sharp breath as her body seized-up and could not now fathom how she would even last longer than eight seconds with this man. Slightly embarrassed she hesitated then, with the misguided notion that she could simply return the favor, reached for the metal buttons of his Levi's. Fingers fumbling, his obligingly abetted; expertly liberating the impossible row of metal buttons for her. She tugged—as he himself pushed—at denim, both working urgently in a combined effort to remove the stubborn material far enough out of their way. She felt instant gratification as his muscles jolted and quaked beneath her fingertips; enjoyed his deep groan of satisfaction as she wrapped them around his thick solid length.

Guiding her hands away, he once again took the lead. She tensed in anticipation, and braced her hands on the round of his shoulders as he elevated her hips, hitching her thong far enough aside before lowering her onto him. His mouth once again fused with hers, and Hannah thought for sure she would go insane with the sweet ache of intrusion as he deliberately took his time torpidly filling her inch by succulent inch.

Jostled, she however gasped in objection; uncertain herself why he would be hastily pushing her away; up off of his lap. The hard curse of disgruntlement hissing past his lips confused her more. In unison, the lights flickered on overhead casting the once enchanted candlelit living room in a harsh sixty watt glare; right about the same time the pesky warble of the doorbell registered in her head.

Realizing herself that somebody was at the front door, Hannah expelled a wretched groan and, squeezing her eyes shut, collapsed atop Mark's chest. The insistent doorbell rang yet again, tearing throughout the tranquility of the house; permanently revoking their spur-of-the-moment excursion to unconditional bliss.

Chapter 11

"Power's back," Mark observed, and on a rather disillusioned yet humorous I'll-pretend-this-isn't-happening-if-you-will breath while now staring at the ceiling.

The shrill of the doorbell, cued that old cliché of a being saved by the bell to chase throughout his head. Painfully aroused, Mark was now convinced that lady Fate herself was not playing with a full deck. Staring at the light fixtures, he grunted. A stroke of luck turned calamity... What were the chances of that happening twice in the same blasted night?

"Um…somebody's at your door…?" was mumbled against his shoulder, and now in that same teeny-tiny voice he remembered from earlier in the barn.

"Yup, somebody sure is," he intoned, then winced with the sensation of her squirming against him as she tried to sidle her way off his lap.

The doorbell warbled once again. There was no way he could ignore it. Nor could he ignore Casper's own barking filtering in through the open windows as—whoever it was—gave up on the doorbell to now pound unrelentingly against the door itself. Sighing, Mark lifted his head off the back of the couch to be confronted by a scarlet complexion. Without comment, she scooted further back, now trying to somehow cover herself with her arms, her hands. Fingertips groping a mountain of toss pillows, Mark located the jersey. Averting his eyes, he offered it up. Letting his head hit the back of the couch, he then squeezed his eyes shut as she expediently dressed, and then groaned once she scrambled off his lap just to bolt out of sight down the hall.

"Jesus," he groused under his breath as another round of knuckles banged against the door to be pursued by the bell. Yanking at his jeans, he refastened the buttons one by one muttering, "This had better be good," in disgust, more so after glancing at the clock to realize it was way beyond that bewitching hour of midnight.

Cranking his neck Mark sent the door, the uninvited intruder behind it, an agitated glare—although he was more irritated with himself and somewhat grateful for the interruption. He hadn't had the willpower to stop her. Nor had he wanted to—let alone had he stopped it himself. And that bothered him. He had more than just a gut feeling that Miss Hannah Bryans was not the type of a woman to partake in meaningless acts of random passion with mere strangers. And neither did he.

Mark knew—and however fabulous that was and would have been to finish—they both would have regretted it come morning. They were both professionals, obligated to maintain an impartial working relationship. She was a criminal defense lawyer; her client was a kid that he as a deputy sheriff had arrested. In essence, they were on opposite ends of the legal spectrum. And, as it stood, letting something like *that* happen would be unethical as well as professionally inappropriate.

Another round of knuckles broke his meditation, and was followed by the rattle of the handle being tested. The doorbell barked when the intruder realized the door was locked. Thank God. Half the time it wasn't, if he was at home. Anyone dense enough to walk in without being a personal acquaintance was likely to get themselves attacked by Casper or just plain shot; then asked questions.

Having had unconsciously locked the door, Mark reckoned he was once again indebted to chance.

A muffled, "Mark? Hey man, you alive in there buddy?" announced friend as it seeped through the window over Casper's own playful yaps.

Mark glanced down at himself as he secured the fly of his Levi's. Yup, he was alive all right. Thriving. Painfully aroused, privileged to a sampling of pure heaven, and now left to cope with that ache of dissatisfaction…the greater smart of guilt.

Frustrated, he dropped his head back against the couch and groaned upon recognition of the voice itself. Pal, poker cohort, as well as co-worker, it was deputy James Tippen who was now pounding down his front door. The man had impeccable timing. Even so, Mark remained on the couch for another few minutes to regroup, hoping his comrade might take the hint and give up. Better yet, just go away.

The warble of the doorbell cued him that Tippen planned to stay—at least until he opened the door and told him to go away. It also suggested he best gather his professional bearings, as Tippen would not be visiting at such an hour if it wasn't work related. Or rather, Mark mused, if Tippen valued his life, then it had damn well better be work related.

Unenthusiastic, Mark pushed himself off the couch. Heaving a sigh, he stalked to the door and swung it wide open.

~ ~ ~

After twenty minutes of hiding out in the bathroom, Hannah took a deep breath and hiked the sweatpants Mark had earlier given her up around her hips. Holding the waist secure, she crept down the hall and peeked into the living room almost relieved to find it empty. The drone of a chainsaw kicking over had her edging toward the front window. Careful not to be detected, she pushed the curtain aside and peered outside. A man, dressed in a deputy's uniform was backwashed by high beams of his own squad car as well as the light bar's spotlight. He was busy cutting into the fallen trunk as Mark himself jumped out of the cab of his idling Silverado. The border collie danced about, tail wagging while chasing between his master and the deputy wielding the chainsaw. Ignoring the dog, Mark was himself now busy at the tailgate. He then disappeared around the front of his truck, and lugging what looked to be heavy cumbersome tow chain.

Curious, Hannah watched their production for another few minutes. A wave of relief washed over her, only to be followed by a twinge of rejection at the realization that they were working to remove that fallen tree trunk. She strained to listen, unable to make out what either of them were saying over the idling engine of the Silverado, the buzz of the chainsaw, and Casper's own playful barks.

Yawning, she glanced at the grandfather clock then padded over to the couch. Gnawing on her bottom lip, she stared at the spot where they had been, feeling somewhat disappointed; more ashamed. Sure she could flirt up a storm to get her way. But, she wasn't one to tumble into intimate interactions, let alone sweltering altercations, with any man at the drop of a hat…or, in this particular case, tears of sorrow.

Hugging herself, Hannah frowned and glanced at the front door. She wondered if Mark thought of her as harlot after that little episode of theirs on the couch. Why wouldn't he? She'd freely given herself to him….well, almost. It didn't matter what she felt or thought. She didn't believe in all that fairytale love-at-first-sight crap anyway. It was a crock. Besides, she'd shunned men all together after Cole. After he'd wrecked not only her reputation, but her life; right after he'd taken her heart and minced it in his blender of callous vengeance before running her out of Wisconsin.

Rearranging toss pillows, Hannah flopped, sinking into the plump comfort of the distressed leather. Restless, she thought about changing back into her halter and shorts, but didn't yet want to part with the jersey; as if wearing it somehow linked her to the man who'd loaned it to her. A man that fascinated her, who habitually called her ma'am in that rich velvet drawl…a hot-blooded male that was nerve-racking to figure out, who'd knocked her senseless with just a kiss, scared her straight with one minor outburst of aggression, and then bared the most vulnerable facets of his soul before knocking her loopy with his own wanton abandon. A man who treated her with old fashion respect. One who someday wanted to have a dozen munchkins… How much more prefect could that get?

Hannah gave herself a hard mental shake. The last thing she need was another complication in her life. And, she had a feeling, dancing the two-step with Mark Bowman could be a tricky hobby. What she needed to do was concentrate on her career; build a reputable name for herself. Not be thinking about prospective husbands, let alone having babies. She'd sacrificed everything remotely close to family the day she'd left Shenandoah Valley. So why fret over having one now? Besides she was better off on her own. Yet at thirty-four she could feel that internal clock ticking away, winding down, exiling her to the destiny of becoming an old-maid.

Hannah closed her eyes and expelled a disgusted sigh. Refusing to think about it any further, she instead deliberated over how long it would take them to remove that tree trunk. What seemed like seconds later, she pried open an eyelid then the other, and much in objection and then closed both of them. The soothing twang chanting her name trickled into her brain stirring a volley of sensations and images to merge and loop lazily throughout her mind. Reopening both eyes, Hannah smiled dreamily at the masculine silhouette hovering over her. Eyelids drifting shut, she floated on a current of warm fuzzy bliss, and assured herself that sexy bronco tamer staring down at her was simply a figment of her imagination. It was merely a part of her dream. And she might have believed that, if it hadn't been for the concrete sensation of warm knuckles gently caressing her cheek.

Panicked, Hannah's eyelids flew open to be greeted by a sexy smile and that penetrating slate gray gaze.

"Sorry, didn't mean to startle you."

Rubbing her face, Hannah propped herself on an elbow. "Why…?" Squinting up at him, it took a minute for her to remember why she was here, on his couch. "Nevermind."

"You were sleeping so soundly, I hated to wake you—ah, earlier that is."

Hannah blinked. *Earlier?* Exactly just how long had he been standing there watching her sleep? Worse, watching her drool; listening to her snore? Mortified at the thought, she squeezed her eyes shut. She wasn't even aware how long she'd been asleep herself, or for that matter that she'd even allowed herself to doze off.

A tad embarrassed, Hannah sat up. Trying to kick-start her brain, she yawned hard in an attempt to wake herself up. Her eyes darted about the darkness, trying to adjust to the gossamer moonlight streaming in through the windows. For some reason she recalled candles, and a lot of them.

She tucked her legs underneath herself when Mark parked himself on the opposite end of the couch; facing her, leaving an arm length in between them. In afterthought he then raised that inquisitive eyebrow as if asking if this was okay with her. Hannah shrugged. The heady aroma of *Irish Spring* coupled with the faint sent of freshly applied *Old Spice REDZONE* deodorant invaded her nostrils. She contemplated a rowdy spike of towel-dried onyx; the clean shaven angles of his cheek and jaw.

Groggy, her gaze wandered over his chiseled chest, drifted to a sculpted abdomen and trailed down the thin ribbon of onyx steeping off his navel. Curious, she studied the deteriorated *PROPERTY OF U OF T LONGHORNS* logo of his shorts then stumbled upon the ample prominence corralled in the flimsy nylon fabric. Her gaze abruptly backtracked, confronted by gunmetal orbs; sluggishly hooded eyes belonging to the freshly showered and real comfortable looking male who was, at present, giving her his undivided attention.

"What time is it?" she yawned.

"Almost four."

"*Four*?" Hannah sat up straight. "As in four in the morning?" When he nodded, she slumped against the couch and squeezed her eyes shut. "Why was that deputy beating down your door?" she then heard herself recall out loud on a harder yawn.

The question triggered heat to crawl up her neck. Hannah opened her eyes to a seemingly unaffected stationary slate gray gaze. Blushing, she averted her own, awash with a torrent of sensations. *Teeth glancing her earlobe; his hot mouth sliding down her throat…*what had been interrupted by the deputy beating down his door.

"Tippen? He was just out on patrol. Stopped by to see if I'd survived. Got worried when he saw that tree in the drive."

Hannah hummed a note of accord then yawned once again.

Stretching, Mark extended his legs and propped his feet atop the coffee table, crossing his ankles. Eyes closing, lacing his finger behind his head, he lounged for a moment, then said, "Tippen could worry the warts right off a frog's butt."

Smiling, she studied his profile. Even at idle rest Mark's compelling features retained that inflexible edge. She hummed a questionable note then probed, "I gather he's more a friend than that of just a coworker?"

"Yup. But a true friend doesn't bang your door down after midnight if an unfamiliar vehicle happens to be parked outside your door," seeped past his lips a low drowsy purr.

Hannah bit her bottom lip spying the smile flirt across his mouth. She was aware that Mark was himself now preoccupied; reminiscing. Intrigued, she studied him for a few more seconds then yawned loudly to remind him of her presence; almost laughed aloud when his eyes popped open and his body lurched to attention. Abruptly sitting up, he dropped his feet to the floor. His hangdog expression suggested that he had not intended for that comment to be publicized.

Now the one avoiding her gaze, he looked away and scrubbed his face, yawning, "At any rate, he's a good egg as well as a good buddy of mine."

"Do all your buddies drop by at strange hours of the night?"

Hesitating, he shifted as if to stand but then decided to stay put. After a moment, he informed her, "Tippen, he said that twister flattened a few barns, took out a couple of silos and tore up a mess load of fields. Neighbor of mine, his was one of those fields with a path plowed right through it. So reckon we're both indebted to chance." His eyes finally met hers as he further enlightened, "He stuck around and helped haul off that trunk."

"Oh...so the tree, it's out of the way then?"

"Yes, ma'am. Reckon you're free to saddle up and head out...at your leisure."

Saddle up and head out at my leisure? Was that a roundabout invitation to hang out? Or just a polite way of suggesting she'd over stayed her welcome?

What welcome? She'd intruded upon his privacy, had invaded his residence. She wouldn't even be here if it wasn't for Monique's own suggestion. *Fraternizing...* Hannah frowned at the notion. She'd fraternized with him, alright.

Scrubbing her face with her hands, she told herself she should leave. Yet the idea of having to get up, get dressed, and drive home just to crawl in to bed, alone, left her somewhat depressed. Meeting those stunning slate gray pools, still staring at her in question, an awkward second zinged between them.

"Since you're already here, might as well stay," he suggested, an inkling of a grin snagging his lips. "At least that way, I won't have to cite you for driving on an expired DL, again, and at such an ungodly hour."

If it hadn't been for the sexy eyebrow coupled with those awesome dimples, his display of censure might have seemed valid. Nodding in agreement, an incriminating giggle escaped her. "Yeah, guess you're right."

"Figured as much." Wagging his head a chuckle erupted. He then glanced about, seemingly on edge himself. His gaze then returned to hers, curious. "Does this mean you'll be taking temporary residence on my couch, Hannah?" he probed; in that same sleepy drawl which left the distinct impression that he wasn't necessarily limiting those accommodations to just his couch.

Hannah considered their earlier encounter. She wasn't sure what to say, let alone what to now expect. Maybe she was waiting for Mark himself to invite her up in to that loft? Or maybe she was just letting her imagination run a riot in thinking that's what he'd meant?

When he did nothing, she scanned the living room a little affronted, slightly confused.

Glancing at him, she realized he was expecting an actual answer. "Sure, okay. If it's alright with you, I mean. But just until morning."

Consulting the grandfather clock, his gaze returned to hers. "It is morning."

Hannah groaned at the idea. "Um...I have to be at the office by eight. So, could you wake me in a couple of hours? I mean, so I have enough time to go home and change?"

"My pleasure."

"Thanks. Monique covered my butt yesterday, but if I—" Cutting herself short, she shook her head. "Nevermind."

Studying her a moment, his lips parted then twitched to a crimp; almost as if he'd meant to say something but had then decided to keep those thoughts private. Releasing a heavy sigh, he abruptly rose. Anticipation wound within her as tight as a top as he leaned over her. That expectation was then pursued by a rush of awkward embarrassment when he simply snagged the throw blanket off the back of the couch.

Shaking the thing out he draped it over her reverently as if tucking a small child in for the night. "Comfy?"

Hannah stared up at him. At a complete loss she simply nodded. Gnawing on her bottom lip, she froze once he lowered his face to hers. Bypassing her mouth all together, however, he whispered, "Thank you," against the shell her ear before tenderly pressing his lips to her forehead.

Confused, Hannah remained still. No dangerous lust. No wanton abandon. Just a simple peck upon her forehead. It was...well, sweet and romantic. Basking in the aftermath that small gesture had sparked, she knew— right then and there—that she was hooked. Before she could even form the words to ask him why he was thanking her, or to even request that he now stay with her, he was gone.

Puzzled, Hannah propped herself up on an elbow. Detecting the distinct creak of stairs, her eyes followed the sound up to the loft. A door sighed shut with a retiring creak and, scanning the murky shadows, she knew that Mark had resigned himself to solitude for the remainder of their sleep-over. Sitting all the way up, the prick of searing tears welled at feeling that slight tug of rejection. Squeezing her eyes tight, she now felt utterly moronic.

Mark Bowman had secluded himself not due to being a

gentlemen, but out of loyalty; because that broken heart of his was still devoted to another woman.

Pulling a hand through her hair then, bloating her cheeks, she sighed at the idea. At least with oh-by-the-way-I-have-a-wife Cole Peyton, she'd had something tangible to cope with. A real person. But this was....this was...well, different. How on earth was she supposed to contend with a ghost?

Chapter 12

After a long morning of pretrial discovery and conferring with her client, inside a stuffy interrogation room lacking adequate ventilation, Hannah found herself loitering at the Law Enforcement Center. Chit-chatting with one of the station's secretaries, she'd used the excuse that she needed copies of the accident and arrest reports, all the while secretly hoping to run into Mark.

She scowled at the notion as she exited; feeling even more foolish than last night. She now had more copies then need be, and she'd wasted valuable time.

Disappointed, heels clapping against the sunbaked black-top, Hannah headed for her vehicle. Like the LEC, the courthouse's own parking lot was nearly deserted. Her own Beemer sat alone on the outskirts; looking like a forlorn straggler left behind by the hurry-up-and-go-get-some-lunch rush. Her stomach grumbled in protest with the thought. Ignoring it, her gaze passed over the gathering of squad cars parked at the opposite end of the lot. She contemplated the dormant light bars, the iridescent emblems reflecting shimmering mirages in the blaze of a merciless afternoon sun. Cupping her brow, Hannah searched the rear bumpers, perusing the assemblage of call tags.

Altoona six was absent from the line-up. He had to be still out on patrol. He hadn't been amongst the officers or deputies who'd abandoned their cruisers to crash the dispatcher's station and lark about. Nor had he been amongst the uniforms playing jab-ass in the hall as she'd made her own way out.

Hannah glanced backwards at the building itself. She wasn't sure herself what she'd been counting on? For him to call? Stop by her office? Perhaps leave a message? It wasn't like they'd exchanged numbers. Nor had he promised her anything of the sort. The only promise that he had made had been to wake her up in a couple of hours.

My pleasure… That pleasure had never been fulfilled.

Too restless to sleep and not wanting to wake him— more leery to venture up in to that loft to let him know that she'd decided on leaving—she'd gotten dressed and had driven home.

She hadn't seen, let alone spoken to Mark since fleeing his couch.

Her left eyelid began its customary tic. She'd see him soon enough. Monique had already begun scheduling the necessary pretrial depositions. All, of which, would begin next week. Deputy Mark Bowman had been penciled in for ten Monday morning.

Heels pausing mid-clap, Hannah scowled. How on earth was she supposed to act, speak to him even, in a professional capacity after that episode on his couch? How was she expected to behave uninterested when what they'd shared kept assailing her with loitering wants? Hannah squeezed her eyes tight and glowered. She didn't need the chronic visuals--the lingering sensations--that kept cropping up to scatter her thoughts every time she thought about that sweltering incident in the pasture, let alone their blistering encounter on his couch.

She'd just have to put it behind her. It was quite obvious that he had, due to his lack of communication. He could have at least phoned her to see why she'd left in the first place. But he hadn't, which was fine with her. He was a deputy. And she was...well, cop repellent. But she couldn't repel the memory, the sensation of his mouth on hers. Preoccupied for most of the morning, she'd found herself so consumed that she couldn't even concentrate on interviewing her client, let alone formulating a plausible defense for him.

Hannah consulted her watch and then groaned at the trill of her cell-phone. She had half a mind to ignore it and let whomever it was leave a message. In afterthought, a rush of giddy excitement had her frantically fishing it out of her purse. She glanced at the caller ID somewhat expectant. Unavailable Number. Almost annoyed, she flipped it open as she walked, answering with a curt, "Bryans."

A bout of eerie static gave birth to an sinister voice, declaring, "Curiosity killed the cat."

"What?" Pausing mid-stride, Hannah readjusted the slim phone, half sandwiching it between her shoulder and ear so she could glance about the lot. "Hello? Who is this?"

Dead air mocked her. The phone then jingled in response; a pleasant little chime which alerted her to the fact that the caller had already hung up. Snapping her phone shut, Hannah glanced backwards toward the building she'd just exited, then toward the neighboring courthouse itself. She couldn't shake the tangible sensation of eyes now upon her. Refusing to display any outward distress, especially to such a childish message, she flipped open her cell phone and hit speed dial—praying that her secretary hadn't abandoned her post in search of lunch yet.

"Brecker, Haley and Merit, Monique speaking, how may I direct you?"

"Good, you're still there," Hannah gushed in a rush of relief.

"Hannah? My Lord, girl…what's wrong?"

"Oh, um…nothing." Wedging the slim Motorola between her shoulder and ear, Hannah debated whether to tell Monique about the call. Just hearing her friendly voice had been calming enough. "Well, I…I just need your expertise again, is all," she fibbed.

Monique's cool, genial, laugh filtered out of the phone, penetrating the afternoon heat. "Don't tell me you're down at the LEC again?"

"Does standing in the parking lot count?"

"What?"

"Nevermind."

"Oki-dokie…? What you need, girlfriend?"

Hannah opened her mouth then frowned. She hadn't actually needed anything. Stalling, she found her keys and unlocked the door. Tossing both her purse and briefcase on the passenger seat, she paused to survey the uniform windows of the courthouse. Whether the person behind that ominous voice realized it, or not, the threat itself had only furthered her assumptions. And she'd be damned if she was going to let some crank caller discourage her from acquiring justice. Staring at the courthouse, she would bet the bank itself on who had been behind that prank call.

"Hannah? You still there?" Monique asked.

"Yeah, I'm here. Sorry. Guess I'm a little preoccupied." Hannah sighed and ducked inside the safety of her vehicle and started the engine, eyes once again roaming the windows of the courthouse. Not mentioning the crank call, she impulsively opted to pursue her latest hunch. "Do you have the address for the Bremer residence handy?"

~ ~ ~

Lost in thought, Mark swung into the LEC's lot alongside an effective demonstration that announced to the public it was indeed hot-- neglected prowlers. Five-fifty-five and the majority of the dayshift were by now inside mingling with nightshift, both parties taking shelter in the air conditioned climate of the patrol room. Half were itching to go home; the other half delaying the beginning of their own tours-of-duty. The majority, in all probability, were playing grab-ass, exchanging jokes and larking about while watching the clock or awaiting that first call which would dispatch them out into night.

Mark didn't blame them. He, right along with the rest of his shift, had endured almost twelve hours of ninety plus degrees. The humidity was again at hundred percent. Despite a slow sinking sun, and the benefit of those air-conditioned cruisers notwithstanding, the evening promised to also be a scorcher. After doling out a handful of miscellaneous citations, scattering a congregation of cattle off highway nine, and mediating an unnecessary domestic, he was ready to call it a night himself. The last few minutes of his shift would be dedicated to filing a couple tedious reports which he'd managed to hen-peck out during his shift. He would then gladly hand over the reins to the nightshift that would have the pleasure of patrolling the county's byways.

He glanced at the clock on the dash. Boring and monotonous had permitted his mind to stray. He'd spent the last twelve hours preoccupied and unfocused. Dwelling, those hours of mind-numbing patrol had been spent mulling over the various reasons of why Miss Hannah Bryans had left. No explanation. No farewell. Not even a departing memo. Just up gone, leaving behind an empty couch and a whole lot of confusion. The only trace evidence that she'd even been there was his borrowed sweatpants and football jersey, folded neatly in the bathroom.

Throwing it in park, Mark killed the engine and snarled. Squeezing his eyes shut he ripped off his Ray-Bans and tossed them on the dash. He screwed the heels of his palms into his eye-sockets. Glancing in the rearview mirror a pair of bloodshot orbs stared back.

If he was fatigued, deprived of sleep--even before her and her unexpected visit--he was now destitute and beyond exhausted. And all due to him thinking about her, how her body fit perfectly to his; all the while trying to rationalize those images himself, while also trying to figure out why she'd then just up and left.

Pinching the bridge of his nose his eyelids slid shut. Feeling duped, he grunted.

He wasn't so sure why he was even allowing himself to get so worked up? Maybe it was because he felt she'd gotten exactly what she'd wanted—ammunition to use against him in court. Or maybe it was the lingering memories of her scent, her taste, that sliver of heaven they'd embarked on—if Tippen hadn't interrupted them— that were jamming his brainwaves.

Whatever it was, it was stoking his ill-mood, leaving him grumpy, short-tempered, and—what the hell had Tippen said? Oh, yeah...difficult to deal with, which supposedly made him even more unsociably unreasonable than normal.

"Difficult to deal with..." he grumbled half under his breath.

Scrubbing his face, Mark told himself it didn't matter. He assured himself he'd be better off not knowing the whys. But he couldn't seem to get past it, get her, or why she'd left off of his mind.

It didn't help that Tippen had broadcasted his own visit to the entire night shift. Mainly the detail that he suspected that he'd interrupted something upon arrival. It hadn't taken long for that information to trickle its way throughout the entire office—PD included. That he'd had himself a guest. That that guest was the same criminal defense attorney who was representing Mr. Holm, the kid that he'd arrested. That same guest had also been the very same woman that he'd hauled in himself that very morning for driving on an expired Wisconsin DL.

He'd become the hot topic of the day; had thus far endured remorseless razzing as well as twelve hours of dodging his coworkers' prying attempts to gain all the juicy-locker-room tid-bits. All because Tippen himself lacked the discipline to keep his damn trap shut.

Mark squeezed his eyes tighter and applied more pressure to the bridge of his nose. He blamed himself. He should have never spouted off those three little words— impeccable timing, Tippen—after answering the door. Making matters worse, out of irritation he'd swung the door wide, giving his pal an eyeful of the candlelit living room. Of course Tippen didn't believe all those candles were actually only due the generator not working. Trying to further explain that the power had been restored at the same exact moment that he'd knocked on the door hadn't much helped either.

The man wasn't stupid. His own mounting frustration, his attempt to keep a tight-lip as Tippen badgered him while assisting him with removing that damn tree trunk…that right there is what tipped his buddy off.

Difficult to deal with… Mark snarled at the notion as he recalled the discussion—no, correction, the argument he'd had with Miss Hannah Bryans. That seems pretty black and white…even for a deputy, Mark. However stated, the problem was they had both hit a home run. He was difficult to deal with. And when it came right down to it he was inept to discern past experience from current events; was harshly judgmental when it came to dealing with drunks. And if Miss Bryans, herself, chose to exploit his black-n-white viewpoint in court…

His gut clenched at the very thought.

He'd taken the scene of the accident at face value; had followed procedure to the letter. He'd processed the entire scene accordingly; had thoroughly investigated. But there was little to nothing to investigate. Holm's had been found unconscious behind the wheel. It was a standard OWI with one fatality.

Mark frowned. Nothing was ever standard, or normal, about an unnecessary death.

But what if...? What if Holm had been telling the truth all along? What if Holm was being bullied into taking the wrap?

Regardless of whether Jake Bremer had been the one driving or not, Mark knew himself the objectionable gossip pertaining to their own county attorney's clout wasn't all mere slander. People county wide knew that his kid's golden-boy image was slightly tarnished underneath. Problem was, up until now, nobody had ever had the guts to express, let alone admit, that publicly.

Hannah Bryans did and was.

Her own personal conviction to go above and beyond in search of the truth was beginning to leave him a little off kilter and not so confident of his own discernment. The idea he'd possibly missed something, that was what was churning his gut and turning him inside-out. The possibility that maybe he'd unknowingly overlooked something because of some so-called prejudice, that's what was eating at him now.

Brooding, Mark glanced at the dash clock then snagged his Ray-Bans and jammed them on his face. He cranked over the engine and snatched up the dash mike. It was six o'clock and he was officially done for the day.

"Altoona six to dispatch."

"Go ahead Altoona six."

"I'm—" Clicking off caused a bout of static. Mark glanced between the courthouse and the jail mulling over the possibilities. *What if...?* "Is Bremer's Porsche still in the south impoundment yard?"

"I think so—hold on, I'll call over and check."

Mark eyed the vacant parking lot, the courthouse, the jail. If Jake Bremer had been driving, then he'd have to come up with some pretty substantial evidence to prove it. Reinvestigating also meant risking not only his reputation, but going head-to-head with the county attorney and a mess load of political clout.

"Disregard dispatch. Altoona six is officially ten-forty-two."

"Ten-four. Have a good one," the dispatcher responded, then paused. "Oh, almost forgot. Vicky has a note here for you. You have a deposition scheduled next Monday with a counselor Bryans at ten hundred sharp."

Heat crept up his neck at the mere mention of her name. A barrage of images stirred residual desire back to life. Embarrassed, Mark glanced at the building as if the dispatcher herself could see him right through the brick wall. Scowling, he wagged his head and grunted.

"Roger that. Just leave the note on my desk."

Stowing the dash mike, Mark stared at the courthouse, gaze transferring to the attached jail. He contemplated the tall barbed-wire topped fence for a long moment. Mentality once frayed by past events blurring with current affairs, his perception however was now lucid; all due to the accidental distraction of one woman.

Cursing, Mark threw it in reverse and peeled out of the LEC's parking lot. In search of redemption he headed south; now compelled to do so by a more simplistic law. Human nature.

Chapter 13

Hannah swiped at her brow then, giving up, stabbed her spade into the dirt and peeled off her gardening gloves. She'd spent the majority of the afternoon on a wild goose chase, interviewing friends, family and the acquaintances of Mr. Holm's; all done after visiting with Jake Bremer himself.

The infamous Jake Bremer who adamantly proclaimed he could not remember anything from the accident itself. An Ivy League frat boy who was following in his father's footsteps by majoring in law and home on summer break. A kid that had mulishly professed he didn't really know Chaz Holm all that well. The same Jake Bremer who'd allegedly handed her client the keys to his Porsche. The county attorney's son who had a colorful reputation for frat house parties, public intoxication and recreational drugs, yet mysteriously persevered his golden-boy image by staying just out of reach of the long arm of the law.

"Couldn't, or wouldn't remember?" Hannah posed the question aloud.

Her impromptu visit to the Bremer's estate had only furthered her speculation that Jake Bremer himself had been driving the night of the accident. It had been an informal discussion as well as an ill-natured interview, cut short by the county attorney himself; right after he'd arrived home from an afternoon of golf to find her questioning his golden-boy without proper representation within the privacy of their own house.

House—Ha! The place was a small mansion, an estate of old wealth and stature; one which reeked of old money and of political clout. And after verbally browbeating her, that so-called upstanding, reputable, county attorney had rudely escorted her to the front door himself.

She'd been tossed out like a bag of fetid trash.

Discouraged, she'd wrapped up the remainder of her day by sifting through old case files and going through medical records. Calling it day, she'd gone home with the intentions of unpacking boxes and working on the tedious task of putting everything away. She still needed to finish painting, hang wallpaper and decorate; do something to at least make her new place look and feel more like home.

What she needed to do was go over her client's case with a fine-tooth-comb, not go off on a tangent of procrastinating. Hiding out in her late grandmother's garden—or rather, trying to revamp that haven of tranquility while subjecting herself to mosquitoes large enough to carry her off—only allowed her mind to wander. And there was nothing therapeutic about mulling over a case and finding herself preoccupied with thoughts of Deputy Mark Bowman himself.

That there would be a waste of taxpayer's good money...and of your time...

Hannah considered his comments, then recalled the prank call she'd received. She rose onto her knees and peeked over the hedges toward the house. She hadn't mentioned the crank call to anyone, not even Monique. And although it had left her somewhat unsettled, she was not about to rush inside and pick up the phone and inform the authorities. What would be the use? They would take her information, merely type up her complaint and then file it away and call it due justice.

She frowned at the notion then eyed her poor wilted blooms, their tomb of upturned dirt. Whoever suggested the art of gardening was therapeutic probably didn't mean restoring inner-self by murdering the actual plants themselves. A snort escaped. Biting her lip, she glanced over the dismal flowerbed. She hadn't murdered them. She'd massacred them. At least, and unlike her poor flowers still suffering within their terracotta pots flanking the porch, these here were pretty much put out of their misery.

Hannah pressed her lips together then laughed even harder. Did even finding humor in that mean she should take up a different hobby?

Sighing, she glanced at the house then plucked up the spade and went back to work. If she couldn't repair the usual disorder in her own life, then she could at least try and somehow resuscitate her poor flowers before the setting sun totally gave up on her.

~ ~ ~

Perched on the hood of his cruiser, Mark for the umpteenth time shot a look at the annoying crows circling above him. Then, and as he had done for the past half-hour, crossed his arms and just sat; gnawing down yet another toothpick, waiting for a pile of scrap-metal to supply him with answers. Now that he'd spent the past half-hour brooding, however, he wasn't too sure why he'd driven out here. Or, what it was exactly that he was even supposed to be searching for. Better yet, why he felt so damn obligated to even look? He'd done his part. His job. It was now up to the courts do theirs. All he really had to worry about was appearing in court; give an accurate account of the details.

Details that he wasn't so sure about himself anymore.

He scanned the impoundment lot, gaze straying over the various makes and models of derelict automobiles. Disheartened, he tipped his face toward the sapphire sky and squinted at a torpidly sinking red-orange sphere. Scanning the tinged pink-mango fluff of clouds scattered across the tranquil horizon, he then glared at the circling crows.

Letting his eyelids slide shut, Mark sighed, "Help me out here a little, will ya?"

The crows cawed nosily overhead; Mark grunted. Perhaps they were mocking him for sitting here roasting in the blazing sun; looking much like the miserable mess load of cars surrounding him? Desolate, awaiting liberation…deliverance.

Caw—Caw—Caw…

Annoyed, Mark reopened his eyes. His face contorted and, cocking his head, he stared at a black crow the size of a cat; the same crow that was now eyeing him from its roost on the crunched hood of Jake Bremer's Porsche. The bird cawed at him once more then pecked about the windshield, scavenging, before taking flight. Baffled, Mark swore half under his breath and pushed himself off the hood of his prowler to scrutinize the spider-webbed windshield. Somewhat humbled he eyed the heavens, then the flock of circling crows, before allowing his gaze to once again rest on the crumpled Porsche.

The answer had been there all along; the missing link, which could either authenticate Hannah Bryans' half-baked hypothesis or could serve to prove her client's guilt.

Mark reexamined the sparse strands of human hair embedded within the spider-webbed windshield on the passenger side of Jake Bremer's Porsche. He grimaced, feeling a vague sense of uneasy dread; fully aware this key may inadvertently unlock a proverbial Pandora's box.

~~~

Gravel popping under rubber tore Hannah from her daydream. The idle drone of an engine nearing summoned her full attention. Peeking over the waist-high shrubbery, she swore and ducked out of sight. Wits scattered, pulse scrambled, she sneaked another quick peek; just to confirm it was indeed a sheriff's prowler rolling to a stop next to her Beemer in the drive. The transmission purred a second longer then was cut, and—clad in those same mirrored Ray-Bans and that tan on tan uniform—Mr. Hunky-By-The-Book himself materialized.

Hannah gaped then, ducking out of sight yet again, held her breath and listened to his boots crunch across the gravel. She popped up to chance another peek then enjoyed the view as Mark strolled across the length of the lawn toward the house. She almost giggled when the screen door was rattled and he called out her name in that rich velvet drawl.

Why on earth? Dumbfounded, it took her a second to regain her composure. "I'm over here. By the gazebo," she shouted, popping up like a jack-in-the-box amidst the shrubs.

Stepping off the porch, he nudged the Ray-Bans down his nose, eyes searching. Her pulse skidded off track once his gaze zeroed in on her location and an involuntary smile tested his lips. She automatically smiled and waved back and then, in a panic, ducked behind the bushes to tuck the wayward escapees of her loose French braid behind her ears. Trying to make herself look presentable, she brushed the crumbs of dirt off her thighs before shooting to her feet, toes stained by rich soil, compost, and in dire need of a pedicure. Glancing herself over she frowned. She wasn't dressed properly for company. She hadn't even expected company—let alone to have that company be Deputy Mark Bowman himself.

Self-conscious she hugged herself as he strolled back across the lawn.

"Hi…ah—?" Mark gestured at his cruiser in curious question while navigating the maze of waist-high shrubbery. "—you didn't hear me drive up?"

Hannah gaped at him. Baffled, she simply shrugged.

"Wow. This is…?" Joining her, he took a quick sweep of the pond, its gurgling fountain, the unkempt bush sculptures, her own pitiful attempts to restore her grandmother's once thriving arboretum. "…different. You do all this, yourself?"

"It's my Grandmother's project, actually—well, was. Guess Grams was into all that Zen mediation stuff. I…I'm just trying to maintain it. Or at least salvage it." Glancing at the uprooted patch of petunias, Hannah grimaced stepping in front of them. Plastering on a brave smile, she then rambled at the speed of light now hoping to somehow defuse the nervous tension churning her gut with small talk. "Had to repair the fountain, added the flowers, the gazing ball—oh, and added those oversized goldfish there in that…well, I guess you'd call it a pond—? Although, when I first got the place it looked more like the creature from the Black Lagoon might crawl out of it. Then, of course, there was—"

"Zen meditation, huh?" Nudging the Ray-bans down his nose, he inspected the flowerbed that she'd negligently mutilated. "Isn't that supposed to be, ah…calming and relaxing?"

Eyes narrowing, Hannah opened her mouth then stopped herself short. Why let him in on the trivial detail that he was the root cause of her torment? Ill managed, however, that torment came across as seething sarcasm, "That's what they say."

Reappraising the massacred flowers, he chuckled, a hint of that sexy analytical eyebrow peeking above the rim of his sunglasses. "Long day at the office?"

"You could say that," Hannah snapped then, looking away, scowled.

Why did he have to look so damn striking in that uniform? And how could he stand there and act so…well, so remarkably jaunty? So relaxed; incredibly sexy. Was he amnesic of their sweltering little tryst on his couch? Or was she the only one having a problem with it? The idea that she was galled her and left her even more bitterly intolerant.

"You were saying?" she prompted, a little too snippy; needing to get whatever this was over with.

"I...ah?" Deliberating such unwarranted rudeness, his casual demeanor evaporated. "I felt it was vital that I see you."

Baffled, Hannah's jaw dropped. The nature of his comment cued a heady cord of longing to spool taut and stirred those damn condors to beat within her gut. She searched his expression and hoped hers now appeared as impassive as that guarded poker-face sporting those Ray-Bans. And for some reason, she now became extremely uncomfortable staring at her own reflection—a skimpy bikini top and baggy denim cutoffs—caught within the mirrored surface of those sunglasses.

If it was so vital that he see her well then he was sure getting himself an eyeful, she mused.

At a complete loss she waited out the restless seconds, secretly wishing he'd take off those Ray-Bans. Nevertheless, she was grateful he hadn't. Either way, she was having extreme difficulty just maintaining eye contact with him.

"It concerns your client, Mr. Holm." The crisp official quality of his disclosure concluded the painful silence, unraveled hope, annulled longing and exterminated any ideas that he'd come just for the sake of needing to see her alone.

"Oh. Um...well of course." She took a stab at being jovial and gestured toward the secluded gazebo, suggesting a place for them to sit and talk. Declining the offer predicted that his visit would be short. Hannah made an effort to sound blasé, failing miserably her tone came across tight and flippant, "What about it? My client?"

Taking off his Ray-Bans he regarded her with incontestable dog-tired eyes; a non-verbal hint, of sorts, that he was in no mood for attitude. Stowing his shades he produced a clear plastic evidence envelope and held it up for inspection. "I found this."

Glancing at it, she shrugged. "Uh, okay. Could you—oh, I don' know—maybe elaborate?"

"Elaborate—?" Lips crimping, his nostrils flared. Mounting agitation wiped out amiable and set his features granite as he stared her down hard. "It's hair."

"Well, I can see that," she quipped.

"Look, I didn't come here to argue. This was in the windshield of Jake Bremer's Porsche--that'd be, on the passenger's side." He contemplated her for a second, jaw muscle flexing. "I thought you should be the first to know. I'm officially requesting to reopen the case."

Stunned, Hannah stood gape-mouthed. He wanted her to be the first to know? And now, after having said his piece, he was simply walking away. Why wouldn't he? She wasn't being that pleasant and had basically blown him off. And by rights, if anyone should feel snubbed it should be Mark. After all, she'd left without saying a single word to him this morning. And here she'd fretted over why Mark himself had not made any attempts to contact her all day?

Hannah squeezed her eyes shut. Humiliation and guilt, blindsided her for having been so impishly moronic, cheeky, so selfish. It took a second for her to gather her wits and regulate her now racing pulse.

"Mark—wait," she called out, cursing under her breath when he didn't. Taking a deep breath, she forced her feet to move and shouted after him, "Please?"

Coming to a full stop, a muddled oath leaked out as he pinched the bridge of his nose. Hannah cringed. The reaction was a habitual reflex. It suggested this man was now grappling to preserve that regimented composure of his; as he waited as she had asked, out of decency and respect.

Not wanting to annoy him any further, she hastily blurted, "You're reopening the case to—" then paused. If she didn't ask, then she would never know. "—to corroborate my own theory?"

"Told you. I always take full responsibility—" Not

wanting to shout, he cut himself short. Optimism arrowed through her and she held breath as he backtracked. Stopping a mere arm's length from her, he stared at her for a moment then finished, "—for my mistakes."

Defeat skewered her gut. It wasn't necessarily the answer she'd been hoping for. Then again, what exactly had she been expecting? For Mark to risk everything just for her? That was laughable. More pathetic was that she allowed herself to even entertain such a notion. They'd only met just yesterday. And, tonight, she'd pretty much ruined the chance—if any—that she might have ever had with this man.

Debating her words, Hannah chased off all romantic fantasy and in a more professional frame of mind probed, "So, you now suspect Jake Bremer might have been the one driving?"

"I'm obligated to investigate all of the possibilities," he supplied. "I just wanted you to be the first to know, ma'am."

Ma'am...it sounded so impersonal, detached. Hannah hugged herself, awash with remorse and surrendered to the idea that she'd also probably just wrecked any form of a professional alliance with this man. "Um...thanks," she croaked.

His lips parted then crimped and for a long moment he regarded her with those critical gunmetal eyes, debating—rather she thought probably tasting his own words before spitting them out at her. Uncomfortable, Hannah looked away and then stared at her toes, bracing herself for what she assumed would be an abrasive reprimand.

"I also pay my debts in full, Miss Bryans," he at last sighed, a peculiar anxiety now thawing his granite features and dissolving the starched quality of his official tone. "And whether you like it, or not, you're one lady I'm indebted to. As you've brought to my attention something that I'd misplaced—rather, a few things I chose to ignore—a long while back. And, beings that's a major feat of itself—" a soft laugh escaped him. "Reckon, if anybody needs to be thanking anyone…it should be me thanking you, Miss Bryans."

Trying to digest the weight of his lecture, Hannah once again studied the chipped mulberry polish on her toes. Taken aback, she still wasn't even quite certain what he was now referring to. "And that something is?" she mustered enough nerve to ask.

"Innocent until proven guilty. For starters."

Flabbergasted, Hannah lifted her eyes to his. As he held up the evidence sachet for proof, the genuine appreciation, the compassion, now radiating from his expression cued her insides to flip-flop. Afraid to ask what this so-called feat of hers all entailed, she took the envelope from him and examined the strands of hair sealed within it.

He could be risking a lot, by bringing this to the prosecution's attention. Not necessarily done for her, but in a sense done because of her. She, herself, had insisted that he reconsider his conclusion, by questioning his own judgment last night. But for Mark to actually acknowledge and admit his prejudices toward drunk drivers, that was true justice. The evidence of him doing so was right now within her very own hand. Evidence which could also serve to exonerate her client.

The value of what that DNA testing could prove suddenly hit her like a sack of bricks. "Oh my God. Do…do you realize what this could prove?"

"Yes. Look, there's something else, ah…that I thought that maybe we could discuss?"

Lost in thought, Hannah nodded, automatically murmuring, "Um, okay. Sure," as she reexamined the strands of hair trapped within the sealed plastic.

The finale verdict was locked in the delicate chain of genetics within her hands. Her client's life teetered in limbo, and all she had cared about was the random encounter that she'd had with Mark Bowman herself?

Now how petty was that in the grand scope of things.

"This…this could prove my client wasn't driving," she exclaimed.

"It could. Now will you let me finish? At least give me a—"

"Oh my god…I, I have so much to do." Energized, she plowed around him on a fevered tangent. Stopped short, she pawed at the hand affixing to her wrist. Determined, unable to break free of his grasp, she simply jerked him along as she wove her way through the hedge maze, rambling on about needing to reformulate her defense strategy. "….and I need to call Monique…and…and…need to reschedule—"

"Hannah, will you stop and just hear me out? At least give me a damn minute to explain?"

"…have to wait 'til morning to file a continuance—Oh, and I'll need to file a motion to…"

Spun around and yanked to her tippy-toes, his mouth intercepted the startled gasp simultaneously censoring her ecstatic brainstorm mid-rant. The envelope slipped from her fingertips. Her knees buckled. For a fathomless second she couldn't think, breathe. Body floating on a current of sheer bliss, her mind reeled with giddy shock, grappling to assimilate the sensation of his influential tongue making deep ardent love to her mouth.

Hannah gulped back an unsteady breath once his lips recanted, ceasing their calculated attack. Eyes locking on his in confused question, she was challenged by an aggressive pair of dark mercury pools, fierce with carnal intent. Detained, thrown by the intensity of his gaze, Hannah pushed unsuccessfully at his chest. When he didn't readily release her, her stomach fluttered as unchecked desire prickled hot across her flesh.

"Now that I have your attention…" The hazardously low rasp of his stern assertion exuded proclaimed entitlement as he announced, "There's something I think we need to discuss."

"And that would be?" she demanded waspishly, aroused yet still a tad flustered.

"Last night might be a good place to start," he declared, mouth again seeking hers.

"What about it?" she quizzed, hemming her fingers at the base his neck to better anchor herself while accommodating those lips.

Grazing her mouth he hesitated then, pulling back all together, choked on an incredulous laugh. "Wh—what about it—? Oh…I don' know, maybe we could discuss this," he clarified, hauling her flush; an effective demonstration highlighting the particulars of what exactly it was that he now wished to hammer out.

"Wh—wh—what's there to discuss?" she managed breathlessly amid a staccato of his sweltering pecks.

Hoisted off her feet in response, their mouths fervently collided. Hannah wound her arms around his neck as imperative hands guided her legs around the cumbersome duty belt hugging his hips. Equilibrium capsized, she clung to him as Mark spun them in a quick semicircle, lips abandoning hers as his eyes now darted about. Sights set, he readily set out, effortlessly swinging one leg, then other, over the waist high hedge.

"Wh—wh—where are you going?" she cross-examined on a giggle, glancing about herself as he continued to hurdle the stout partitions of winding shrubbery.

"Mercy woman." Mouth once again mugging hers, he deftly tore the scrunchy from her French braid. Fingers sifting then fisting within her hair, he angled her head back to greedily ravage her throat as he questioned, "…do you have to argue everything?"

Hannah squealed in delight, "What do you expect? I am a defense attorney," as his lips nipped playfully up the side of her neck, teeth gently capturing an earlobe.

Bulldozing the last bit of her sanity his husky drawl buttonholed her eardrum, "Well then, care to elaborate your defense on why you left without saying goodbye, counselor?"

"My de—what?"

Hannah glanced about as Mark mounted the steps of the gazebo, where the setting sun poured through the lattice-work diffusing the onset of dusk. Unsure why he'd chosen this over the air-conditioned comfort of her house, she simply played along. "Oooooo-oh, that. Now you want to sit down and discuss that, right this minute?" she panted amid a staccato of his hit-and-miss kisses, holding her giggles back—and onto Mark for dear life—as he toed off one boot then wrestled out of the other mid-stride.

"No. First we're gonna finish what you started last night," he declared.

"Oh really, well…" Amused, she glanced about then snorted against his lips, "Right here? Right now?"

His tongue hijacked hers, hotly possessive. To make his intentions clear, a succession of quick tugs freed the strings of her bikini top. Setting her on her feet, another tug had her denim cutoffs puddled around her ankles. She stepped out of them as his hands explored, leaving her woozy and desperate.

His hands then abruptly stilled. And as if in afterthought, he paused, his own frayed breathing mingling with hers and bathing her lips. "Any objections, counselor?"

"Just one."

Shoulders sagging, he drew back, eyes trapping hers; pupils so dilated and black it accentuate the pewter specks, the liquid mercury shards, within those steel gray halos now vivid with rampant untamed desire. Tamping down an oath, that incredibly sexy eyebrow shot skyward. A dubious, "What now?" eluded his throat.

Hannah grinned wildly then whispered, "You still have all your clothes on," against his lips as she unshackled the buckle of his duty belt, mastered a button, and jerked down the zipper. His shuddered groan vibrated her lips as gravity confiscated the duty belt, taking the attached uniform slacks along, landing with a loud hefty thunk. Under extreme duress, the portable radio cord—attached to the mike—stretched taut until the thing clipped to his shoulder sprang free and bounced hard against the floor triggering a bout of static.

Hannah giggled as Mark swore outright then snorted himself once the dispatcher's voice belched forth; asking if anybody had traffic as they both tackled the buttons of his uniform shirt. Shoving it half off his shoulders, fingers eager for warm flesh and hard muscle, Hannah pouted hampered by the stiff barrier of body armor. Shrugging out of the shirt himself, Mark flung it aside as Hannah went to work on figuring out the confusing matrix of Velcro binders securing the bulky bullet proof vest.

Cursing it, Mark assisted her by simply ripping the thing off and then flung it.

Their fingers collided on a desperate mission to remove his cotton undershirt. First stealing himself a blistering kiss, he allowed her to tear the t-shirt over his head. Letting it drop and, commandeering the waistband of his BVD briefs, Hannah dropped to her knees, mouth plummeting along the directional patch of black onyx. Hastily towed back up, a rumble of instant approval snagged deep within his throat once his palms mugged her bottom, greeted by her bare flesh and the thin slice of her lacy silk thong.

"Thinking about you drove me crazy all damn day," he whispered against her lips. "Couldn't concentrate, couldn't stay focused…couldn't think straight…"

Nearly driven mad by the seductive pull of his words, his hypnotic drawl and his teasing nibbles, Hannah moaned, "Me too—now shut up and just kiss me."

Interrupting them, the dispatcher's voice once again inquired if anyone had traffic. Hannah snorted when Mark freed his feet and punted the duty belt--with radio, uniform slacks and underwear intact--across the gazebo.

Crashing in a heap cued another bout of static to belch forth from the portable radio. Rightly annoyed, the dispatcher bypassed anymore queries and now demanded that all units on duty check in, activating a hectic stint of radio transmissions.

"You're not on duty, I hope," she giggled.

"Nope," he answered, his hot hungry mouth taking full custody of hers as he pressed the solid ridge of his arousal against her abdomen. Infected by the urgency of his own wanton abandon she wound her arms around his neck. Hoisted off her feet once again, Hannah feasted on the round bulk of his shoulder, his neck. He tasted male, vaguely salty, and stimulatingly scrumptious. Nibbling on an earlobe she was rewarded with a guttural growl; the action itself prompting Mark to level a wrought-iron chase lounge with one efficient sweeping kick.

Deposited atop its thick floral print cushion, her thong was confiscated and tossed. Muscular thighs were then segregating her own as his athletic build pinned her beneath him and he piloted her legs around his swift sinking hips. Her mind blanked for an immeasurable second, fingernails digging into his back with that first potent lance. Accommodated by her slippery wetness, his hissing oath vibrated against her lips. His body momentarily stilled; as if to savor the reception. Then the glorious sweet ache of intrusion lashed throughout her when he drove himself deeper yet. Her breath leaked passed her lips at the sheer shock of his powerful thrusts, each pass generating an escalating title-wave of intoxicating pleasure.

Greedy, Hannah cinched her legs tight and rocked. The sultry heat was suffocating, and scarcely able to breathe, she dragged her lips from his, grappling to just gather her wits. Her breath snared in her lungs and her muscles instantaneously tensed as his mouth recaptured hers, and she free fell on a wave of incinerating heat that buttered the thickness of his ample girth with seismic aftershocks of a powerful climax.

Tearing his mouth from hers, he sucked at the air like a man no longer able to contain himself. Muttering an oath, he took firmer hold, propelling her hips in perfect sync with his. A cry ripped from her throat as he drove himself harder, devastating the last bit of his own control while steering her beyond the threshold of one mind-altering euphoria to another. The harmony of their sweat glossed flesh clapped in frenzied cadence until the muscles of his back grew rigid beneath her fingertips. And when she thought she couldn't go any higher, her entire body seized, soaring through the levels of yet another blinding climax alongside the pulsing torrent of his.

Spent, her legs fell limp, her body a quivering mess beneath his. Mark relaxed himself, his sweat varnished chest collapsing atop her glistening breasts. In unison they struggled to regulate their ragged breathing as their adjoined bodies trembled in the glorious aftermath. As she floated back to earth on a current of sheer bliss, Hannah lazily opened her eyes. Moonlight now reigned and streamed through the lattice work draping the gazebo in its surreal gauze. The sounds of nightfall filtered in around them. A gurgling fountain. Chirping crickets. The occasional squawk of a night bird; the low bugle of a hoot owl; the flickering fireflies which sporadically illuminated the night.

Taking it all in, she mused it would have been perfect, if it wasn't for the heaviness of dread now assailing her better judgment. She stared at the rafters of the gazebo and wondered what on earth she'd been thinking as she now contemplated what it was she had just done, had let happen.

She hadn't counted on yet again falling so quickly for a man who could never really love her back.

Closing her eyes, Hannah pushed all misgivings aside and concentrated on the contentment humming throughout her, the sensation of Mark still deep inside her.

If she couldn't have it all, she would then at least enjoy this, these few moments of bliss.

After catching his own breath, Mark shifted and resituated them both on the chase lounge, legs intertwined. Despite the sweltering temperature, she allowed him pull her closer and automatically snuggled against his chest; relished the feel of his masculine body stretched out alongside hers. She frowned once he began idly tracing his fingertips through her sweat dampened hair and then closed her eyes tighter against the surge of searing tears once his lips brushed tenderly across her temple. She told herself the gesture was simply done in reflex, probably done out of appreciation most likely...not out of loving admiration--something she'd only witness from afar--which real couples shared.

Physically, the sex had been phenomenal; emotionally, she couldn't handle this...him.

Needing to flee, Hannah untangled her legs from his and tried to pry herself free of his embrace. Unsuccessful, a muscular thigh trapped both of hers delaying her escape. She then felt foolish when Mark propped himself on an elbow and playfully tweaked the tip of her nose before tracing his fingertip across the swell of her bottom lip.

"Penny for your thoughts...?"

Staring at him, she knew those words could have very well been: *And where do you think you're running off to so quick?*

"The mosquitoes are going to eat us alive," she muttered; wishing they would just carry her off instead because she was incapable of masquerading her sullen pout.

Brow furrowing, his drowsy smile vanished. "Something wrong?"

Dodging his eyes, she turned her face away cursing herself for having been so impulsive, so foolish. She blinked back the onset of tears when he ran his knuckles down her cheek. Hooking her chin, drawing her own eyes back to his, he studied her with those almost too insightful analytical gunmetal orbs.

"What's wrong?" he then asked.

What's wrong? Where do I begin? I just allowed myself to have the most phenomenal sex in my life with yet another man who can't love me back...? Or, better yet, was a reckless moron for having just done that without thinking about contraception...? Hannah groaned and squeezed her eyes shut. It was a little late to bring that up, let alone debate it. And wouldn't that be just her luck. She may be cop repellent, but she sure as hell wasn't munchkin proof.

"Nothing," Hannah croaked then, shoving his leg off hers, attempted to get up. "Let go. It's hot out here."

Before he could answer, or protest, she shimmied out of his embrace and bolted off the chase lounge. Groping around the floor, she located her shorts and bikini top.

"Hannah? Where are you going?"

"Inside." Grateful for the cover of night cloaking the gazebo in semi-opaque shadows, she hastily dressed, then exited just as fast, fibbing, "I have a defense to reformulate."

Chapter 14

Stymied, Mark stared at the gossamer pattern of moonlight streaming through the lattice work, dejection displacing contentment; sinking heavy within his gut. Sitting forward, he braced his elbows on his knees and scrubbed his face. He then glanced around the empty gazebo a little rattled, more bamboozled.

He thought he was accustomed to solitude; had gladly welcomed it over the past six years. Yet, he'd just become acquainted with a new level of seclusion. The isolation of being shut-out, cut-off, and dissociated from Hannah Bryans and her own private wealth of emotions.

Mark pinched the bridge of his nose and snarled. What the hell did he expect? They'd only met a day ago; hardly knew each other. Yet, for some reason, her indifference stung to the center of his core. He applied more pressure to the bridge of his nose and grunted as blips of jargon mixed with static drifted from his discarded radio.

He sat a moment longer then, collecting his uniform, dressed. Using his flashlight he searched for then located the evidence envelope as he wound his way back through the hedge maze. Dumping his undershirt, bullet-proof vest, and duty belt in his squad car he then made his way toward the glowing windows of the house.

Mounting the steps he loitered on the porch then, rapping his knuckles against the screen door, let himself in. "Hannah?"

"Sorry, you'll have to excuse the mess. Bathroom's that way through that door around the corner and down the hall to you're right, um, that is if you need to use it."

Mark followed her vague gesture to a labyrinth of cardboard moving boxes within what appeared to be a living room. "Thanks. I'm good," he murmured, scanning the disarray of the kitchen.

A wadded up drop cloth speckled with various colors of latex took up one corner. Gallon paint cans, thinner and a slew of painter's paraphernalia had been left scattered across counter tops as well as cluttered the cracked and peeling linoleum floor. Half melted candles, sometime ago extinguished, dotted the counter, table, and squatted atop an ancient avocado green stove.

Mark deemed it a fire hazard waiting to happen. Not mentioning it, he surveyed the thick spools of wallpaper still encased in their plastic sheaths. Jugs of adhesive waited next to a pyramid of shorter spools—border, he assumed—that had been left atop the farmer style table.

Sizing up the mess, he glanced at his hands. Uncertain why he'd even brought it in, Mark set the evidence envelope on the table. "Hannah, I—"

"I've been so busy lately, well, I mean, I just haven't had the time to do much of anything. Still need to unpack half this crap and finish decorating…but now with this case…"

Taking a step toward her, Mark halted when she unconsciously flinched at his proximity. "Hannah, if there's something wrong, I think we should at least discuss it…?"

"There's nothing to discuss." Jerking around, her cheeks were flushed, lips still swollen and ruby from their shared lust. The stilted expression, however, matched her aloof body language and complemented the frostiness lacing her tetchy tone, "I think we pretty much covered just about everything you wanted to discuss. Or was there something you missed?"

Mark narrowed his eyes, nostrils flaring at her accusation, the rejection it conveyed. "An explanation maybe, to why you high-tailed it out this morning—or just now from the gazebo—for no apparent reason?" he interrogated point-blank, unchecked anger surging through his veins.

Toying with a castaway scrunchy she plucked it off the counter-top, her gaze not quite meeting his. "I already told you. I have work to do," she commented, carelessly bunching up her hair and knotting it in a makeshift pony-tail-half-bun atop her head. She then shrugged, a curious quaver undermining her dismissive approach. "Nothing's wrong. Really. I…I just have a lot on my mind right now, is all."

Turning away from him to commit her full attention on making coffee, gave Mark the distinct feeling that she was now trying to avoid him. Raising an eyebrow he observed her a second longer then, coming up behind her, seized both of her wrists, crossing her arms over her chest beneath his in a gentle but secure embrace. "Nothing's wrong, huh? It's just this case?"

"Let go," she quietly implored after a second or two.

Refusing to comply, Mark stood his ground. "Is that why you're dumping Folgers in the water reservoir, to make coffee, Hannah? Because you're so hyped up about reformulating some damn defense you can't think straight enough to put the coffee grounds in the filter? Ask me, I think all this ruckus is due to what just happened in the gazebo between us."

A muffled curse leaked from her lips realizing that he was right. She squirmed then stiffened against him. "Let go of me, Mark. Please."

"No. Not until we talk about this."

"Mark…" her resolve hiccupped on a jumble of desperation and defeat, "don't do this."

"Do what?" Turning her around, he cupped her chin in one hand and affectionately lifted her face to his. "Regret? Or worse, write-off what we just shared? Pretend it didn't happen, or that it doesn't—"

"Please, Mark…I, I just can't—not now, not—"

"Don't count on it," he told her then tenderly glancing her trembling lips with his, sighed when she turned her own face away denying him. Maddened, he studied her a second, then barked on a half laugh once it dawned. "You...you actually think I'd—"

"Leave!" she demanded, flinching herself as the tactlessness of her own outburst echoed throughout the kitchen.

Backing-off, an alien pang of disillusionment skewered his chest once she dropped her eyes from his; dismissing him and, oddly enough, as if taking back something of great value which had never really belonged to him to begin with. "Hannah, I don't think you understand. I—"

Not letting him explain, she amended in a quavering whisper, "Please, just leave, Mark."

Irrational reasoning egged him to stay; astute logic warned him to make tracks. Respectful of her wishes, he obeyed. Collecting the evidence packet, Mark stowed it safe within his breast pocket. Pushing through the screen door, he then hesitated. "Don't cheapen what we shared tonight, Hannah." Half turning, he waited until their eyes touched. "It wasn't premeditated."

He exited on a brisk pace, not allowing her the opportunity to question him or dispute it. Moreover, he was unprepared himself to now identify the very reasons of why he even desired such a debate.

~~~

"Holy Moses, Bowman." James Tippen rubbernecked the document within his hands. "This here's a…this is a seizure warrant—?"

Mark grimaced at Tippen's announcement and, after glancing about the empty patrol room and snatching the warrant back, headed out. He'd just spent the last three hours obtaining the necessary saliva swab from Holm, preparing the sample as well as the evidence itself to be ship off for testing, and had typed and filed the necessary reports to reopen the case itself. Phoning the honorable Judge Ramkie at home and rousing him from slumber to request the warrant—prior to the sheriff's own knowledge—pretty much guaranteed he'd just committed himself to outright pandemonium once his boss found out.

Holm's own sample would be more than sufficient to compare against the evidence and give them an answer to whom the hair belonged to—but, he wanted Bremer's as well. If he was putting his job, his own reputation on the line, then he was going to make sure to do it up right.

"Mark? Hey man, hold up a sec." Jogging the length of the corridor, Tippen snagged his shoulder and lowered his voice. "Have you thought this completely through? What you're about to—"

"Get off my back, Jim," Mark warned, shrugging off Tippen's misguided attempts to coddle him. "I'm a big boy. I know what I am doing. Trust me you couldn't even begin to under—"

"Know what you're doing? Do you? You're serving a search and seizure warrant at…at…" Once again falling instep beside him, Jim quickened his own pace in order to block the exit, then glanced at his watch. "It's after one in the morning, Mark…?"

Delayed, Mark scowled. "Thanks Jim. I know what time it is." Not wanting to waste the energy or the time it would take to explain, Mark tucked the warrant in his back pocket and, pushing Tippen aside plowed through the double doors and kept walking.

"C'mon man, think about what the hell you're doing.

Forget what time it is…jeez, Mark that warrant there is for Jake Bremer himself."

"I know. I requested it myself. Remember?" Mark intoned sarcastically on a heated growl. Nearing his prowler he fished out his keys. "And I'm doing what I should've done the first time."

"The first time? Should've done *what* the first time?"

"My job!"

"You're job?" Jim barked on a snort then, wagging his head, laughed, "Jeeze Bowman….if the boss didn't have high blood pressure already, he's sure gonna now. Especially once he finds out you're…"

Ignoring Jim, Mark unlocked the driver side door of his cruiser and swung it open.

"Come on, Mark. Think about what you're doing." Determined to reason with him, Jim stepped in between him and the opening, bracing one palm on the door not permitting Mark to get inside his vehicle. "You're going off half-cocked—not to mention, jeopardizing that job of yours. And for what? I gotta guess it's all because of some pretty little criminal defense lawyer and—"

"This has nothing to do with Hannah."

"Hannah? First name basis are you? Sure sounds like it has everything to do—"

"This doesn't concern you, Jim," Mark warned.

Not heeding his advice, Jim needled, "The other night must have been real good— 'cause it sure sounds to me like she's already managed to cloud your better judgment."

Snarling like a rabid dog, Mark's tolerance snapped. Grasping fistfuls of Jim's uniform shirt he forcefully pick the man up and moved him aside, all the while growling, "Back off!"

Chapter 15

"Got a minute?"

Lost in thought, Hannah glanced up from the canary yellow legal pad she'd been jotting down notes on. "Sure." She gestured with her pen, waving Kender inside her office.

Entering, he toed the door shut before giving her his full attention.

Hannah sat up a little straighter and, now uneasy, glanced between him and the closed door of her office. "What's up?" she inquired trying to sound nonchalant.

"Wanted to extend my condolences," he began. His comment was chaperoned by a raw lopsided simper of fabricated empathy.

Hannah stared at him for a blank second, then stiffened, heart racing. She assumed—if they were going to indeed fire her over her mishap, that was—they would have summoned her to the conference room to do so; just as they had done when they had interviewed her and had offered her the position. Then again, maybe Kender hadn't gotten the memo...? Or worse, he had and had drawn the shortest straw, and was now doling out his brand of simulated sympathy in order to lessen the blow;

before requesting she accompany him to the conference room where they would, together as a pack, give her career here the ax.

Wonderful. Her left eyelid began to twitch.

"Um…okay…?" Swallowing the anxiety clutching her throat, Hannah plastered on her bravest smile and tried sounding positive, even jolly. She half laughed, "I give up. For what?"

"Heard you caught the Holm's case."

"Oh…that. Um, yeah," she replied, more than relieved. She tapped her pen against the canary yellow legal pad. "Actually, I was just working on reformulating my defense strategy since--"

"Don't waste your time," Kender chuckled then, perching a hip on her desk, exclaimed, "It's a dumptruck."

"Oh, well…I…?" Following his snooping eyes, Hannah set her pen aside and began causally gathering up the documents spread out across her desk. Apparently, Deputy Bowman's intent to reopen case had not yet been made public. Not wanting to disclose any vital specifics herself, she simply announced, "Well regardless, it's my case and my duty to be prepared to take it to the box."

He raised an eyebrow as he considered her point blank assertion to take the case to trial. Wagging his head, the somewhat shocked expression toggled to affected concern. "You might want to rethink that gung ho attitude…" Smiling at her with that same phony expression, he sighed heavily.

Recalling some previous catastrophic court room experience, he embarked on a long winded I-too-was-fresh-out-of-law-school-once story. Subject to a more than belittling air, Hannah sat back and crossed her arms; half listening and becoming increasingly affronted the longer he spoke down to her. Instead of correcting him on the minor detail that she wasn't fresh out of law school, she simply waited for him to finish his annoying I'm-a-senior-you're-a-peon-so-heed-my-advice spiel.

"Can't say that I blame you though--thinking a case of this nature might advance your career somehow. Guess it could—that is, if Holm's wasn't guilty. Really, Hannah, it's a barking dog—a howler at that. One with no plausible defense for you to even worry your pretty little head over formulating. Save yourself the headache. Not to mention, the embarrassment. Apply that clever energy of yours towards a client who's not actually guilty." Glancing at his watch, he frowned. "Oops. Gotta run. Can't be late for tee time."

Pushing off her desk, he reached for the door then paused before opening it. Studying her briefly, he advised, "Really, Hannah, if you expect to survive around here...I'd pick my battles more wisely."

Hannah held his gaze, and then bloated her cheeks and blew out a long silent breath after he'd sauntered out. *Save yourself the embarrassment...? Pick my battles more wisely...? If you expect to survive...?* Strange. An odd choice of wording, Hannah thought. More peculiar, was the strong sense of paranoia those parting words of his now evoked.

*Curiosity killed the cat...*hit automatic reply within her head.

Picking up her pen, Hannah tapped it pensively against the pile of documents that she'd attempted to hide from his seemingly prying eyes; a little unnerved. To be more precise, she was slightly apprehensive of the unspoken message which in a round-about way Kender's so-called friendly advice had conveyed.

Hannah sat forward and glanced out the open doorway then, sitting back, gave herself a hard mental shake. Jeez...what was wrong with her? One prank phone call and she was jumping to conclusions? Questioning Kender's own intent? She was a tad spooked due to that crank call. But now even more rattled because of a coworker's rather strange choice of words? He was a sniveling little man who'd initially struck her as being rather meek and docile. He'd been the last senior to welcome her, and had done so with a simple potted plant along with a memo of greeting when she'd accepted her position within the firm.

She never once regarded Kender as being...well, dangerous, let alone intimidating.

She assured herself there was no way Kender had meant that parting comment of his literally. Nor could he have been the crank caller. Why would he be? Although, she had to remind herself that Kender did have access to her cell phone number. But then again, so did any one of the numerous office personal within their firm. Not to mention, those who worked at the LEC and within the courthouse itself.

The call could have been made from anyone.

...it's a barking dog—a howler at that, with no plausible defense for you to even worry your pretty little head over formulating...

Hannah contemplated Kender's words of advice as they chased throughout her head. Why would Kender feel compelled to force his opinion on her? What would be the point? He'd dropped the case himself. Since he had, why was he now so interested to steer her towards dump-trucking the case? And why exactly had Kender dumped it himself?

Although his mannerisms were tame compared to the rest of the seniors, Hannah could not discount that he had managed to leave her in an ambiguous cloud of paranoia.

Holding her breath, she leaned forward and peeked to hallway once again. Telling herself it was simple curiosity, she plucked up her phone and hit the intercom button; cringing at the loud buzz it triggered just outside of her office.

"Yes darling?" Monique answered.

"Pick up the receiver," she instructed on a hurried and somewhat guilt riddled hiss.

"Okay...but why are we whispering?" Monique quizzed, sounding somewhat amused but now using the same conspiratorial decibel.

"I need your expertise again."

"Fire away, girlfriend."

Glancing out her office door, Hannah rolled her eyes at her secretary's choice of words. She cupped her hand around the receiver as if to better conceal the whispered request itself, "Find out who Kender plays golf with, for me, will you?"

"Oh," Monique exclaimed out loud then, giggling as if they'd just shared some wonderfully amusing gossip, went back to whispering, "That's an easy one. Paul Bremer. Why?"

- - -

"Are you insane—?"

Knowing better than to comment, Mark stood at full attention, listening without flinching, as Sheriff Lynn Schmitt bawled him out. He could almost feel the quiet hush outside the confine of Lynn's office, as well as the curious eyes; the ears, cocked and straining to decipher every word now shouted at him.

Not once glancing away, Mark endured the Sheriff's thunderous dressing-down.

When the sheriff took a much needed breath, Mark took the opportunity to speak, "Sir, I can understand why you're upset. But at the same time, I—" he hesitated, unsure if he should share the particulars. "Last night I felt it was vital that I secure samples from both, and therefore I—"

"I understand the whys. What I'm having a hard time digesting is the fast-and-loose manner you went about going about it," Lynn barked, then shaking his head in disgust, grumbled half to himself, "not at all like you, Mark...not at all."

He then jabbed a finger at his phone, tone once again exceeding thunderous. "First thing this morning, I got Bremer on line one, breathing down my goddamn throat telling me I oughta can you—not that I would—Not to mention, Ramkie on line two, informing me that he wasn't too pleased that you'd woken his whole blasted family up at one in the morning and all for—never mind that you wasn't officially on duty—a warrant an' affidavit that he felt he could've signed during normal business hours. Not even going to mention the fact you went ahead and done so without my goddamned knowledge or consent! Let alone disregard procedure by going ahead and serving the blasted thing at two in the morning!"

Face now a rather unbecoming hue of purple, the Sheriff sat back, shook out then gobbled down a handful of Tums, and then pretended to shuffle through the papers atop his desk. Going about his daily business, he grumbled, "Normal business hours my ass. Be nice if crime stopped at five, county wide, therefore we could all operate within normal business hours ourselves…"

Accepting the reprimand at face value, Mark stood at attention; silent and uncomplaining. Lynn hadn't yet dismissed him, officially. And although he wanted to know the status of Bremer's warrant, he remained tight lipped. He was not about to ask any questions.

Upon serving it, Paul Bremer had laughed in his face and had slammed the door shut upon his attempt to explain the specifics of the affidavit; right after the man had advised him that he would be filing a motion, himself, to contest the warrant at first light. Which in all truth, he assumed would be the county attorney's reaction. He had counted on it; just as he had also known Bremer would phone the Sheriff to complain about it. Requesting that he be fired over it, without doubt, only corroborated the hearsay regarding Bremer's manipulative business practices.

Mark now wondered, however, who amongst their tight-knit community supported such underhanded methods. Considering that the Sheriff was an elected official—in a way, making him a politician of sorts himself—he kept his mouth shut. He had to be certain.

Lynn glanced up after a moment and then, gesturing

for him to sit, asked, "You get Holm's sample sent out?"

Mark relaxed somewhat and cautiously felt the Sheriff out with, "Ah, I was waiting to secure Bremer's sample, first."

"Hell…might as well send in what you got. Idiot already filed a motion to contest this morning--Now there's a shocker. Probably manage to tie the damn thing up, if not annul it completely. Know as well as I do—even if the damn thing goes through and the cotton swab itself was plated in pure silver—he'll make sure it'll take months before any of us even get a blasted swab near that golden-boy-of-frat-brat's mug." Glancing at the closed door of his office, he dropped his voice another decibel. "You ask me, that whole damn gene pool is corrupt."

Satisfied with Lynn's candid opinions, Mark sat forward ready to expose his strategy.

Lynn continued to vent, "Burns my hide. He's as crooked as they get. Wouldn't surprise me if that Holm's kid was telling the truth. Apparently it don' matter. Seems no matter what that frat-brat-of-a-golden-boy does, us peons can't touch him. Everybody always says that kid of his could get away with murder around here—" a disgusted snort of irony escaped. "Just never thought myself that it would be literal."

"Not exactly." Having deemed the Sherriff trustworthy, Mark enlightened, "All we need is for Holm's own DNA to work for us." Giving Lynn a few seconds to grasp the full gist, Mark glanced at the closed door and then lowered his voice as well. "Just reckoned I'd launch a little diversionary tactic with that warrant. Ought to keep Bremer busy for a while, at least."

When it clicked, approval scrolled across the sheriff's craggy features. "Genius—sheer genius, Bowman. It's 'bout time somebody shook out the rug." His smile widened, and on even more confidential tone he admitted, "You had me right worried there for a spell. Should have figured you were up to something. Never known you for fast-and-loose, to disregard proper procedure."

"Sorry 'bout that, boss. Won't happen again."

"Rightly so," Lynn stated, appreciative of his deputy's recent atypical behavior. After a brief moment of meditation, he quizzed, "So what's next on our agenda?" outwardly eager to participate in—well, what Mark guessed the Sheriff deemed some covert cloak-and-dagger operation.

Thinking about it, Mark wagged his head. "Reckon I'd best be apologizing to Tippen. We sorta had ourselves a minor scuffle regarding this whole matter." Reading Lynn's unsatisfied expression, he then suggested, "I reckon we sit tight, ah that is until the DNA report comes back. I'll ship it out today. Probably take four to six weeks before we get any results back. Unless, you yourself, make a call to the lab—see about getting it expedited?"

Smile returning, Lynn nodded in agreement. Leaning forward, he asked on hushed and now rather gung ho breath, "So do we pretend I fire you now?"

Mark almost laughed, then entertained the Sheriff's suggestion. Brilliant as it almost sounded, it was little too excessive. Even if it was only for show, it would be out of character for Lynn to do so, and everybody would know that. Which, in turn, might serve to tip Bremer off that something was indeed afoot. He might have been preoccupied these past six years, but he wasn't stupid. There were too many eyes and ears within their office; PD included. And Mark would bet, a select few of his coworkers were enrolled in Bremer's private pay-roll package.

"Naw. Too extreme." Mark chuckled when Lynn's spirited enthusiasm waned to sulky disappointment. Half liking the idea, however, he recommended with conspiratorial wink, "But I reckon a suspension might be proper. I could use a few days off."

Chapter 16

Holed up in her office, Hannah had lost all track of time. Glancing at her watch she grimaced. She'd spent a good part of the afternoon, and now the evening, reworking her defense for the Holm's case. Pushing away from her desk, she stretched then, grabbing her coffee mug just in case, wandered outside her office. After confirming for herself that the entire building had been cleared out—and most likely hours ago—she deposited her coffee mug next to the guts of the already washed and squeaky clean coffee machine which had been set out across the counter to air dry. She then marched to the basement door and after taking one last look around, swung the door wide to now moonlight as a sleuth to investigate her most recent hunch.

Flipping on the light, Hannah examined the rickety wooden stairwell then crept down them in to the basement of their building where inactive client files were warehoused. Earlier, she'd entered Jake Bremer's name in to her computer, searching their own interoffice network to find that he had indeed been a frequent-flyer of their firm. While she had a feeling the county attorney's son should have a rap sheet the length of a young child's

Christmas wish list, snooping in hopes of viewing his full client history, she had been denied by a password prompt. The only information she was provided were court dates and case numbers; all earmarked with similar notations. Charges dropped. Case dismissed. Case sealed. Et cetera, et cetera. She'd even searched the database of public records via the world wide net and just to learn that every single complaint ever filed against Jake Bremer had somehow been reversed, annulled, or had magically disappeared.

Apparently, the Bremer's had found themselves a magician. An extremely cunning and reliable criminal defense attorney who, interestingly enough, provided such phenomenal services from within the same firm as her. Which in a way she felt was odd, considering the Bremer's could afford to hire a big-gun from one of the numerous law firms operating outside their small community. Instead they hand picked a local yokel, from Brecker Haley & Merit, no less. And she was now determined to find out who that person was.

Staring at the line of tall filing cabinets, Hannah bit her bottom lip, then grimaced at the dusty veil of cobwebs before actually prying open the correct drawer. Eyes zeroing in on the systematically alphabetized tabs, she flipped through the legal sized file folders to find absolutely nothing. Not one file, document, or even a memo, with the name Bremer attached to it.

"Odd…" Hannah whispered, going through the files once again. Thinking the file had been misfiled, she began an all-out search of the entire line of filing cabinets. Pulling open drawers at random, her fingertips tip-toed, file by file, as her eyes searched. Engrossed, her heart lodged in her throat; startled by a hard thump ensued by a jarring rattle. Glancing up, she sighed and then laughed at her sudden bout of skittishness once the labyrinth of ductwork above ticked and the air conditioning system kicked on overhead with an enormous hiss.

Going back to work, she rummaged through the entire alphabet, and then the odd-ball batch of files marked MIS for miscellaneous—just for good measure—before giving up all together. Stumped, Hannah shut the last drawer and gnawed on her bottom lip. Jake Bremer was in their client database, therefore there had to be hard copies of….well, correspondences, billing invoices, or at least something with his name on it somewhere.

Pensive, she eyed the cabinets then somewhat panicked noticing the helter-skelter map of smudges and fingerprints she'd left in her haste now marring the fine veil of dust. Glancing around, she was seized by the urgent necessity of finding something to wipe the filing cabinets down with, to erase any indication that she'd even been down here snooping. Rolling her eyes, she then snorted; feeling like a complete dimwit for having even allowed herself to entertain such an idea. She was not doing anything illegal or wrong. Client files, whether active or inactive, were readily available to anyone within their firm. It appeared, however, that nobody--until now that was—had utilized the wealth of information warehoused down here for a while.

Unsatisfied, Hannah made a small circle and surveyed the basement. She scanned the utility shelves. One housed neatly stacked boxes of Kleenex, various cleaning supplies, and spare rolls of toilet tissue. The other posed as a graveyard for broken and, or, out of date office paraphernalia. Equipment in need of repairs, sometime ago forgotten and, or just simply replaced.

Not yet ready to surrender, she eyeballed the waist high pillars of cardboard storage boxes. Prying a lid open, out of curiosity, she unearthed an assortment of meticulously packed Christmas and New Year's Eve decorations.

Glancing about the neat and tidy basement, Hannah bloated her cheeks then blew out a heavy breath of dissatisfaction. Dusty cobwebs notwithstanding, the basement was—for the most part—as immaculate as the offices above it. Nevertheless, it appeared that whoever had represented Jake Bremer had poor filing skills.

"Or, had been paid off to make it appear that way," Hannah construed on a quiet murmur recalling that the computer history itself had been password-proofed. The idea that Bremer's client file had also been simply misplaced due to human error just didn't quite sit right.

Whoever had represented Jake, knew enough to keep that client history secluded. But by who and why? And what was the price tag for those who dared to snoop, or worse meddle?

Curiosity killed the cat, looped throughout her mind, cueing Kender's own parting comment…*if you expect to survive*… Idle threats so far. The prospect of them becoming valid however sent an icy shiver down her spine. And considering the parties in question, Hannah now wondered just how far they were willing to go to see that she did not take Holm's case to trial.

Hannah crept back up the rickety stairwell; now with an even more overwhelming sense of paranoia. Suspicion which triggered a strong intuit of reservation to churn within her gut. Preoccupied, she quickly collected her purse and briefcase, flipped off the lights and locked up. Heading out and now on a mission, she trotted to her Beemer; heels clapping purposely against concrete. Her destination: the halls of justice. Specifically, the clerk's office where a wealth of confidential information was kept; that of which as an attorney she was privileged to.

~ ~ ~

"It'll only take a minute or two," Hannah cooed sweetly in a syrupy voice while batting her eyelashes at the rather repulsive and still unconvinced looking, security guard. "I promise."

Scrutinizing her Bar ID, the security guard glanced her over again, puckering his doughy chops while now rubbing a chunky contemplative hand across the portion of his

Buddha sized gut that protruded over his duty belt. Rocking from heel to toe, toe to heel, he went back to inspecting the identification card she had provided him.

"So you're that new guy at Brecker, Haley and Merit," he surmised after another annoying moment of heel to toe, toe to heel.

"Yep." Swallowing repulsion, Hannah grinned flirtatiously, and then covertly eyed the thick heavy ring of keys dangling off his belt as his chunky paw settled atop of them, setting the keys a jingle then muting them with his grimy sausage-link like digits. "Like I said, I just need to sneak in and look up some priors for that case I'm working on…then poof it'll be as if I was never here."

He glanced at her, then winked. "Wanna sneak in, eh?"

Impatient, Hannah forced herself to remain calm and pleasant. After all, he knew she wasn't really sneaking. Any and all types of records kept within the clerk's office were available to her, for her viewing pleasure. Apparently, just not twenty-four and seven. The courthouse had been sealed up as tight as Fort Knox at five sharp. At present, it was past eight. She'd been lucky enough that the man had been outside, taking a smoke break. Or as he'd put it, was *checking the grounds* when she'd arrived.

"I would've come earlier today but I was so busy at the office, lost track of time," she began to explain.

"So how much time you think that Holm kid will get?"

"Huh?" Caught off guard, Hannah shrugged, then fibbed, "Oh. Probably twenty-five, without parole." It wasn't necessarily a lie. The maximum sentence was twenty-five years.

"And you just need to check on this Holm kid's priors?"

Being economical with the truth, Hannah nodded in agreement. She'd never mentioned whose priors she was hoping to check, and the man merely assumed it was her client's. While still waiting for him to decide, anxiety stewed at the possibility that he could tell her to come back during normal business hours. Her smile then widened, relief chasing away the cloud of nervous tension once he shrugged and unhitched the thick heavy ring of keys from his duty belt.

Ushered inside the now quiet as crypt courthouse, Hannah glanced over her shoulder, then tagged behind the security guard. "Thanks a lot. I really appreciate this," she told him.

"Yeah, yeah. Just make it quick." Unlocking the clerk's office, he swung the door wide, then toed a well-used wedge of wood underneath of it in order to keep it open. "Fights gonna start and I don'wanna miss the pre-show, so fetch what you need and then get."

~ ~ ~

Almost home Hannah squinted, then adjusted the review mirror against the annoying glare of high beams coming up fast behind her. Assuming the idiot manning the helm of that beat-up truck intended to pass she edged her Beemer closer to the gravel shoulder while slowing her speed. Despite her generous cooperation, the truck loomed even closer, menacing high beams now flooding the womb of her Beemer, half blinding her. Distracted she wound-up missing the turn off that lead to her own gravel lane.

"Figures," she grumbled. Irritated, she glanced at the driver side mirror and shouted for her own satisfaction, "Why don't you just crawl inside my trunk, you jerk!"

Fed up when they still didn't pass, she tapped the brake pedal in rapid succession singling for them to pass, then yelped in startled shock as the truck sadistically kissed the rear of her Beemer in response. Thrown forward, gripping the steering wheel in sheer panic, Hannah floored the accelerator then glanced over her shoulder. She was more traumatized to find the truck still nipping at her heels like a mangy rabid mutt. Pinning her sights on the road ahead, her headlights illuminated an iridescent triangle warning her of the approaching S curve. The next displayed fat black numbers recommending a top speed of forty-five.

She glanced down at the speedometer needle as it skipped past eighty, then once again at the malicious truck on her tail in hot pursuit. Fear curled inside her as cold as an icy fist. There was no possible way that either one of them could take the fast approaching S curve at this high rate of speed. Proving her theory wrong, the truck plowed into her bumper yet again, the force pushing her vehicle forward and pitching her hard against the steering wheel. She snapped back against the seat, her skull hitting the headrest then bouncing off. Stars scattered her vision as her Beemer skated across the pavement, still bullied by the truck.

Blinking hard, she concentrated on the yellow smudge of the center line while wrestling with the steering wheel to keep her Beemer on the road. Relentless, the truck sped up, this time jumping lanes as if to pass, then swerved its front fender clipping the rear panel of her car in a brutal attempt to send her spinning out of control.

Counter steering as her vehicle fish tailed then skidded almost sideways through the first half of the curve, Hannah gunned it and somehow managed to right the nose of the Beemer. The truck took another swipe, and this time didn't let up, flicking her smaller car like a pesky gnat off pavement and onto the shoulder. Tires kicking-up a plume of dust, Hannah fought to keep the steering wheel steady as the truck sped up nearly neck to neck beside her to take a crack at completely shoving her car off the shoulder.

Jerking the wheel hard, she slammed in to the truck to avoid crashing into the stout stretch of guardrail as it rose up from the earth. She knew herself that it was crazy, but there was nowhere else to go. It was either counter attack, or chance the sturdiness of those steel cables stretched taut across the squat wooden post. At this particular moment in time, she did not want to chance her luck with such a flimsy looking guardrail. She'd probably wind-up breaking her neck, after snapping those steel cables; just to flip side-over-side—or worse front over rear—in her ragtop down the steep rugged incline, to crash into the overgrowth of the ditch below.

Unnerved by such a dismal prospect, Hannah held her breath as their vehicles continued to bounce off each other just to kiss yet again. Gravity began working against her own efforts, sucking her Beemer toward the steel cables of the squat guardrail. The truck took advantage of it, thumping her over inch by inch like a pinball machine lever. With no room on either side to budge, sparks erupted. Sandwiched, beat-up metal bullied the sleek glossy finish of the driver's side; all the while, the steel cables of the guardrail itself engraved grooves along the length of the passenger side panels, as they both skidded violently around the tightest stretch of the curve.

When the structure of the guardrail itself ended, Hannah seized the split second opportunity and quickly steered her Beemer away from the truck, veering hazardously toward the drop-off of the shoulder. The tactic, however crazy it was, gave her just enough room to bolt forward. Cranking the steering wheel hard, tires gobbling up then inadvertently spitting loose rock at her aggressor, Hannah cut in front of the truck as it was swallowed whole by the dense plume of gravel dust.

Energized by her small victory, Hannah glanced in the review mirror and boasted prematurely, "Yeah, that's right, jerk....eat my dirt," then squeaked out a yelp and slammed her foot harder on the accelerator as soon as the high beams sliced through the dust and the outline of the beat up truck emerged. Swearing, she gripped the steering wheel white knuckled and, defying the laws of physics, sling-shot her Beemer around the second curve.

Mind racing, her eyes searched the dark landscape as the lumbering truck rounded the last curve, lethargically picking up momentum. Taking advantage of the short distance she'd managed to put between them and the long straight stretch of highway now before her, Hannah held her speed while attempting to read the road signs as they blurred past. She wasn't certain what she was even looking for, but knew she needed to do something and fast.

Several rail-road crossing markers dotted the way, alerting her—a little too late—of the tracks cutting across the highway; indirectly, also jarring her memory to events which she'd rather just forget, but for some reason she now equated with safety. Bracing herself as she barreled over the tracks, she automatically tapped the brakes. That distraction, the road which lead to it—she now realized—was way before the actual railroad crossing.

Groaning at the very idea, she glanced over her shoulder just to see the cross-bucks light up as the menacing high beams bounced over the tracks in hot pursuit. And right before both of the wooden barricade arms began their lazy decent, red strobe beacons flashing madly.

Crap...

With the truck gaining on her, Hannah knew she had to act fast. Holding her breath, she slammed on the brakes then just as hastily threw it in reverse. Whipping the Beemer around, rubber screeched against blacktop as she came to a rocking halt. Pausing only long enough to regain her bearings, she shoved the gear shift back in drive and simultaneously floored the accelerator. Baffling her aggressor yet again, she ate up the yellow center line while aiming her own headlights point blank at the oncoming truck. Not letting up, she jerked the steering wheel hard at the last minute to avoid a head on collision and, leaving a mere hairbreadth in between them, rocketed past the truck.

Her mind was made up. The concept had seemed viable. The objective—the spontaneous plan itself, had sounded...well, reasonable in theory a second ago. Speedometer needle surpassing ninety, Hannah held her breath. There was no room for second thoughts. Full attention focused on the stretch of highway beyond the tracks themselves, she was already committed to her own harebrained plan: escaping her tormentor by playing chicken with the rapidly approaching freight train itself.

Plowing through both of the wooden barricades as she flew back over the tracks, Hannah squeezed her eyes shut and cringed at the close proximity of the train; its roaring engine, the earsplitting screech of its warning whistle—moreover, the sheer recklessness of her own improvised and foolhardy tactic. Opening her eyes, going miraculously unscathed, she released her breath on howling whoop, hips doing a little victory jig in her seat as she zoomed down the highway. However insane that maneuver was, she had successfully placed a long line of rambling boxcars between her Beemer and that sadistic truck; ultimately putting a halt to its vicious harassment.

For the time being, that was.

Adrenaline pumping, heart still hammering against her ribs, aware the train would not act as a permanent barrier, Hannah once again slammed on the brakes. Whipping her Beemer back around she edged onto the gravel shoulder and sat a moment to gather her wits. She could not chance driving all the way back in to town. Nor could she afford to go home. The only option now was the distraction of which those stupid railroad signs had reminded her of. A winding gravel road named Picnic Woods Lane which would lead straight to Deputy Mark Bowman himself.

Praying to God that she didn't cross paths with that sadistic truck in the process, Hannah threw it in drive and crept along the shoulder doing a mere forty-five hunting for the exact turn off that would take her to Mark's house. Relief flooded her spying the correct marker. Stationed right next to it was the first railroad crossing sign. Grateful, she piloted her battered Beemer along the dark and lonely, but already familiar, gravel lane that wound its way   deep   in   to   the   remote   countryside.

Chapter 17

Ambivalent, Hannah surveyed the house, the outlying fields, and the dark rolling meadow where the crest of the landscape radiated with the soft artificial glow of halogen lamps. Piloting her Beemer up the narrow trail leading to the barn, she pulled up just in time to witness Mark being tossed in the air like a rag doll. She cringed as he landed hard in the dirt. Liberated, the steed Mark had been riding fled, nostrils flared, eyes wild. Slowing to an easy trot, the animal then stopped at the opposite end of the corral to stomp at the earth and eye the human of which it had just tossed; as if arrogantly unimpressed, yet still somewhat aggravated by the entire ordeal.

Hannah shut off the engine. Unaware of her arrival—or maybe he had been knocked unconscious?—Mark remained sprawled in the dirt, a stationary heap. When he didn't stir, she felt a rush of alarm and, unclipping her seatbelt, attempted to exit her car. Battered, the driver side door wouldn't budge. Frustrated, Hannah scrambled over the seats to exit on the passenger side, somehow nicking the horn in her rush; unintentionally further spooking the horse.

"Mark?" Hannah called out then eyed the overly

anxious horse; it's owner who was still lying in the middle of the corral. Panicked, she kicked off her heels and hauled herself onto the metal fencing with intentions of...well, she wasn't quite sure yet. If Mark was unconscious—or worse, injured—she'd have to do something. She couldn't just let him lay there in the dirt to possibly be trampled by some horse.

"Stay put." Halting her off-the-cuff rescue, the command itself delayed her from actually hitching a leg up over the top rung of the metal fence. Rolling over, Mark jumped to his feet, his undivided focus on the horse, voice calm yet stern, "I'm fine. And No Limits is skittish enough. Don't need you jumping in here to further rile him up—honking your horn didn't help."

Feeling more than a tad ridiculed, Hannah open her mouth to argue, but then thought otherwise. Although she hadn't purposely honked the horn, it wasn't worth the argument. Truth be told, Mark was right. She had no clue what she would have done once inside the corral itself. Leaving him to tend to the animal, she eased herself down off the metal fence. Adjusting her rayon cowl-neck tank top, she smooth her palms down her signature Moulinee herringbone trousers before collecting her heels and wandering toward her battered vehicle to digest the brunt of the damage.

"What exactly—better yet, when exactly did that happen?"

"Oh...that?" Hannah made a face and shrugged, then estimated aloud, "I don't know. Fifteen, maybe twenty minutes ago...?"

"Fifteen, twenty minutes ago—?" was parroted after a brief moment of silence, then was followed with what sounded like a soft snort of sheer astonishment. "Most people usually call and then wait for the law to show up, at the scene of the accident itself…not come find them…?"

Hannah frowned and gnawed on her bottom lip. Lost in thought, she wasn't sure how long he had been standing beside her, surveying the damage himself. Absent of a snappy retort, she sighed and simply continued to stare at her mutilated Beemer. She had no clue to what she had been thinking by coming here, to Deputy Mark Bowman's house.

Seconds lapsed to minutes as they both just stood in silence, staring at her car.

"No PIs then, I take it," he assumed aloud, breaking the silence.

PIs...cop talk for personal injuries. A pang of hurt needled her that the question was in general, and not regarding her own individual wellbeing. Without further comment, Mark himself stepped forward to squat in front of the driver's side door. Hannah crossed her arms and half listened as he mumbled something about repair shops while studying the shell of what used to be the driver side mirror dangling from metal; to then testing the mangled door handle to no prevail. She contributed his fascination—the determination to try and somehow fix what was otherwise unfixable—to simple male disposition.

"Neither of you thought to call this in at the scene of the accident itself?"

Irritation bubbled to mingle with disappointment, causing her to pace. She felt like an idiot. Worse, she felt like a teenager being scolded by a parent after dinging up the family sedan. What on earth had she expected, for Mark Bowman to sweep her into his arms? Maybe show her the same attention that he was right now giving to her disfigured car? Why would he? They weren't connected romantically in any way shape or form. She was a defense lawyer. He was a deputy. They had had sex. That was it. The only thing that linked them was a case—a surly punk of a kid, of which she just happened to be defending.

Leave it to her to try and parlay spilt morals into something resembling a relationship...

"I was a little preoccupied. And I don't think it crossed their mind either," she quipped, still pacing, hoping to somehow walk off the disenchantment she now felt.

"You at least exchanged insurance info, right?"

At that she stopped mid-stride and sent him a long sideways glance. He was still too engaged with sizing up the damage to even take notice. Heaving a helpless gesture toward the night sky, she sardonically snorted, "Slipped my mind....and seeing how they were hell-bent on running me off the road, I don't believe exchanging info was top priority on their agenda."

With some satisfaction, she noted the instant his relaxed posture tensed. Straightening, he turned and drilled her with questions. The typical gambit of: what-where-how-why and when? Before she could even provide answers, his astonishment then shifted to authentic alarm as he suddenly demanded, "Who did this—?"

"Good question..." Hannah shrugged, wincing at the subtle bite of pain starting to radiate throughout her shoulders. Exhausted she closed her eyes and dropped her head to gingerly massage the base of her skull and neck. Her temples throbbed. Her entire body ached. Now that the adrenaline rush itself had ebbed, the slight tremor of fear eclipsed the arctic sarcasm in her voice. "A couple names come to mind. Although, I didn't think it was in my best interest to stick around to ask questions."

"Christ, Hannah—Are you hurt?"

Opening her eyes, she focused on his sober slate gray orbs. She didn't have the strength to protest as he cupped her chin, tipping her face up to his as if to better gauge if she had sustained any injuries.

"I'm fine," she assured him, and then confessed, "A little rattled, maybe...but at least I'm in better shape than my car."

"We'll see about that. I'm taking you to the ER. Have the doc look you over," he decided, his tone stern and official, yet as soft and tender as the thumb now absentmindedly caressing her jaw. "Afterwards, we'll file a report at the station and—"

Hannah reassured herself that it wasn't incontestable concern that she'd detected within his voice, his eyes or his very touch. Even though a tiny part of her knew this is exactly what she had wanted, hoped for, had come here for, she stepped away to dispel the longing, the lingering desire, the growing ball of want within her gut. Moreover, she did so to avoid the potential of either one of them taking full advantage of the moment. Allowing him to be charitable enough to fulfill her fantasies would be wrong. Permitting it would only leave her wanting more. Things, of which, she already knew she could never have, or acquire, from this man.

"That won't be necessary," she announced.

"The hell it isn't." Anger flashed, erupting from out of nowhere. "Somebody runs you off the road, leaves you for dead and—"

"That's not exactly how it happened," she interrupted, matching his tone, willingly unleashing the restlessness of her own pent up distress.

Barking out a deranged laugh, Mark shot a backward glance at her Beemer. "Then what exactly did happen?"

I got lucky...Hannah thought, but countered, "I managed to get away before that could happen. And I'm fine. See? So you're not carting me off to the ER like some helpless victim. All I need right now are a couple of Ibuprofens and—" ...*and what? For him to not be a deputy right now? For a man—if not him, then any man—to actually for once give a damn about her....just her, and without that association being due to some case she just happened to be defending, or what they might get out of it in return?*

Having stopped herself short, only gave him the opportunity to continue his own case of why she should see a doctor. Infuriated, Hannah squeezed her eyes shut and pressed her fingers to her temples as his words drifted above the buzz of static in her head. For a fleeting few second she allowed herself to believe it was genuine concern, not annoyance, thickening that Southern drawl of his. It was that off-chance that this man might actually give a damn, which defused her ire and nullified her own argument. If it was only friendship that Mark Bowman could offer her, then why stand here and sabotage the only association she did have with this man?

Sighing, Hannah combed her fingers through her hair. She didn't have the energy to bicker with him. "It's not a big deal. I'm fine. I don't need a doctor. And I can file a report in the morning and..."

"Not a big deal," he parroted half under his breath, while glancing backwards at the Beemer. "Right." Again pinning those staggering sober slate gray eyes on her, and after scrutinizing her for an unbearable moment, he mockingly construed, "Somebody tries running you off the road and so you just happened to stop by, on the off-chance, that I might have a couple of Ibuprofens— ?"

Hannah glanced away from his penetrating, and somewhat patronizing, gaze. However unfair that last remark was, in all truth, she'd deserved it. Not wanting to voice the obvious herself, she told him, "Something like that." Meeting his still dubious gaze, she simply sighed then asked him, "So...do you? Um, have any Ibuprofen?"

Releasing an amazed you-got-to-be-kidding-me grunt, he tossed a vague gesture toward the house. "If I do, they'd be in the bathroom, I reckon."

~ ~ ~

"So are you going to tell me why somebody would want to run you off the highway?"

Hannah swallowed four pills then, taking her time, refilled the plastic tumbler with water and drank greedily before setting it aside. Aware of his proximity behind her, she busied herself with turning off the faucet and placing the bottle of Ibuprofen back inside the medicine cabinet where she had found it. Shutting the cabinet door at last, she noted her hands were trembling. Avoiding Mark's own reflection in the medicine cabinet's mirror she busied herself with wiping up the splatters of water around the sink.

"Hannah? You going to tell me what's going on, or do I have to stand here and guess?"

"Apparently, curiosity killed the cat," she quipped, poorly covering the tremor of fear that rose to constrict her throat. Clearing it, she then attempted to calmly explain, "I have to assume that somebody doesn't like the idea of me representing—or maybe I should say, investigating the Holm's case."

"Curiosity killed the cat?" he echoed in perplexed question.

"That's what they said." Hannah made a face as panic twisted her gut. In desperate need of regrouping, she squeezed past him to escape into the open space of the living room.

Mark followed, nipping at her heels. "That's what who said?"

"Beats me. It was a crank."

"What—? Hold up just a damn minute." Grabbing her arm, he stopped her and turned her around to face him. "What the hell are you talking about, Hannah?"

Hannah squeezed her eyes shut in an attempt to regain her bearings. With the adrenalin rush pretty much spent, and her trusted coping mechanism of sarcasm now proving ineffectual, she knew the falling-apart phase would be next and it was coming up fast. She'd rather had privacy for that portion. But there was nowhere to hide, or go, and the hot surge of tears was already beginning to sting at the backs of her eyelids. Meeting his gaze didn't help. The concern was genuine. The alarm was just as valid. Crank calls notwithstanding, someone had just tried running her off the road; with intent to possibly leave her for dead. This was serious. And she knew she could not try and down-play the facts, let alone the situation, any longer.

"I...I just need a minute," she admitted on shaky breath. In attempt to steady the quivers of fear she drew in a long deep breath, but the tears sprang forth and the tight ball of anxiety unraveled rendering her a blubbering mess.

Not saying a word, Mark gathered her into his arms and held her in a protective embrace. Swaying gently, he stroked her hair and allowed her as much time as she needed. Grateful that he wasn't the type of male to offer awkward pats and shushing, Hannah buried her face in his chest and let three months-worth of pent up frustration along with tonight's fear drain from her system.

Once the majority of that fear and frustration had been purged, she took a deep breath and then feeling somewhat embarrassed half laughed against his chest, "Um, I'm getting mascara all over your shirt."

Shrugging indifference, Mark cupped her chin and lifting her face brushed the remaining tears off her cheeks with his thumbs. "Feel better?" he then asked, eyes roaming her face.

Hannah nodded still slightly abashed she was unable to keep eye contact with him.

"Hold on a sec." He disappeared down the hallway and into the bathroom. Returning he offered her a cool wet washcloth and set a box of tissues on the coffee table. Then just stood there, still waiting for an explanation.

Hannah perched on the arm of the couch and took the washcloth from him and then covered her face with it. Sighing heavily she pressed the coolness of the washcloth to her skin. She had to look a fright by now. Her eyelids felt swollen and were sticky with clumps of mascara. Shaking her head at the vision of raccoon eyes and streaked mascara, she pulled the washcloth off and glanced at Mark. "Sorry and thank you. I mean…well, I don't usually fall apart like that in front of strangers," she confessed.

A half smile hitched the corner of his mouth. That sexy eyebrow shot skyward. "Strangers, are we?"

Hannah blushed at his question, at the very the thought. When she didn't readily answer he took a deep breath and then pursed his lips as if wanting to say something more. Maybe he was debating whether or not to even pursue the subject? He instead switched gears and requested, "Tell me about this crank call."

"Yesterday afternoon, I was leaving the LEC when I got the call on my cell," she explained in between sniffles. Folding the washcloth she stood and laid it next to the box of tissues before plucking one up to blow her nose. Glancing about, she sighed heavily then simply wadded the tissue up and tossed it next to the washcloth and then hugged herself. "Curiosity killed the cat. That's all they said."

"Any idea who it could've been?"

Hannah shrugged, and then rolled her shoulders, wincing at the bite of pain the motion itself produced. She didn't object when he step forward and began kneading the base of her neck and shoulders; nor did she protest when his thumbs began delicately tracing the crook of her jaw and neck in a rhythmic motion as his fingers did magic on the tight knot at the base of her neck and shoulders. Enjoying it, she closed her eyes and letting the tension escape, relaxed and heard herself say, "At least a dozen or more people have access to my cell number. It could've been anybody. Whoever made the call disguised their voice, because—" Lifting her face, Hannah stopped mid-sentence once her eyes locked on his.

Somehow, somewhere between all of his coddling—the caressing of her jaw to the kneading of her shoulders and neck—the scant distance between them had again dwindled to nothing. Hannah dropped her gaze and forced herself to step away; before she could actually decide to let that carnal mouth of his possibly cloud her train of thought, let alone her better judgment.

Pushing his fingers inside his front pockets, Mark stood a moment and watched her. Sounding a tad annoyed he asked, "Anybody threaten you? Other than the crank call, that is. Anything out of the ordinary occur recently?"

"No, not really," she mumbled. Still pondering the

question, she began to pace, wandering aimlessly about the living room. Stopping in front of the stone hearth of the wood-burning stove she stared at nothing in particular, then suddenly turned toward Mark and exclaimed, "Actually, there was. Something odd, I mean…Kender, well he said something really strange to me today. He suggested that pursuing the Holm's case would be a waste of my time. Then tells me that if I expect to survive around here—I assumed he'd meant the office—that I should pick my battles more wisely. I mean I could be wrong, but that's sort of strange…could be construed as sort of a threat, don't you think?"

Mark hummed a note of contemplation. "Could be," he said almost to himself. Consulting the grandfather clock, he then blew out a long sigh and informed her, "Here's what we're going to do. We're going to head into town, stop at the station and file that report. Then we're—"

Hannah crossed her arms and laughed out loud at his sudden and rather possessive not to mention overprotective demeanor. "What's with all this we stuff? I am perfectly capable of driving into town and filing a report, myself, you know."

"*Really*—?"

Reading what she thought was skepticism scroll across his handsome features, Hannah squared her shoulders; prepared for an argument she thought would for sure ensue. "Yes really. And, I'll have you know, I can take care of myself."

"Might be right so. But tell me—" Mark chuckled and then grinned as he trumped her most recent assertion with, "—did you ever get that driver's license of yours renewed yet, Miss Bryans?"

Maddened, Hannah narrowed her eyes, but then found she had to press her lips together just to curb the incriminating grin. "Fine. You drive," she replied as he ushered her outside. "But I'm still not letting you cart me off to some hillbilly ER," she warned as he now opened the passenger side door of his Silverado for her.

Crawling in, clipping her seatbelt in place, Hannah flipped down the visor to peer at her reflection within the tiny lighted mirror. Hell, forget raccoon eyes, she looked horrendous. Flipping the visor in place as he slid behind the wheel, she stifled a giggle and promptly informed him, "And before we go anywhere, *we* need to get my purse and briefcase. They're still in my car. Oh and then *we* need to stop at my house. I'd like to change out of these heels and work clothes, please. My feet are killing me!"

Chapter 18

"Give me your keys," Mark requested killing the lights while easing onto the grass and putting the truck into park. Shutting off the engine, he scanned the area and then reached over to unlatch the glove compartment door.

"You could've parked up by—" Hannah began, glancing about uncertain why he'd chosen to park so far away. Her mouth then snapped shut and her eyes grew large as Mark retrieved a handgun out of the glove compartment. "What's that for?" she hissed watching in horror as he skillfully manipulated the thing to…well, she guessed, to confirm that the weapon was indeed loaded. She cringed at the idea.

"Back-up," he told her and then popping open the center console hatch, pulled out a small Mag flashlight as he explained, "Somebody tried offing you tonight on the highway. Who's to say that same somebody isn't right now waiting for you in the shrubs, or inside your house, to finish the job?"

"Oh…well…that's just silly. Whoever it was, was just trying to scare me is all."

"Silly is you not taking this seriously. Somebody tried running you off the road for a reason, Hannah, and I don't believe for one minute that reason was to merely scare you off some case."

Wide eyed, Hannah searched the darkened windows of her house and then shuddered at the idea. She then sat forward, squinting, as if to better survey the vast stretch of land that surrounded her house. It had never crossed her mind that somebody might possibly want her dead, would hide in the shrubs or break into her house with the intent to do her actual harm. Then again, she never thought someone would try and run her off the road…until tonight that was.

"So…we're going to—"

"We aren't going to do anything. You are going to stay put right here. Got it?"

Hannah nodded then rifled through her purse to locate her keys. Placing them in his out-stretched hand she then simply stared at him saucer-eyed and now anxious.

"I put the truck keys in the cup holder, just in case. Lock the doors once I'm out of sight, okay?" He opened the door but then paused. "You got your cell phone, right?"

Hannah searched her purse, and then looked around the cab. "I…I think I left it in my car," she whispered in a panic.

"Not a problem," he assured her while digging out his own from his pocket. Grabbing her hand, he pushed the cell phone into her palm and curled her fingers around it. Giving her hand a gentle squeeze, as if to better gain her full attention, he then waited until she made actual eye contact with him then instructed, "Dispatch is number one on speed-dial. But only if you need to contact them…okay?"

Hannah nodded, but made a face. "Um, how will I know?" she quizzed, feeling the blood drain from her face at the very idea that he was serious, that this was serious.

"Give me fifteen minutes to make sure everything's okay. I'll turn on the porch light, if it is. If I don't, then I need you to hit speed-dial and request back-up—and then you drive away. Got it?"

"Okay, okay." Scared completely out of her mind, she sat forward squinting to glance over her house yet again while reciting his instructions on a shaky whisper, "I stay put. Lock the doors. Truck keys in cup-holder. Dispatch on speed-dial, number one—but only if needed. If no lights after fifteen then I hit speed-dial, request back-up and drive away. But what—" Turning to face him, Hannah sucked in a startled breath when his mouth greeted hers and he stole an urgent surprise peck. Letting the air swelling her lungs rush out once the sensation of those warm persuasive lips vanished, she breathed, "—about you?"

"I'll be fine. I promise," he murmured, his mouth once again settling over hers; this time it was a methodical knock-your-socks-off kind of smooch, which pretty much calmed her frayed nerves and reassured her that this man indeed knew exactly what he was doing, and in more ways than one. "Now sit tight—and lock the doors. I'll be right back."

Knocked for a loop, Hannah nodded and did so. Clutching the cell phone white knuckled, she watched as Mark snaked around the trees to be swallowed by the black of night as he hastily but covertly made his way toward her house.

~ ~ ~

Still somewhat spooked, Hannah listened for the comforting twang of Mark's voice. Relieved at hearing it, she resumed hastily scrubbing her face; successfully washing away the tear stained streaks and clumpy mascara as well as pretty much any trace of make-up all together with soap and water. She then raced back into her attached bedroom and just stood a moment to catch her breath. Glancing at the bedroom door she'd left ajar, she could still hear Mark's voice filter up through the old-fashion floor vent which confirmed that he was still downstairs talking on his cell phone, before quickly stripping off her slacks and top. Tossing her work clothes across her unmade bed, she swung open her closet door and yanked out whatever her fingers came into contact with first and pulled it over her head. She then jerked open a drawer and pulled out a pair of jeans, stepping inside them, hopping on one foot then the other, to hike them up as she rushed back into the bathroom. Reaching for a French clip, she swept her hair up with the other hand and secured it. Pushing her bare-feet inside a pair of worn multicolored espadrilles—that she'd some time ago abandoned in the corner of her bathroom, she headed out and then paused to check her overall reflection.

"Good Lord," she groaned after inspecting her choice ensemble. A simple tee-shirt which she kept on hand for such tasks as painting and wall-papering—that ironically proclaimed: 'I'm just going to nod and act like I'm listening'—tucked into a pair of faded Levi's. Making a face at herself she then sighed and scolded her reflection, "Good Lord is right. It's not like this is a date. You're simply going to town to fill out a police report."

Turning to head out, in afterthought Hannah snatched up a tube of gloss and swiped the wand across her lips. Flipping off the light, she flipped it back on and this time reached for her perfume, spritzing it about her sparingly before finally turning off the light and heading downstairs.

"Okay, I'm ready," she claimed, slightly out of breath and for some reason now as nervous as a virgin prom date.

Standing, back half to her, amid the maze of unpacked moving boxes stacked within the living room, Mark held up a hand to signal that he was still on the phone, mid-conversation. Hannah felt her heart thump watching him; reading his causal stance; eyeing his masculine physique. Spying the handgun tucked within the waistband of his jeans she swallowed hard. She didn't much care for firearms, but for some reason staring at the gun tucked safely away at his back, she thought it made him look both dangerous and sexy. Heat stirred at the idea.

After agreeing to meet whoever it was at the station, he ended the call and was now giving her his full attention. Hannah felt acutely self-conscious as his gaze swept down the length of her; for some reason she now wanted to race back upstairs and change.

"That was quick. Ah…you aren't bringing anything else with you?"

Hannah stared at him a moment. Unsure of what he was now referring to, she somewhat laughed, "Was I supposed to bring something else?"

"An overnight bag might be good," he suggested, deadpan.

"Um…" Making a face, she crossed her arms and cocked her head as if that last statement of his didn't quite compute. "I don't remember discussing anything about a sleepover?"

"We didn't. And it's not. It's protective custody," he said, his tone official and all business as he further informed her, "Got a problem with it, take it up with the Feds. Apparently we're meeting them at the station…ah, as soon as you're packed and ready to go."

"*Feds*—?" Hannah gasped and then stared at him, panicked yet dubious. She half hoped he was pulling her leg and waited for him to tell her so. When he didn't, and when she didn't readily move or say anything more in return, Mark then added, "Unless of course you wish to stay out here all by yourself and chance it?"

At that, Hannah swallowed the first phase of what was going to be her argument and turning on her heels raced back upstairs to pack an overnight bag.

~ ~ ~

"I sent Darryl's Towing out to your place to pick up the vehicle. Tippen followed him out. Probably on their way back by now," the Sheriff reported to Mark as he and Hannah settled themselves inside the man's office. Shaking out four Tums, tossing them into his mouth he paused to chew, then washed the glob down with a long swallow of cold coffee before leaning over his boxy desk to address his visitor. "Miss Bryans, it's nice to meet you—I'm sorry that it's not under better circumstances, however."

Hannah managed a half smile. Leaning forward herself to match the Sheriff's firm handshake she inquired, "Where is my car being taken? I'll need to notify my insurance company so that they can send an adjuster out for an estimate."

The Sheriff and Mark exchanged looks. Settling himself in his worn leather office chair, the Sheriff explained, "Your vehicle will be towed to the impound lot and will stay there during this investigation, or until I hear otherwise, Miss Bryans."

"What? But I—" Hannah looked between the two of them, dumbfounded. Just because some maniac tried running her off the road didn't mean she had to halt everything about her life, did it? If they were going to hold her vehicle captive, then they should at least offer her a replacement. "How am I supposed to get back forth to the office?"

"This is out of my hands, Miss Bryans. I've recently been informed the incident you were involved in earlier tonight, may possibly be connected with an ongoing federal investigation. Your vehicle will be released to you just as soon as the FBI crime lab finishes with it," he assured her.

Hannah glanced at Mark. Were they serious? "Federal investigation—Crime lab? What *exactly* is going on?"

"They'll be looking at your car come morning," the Sheriff informed her without commenting on the rest and then asked, "Do you recall the make, model, possibly the year, of the vehicle that assaulted you tonight, Miss Bryans?"

Annoyed, and now beyond confused, Hannah glanced at Mark. Frowning she told the Sheriff, "I don't really know all that much about vehicles. All I can tell you is that it was a truck." She took a minute to think about it, really think about it, and then held both hands up in somewhat of a helpless gesture. "It was a truck. Just an old beat up truck. I don't know. It all happened so fast, I...I can't remember."

"Do you recall what color it was? Happen to catch the license plate? Anything at all...anything that you can remember could be useful."

Left eyelid beyond its tattletale twitch, Hannah stared at the Sheriff. Which part of I don't know did this man not understand? Sighing, she cradled her head and pressed her fingers into her temples. She suddenly felt nauseous and needed air. "I'm sorry. I don't recall...other than what I've already told you. It was an old beat up truck. It came from out of nowhere. I don't know a make or model or year. Color wise, um, possibly light blue or tan, maybe white...it was rusty...and just looked hideous. That's all I can remember. I...I think I need fresh air...?"

Throbbing debilitating pain consumed the left side of her head. Rocking forward Hannah reached for her purse but missed it. She felt movement beside her, heard the quick scrape of a chair, the shuffle of boots as Mark steadied her from actually falling off her own chair. She then saw a trash-can appear within her peripheral view.

Hannah glanced up, wishing she hadn't as the quick motion itself only propelled the symptoms of her migraine, causing the swirl of nausea to amplify and the throbbing pain to worsen. She moaned, prompting the Sheriff himself to pick up the phone and depress a button. Within seconds a woman—possibly a dispatcher or secretary? Hannah wasn't sure—was standing in front of her, shoving a Styrofoam cup at her. She shook her head and waved off the cup. She didn't want water or a wastebasket, she wanted her purse; needed the Imitrex injection pen within it in order to help stop the symptoms before they got any worse.

Vision blurred by a white cluster of blinding spots,

Hannah insisted, "Purse…I need my purse." She hastily stood and covered her mouth as a torrent of nausea consumed her and somehow managed to mumble, "…medicine—in purse…oh I think I'm gonna be sick…"

~ ~ ~

"So what's going on?" Mark asked staring at the closed door of the Sheriff's office. Restless he tamped down the urgent desire to go to Hannah, as he was forced to stay put as the Sheriff now debriefed him.

He'd learned of the FBI involvement during his brief phone call with the Sheriff after searching Hannah's house for possible intruders. He just didn't have all the details…yet. Now that Hannah was absent—for the time being—he knew the Sheriff would use this opportunity to fill him in regarding the issue.

"Federal agents are already here," the Sheriff told Mark in a hushed tone. "Seems there's been an ongoing investigation concerning our very own county attorney and at least four cases—possibly more—in which people allegedly paid large sums of money to have charges against them dismissed, or at least greatly reduced…" he paused a moment and then disclosed, "I was told that at least two of those cases involved repeat drunk drivers."

Mark stiffened at that last statement. Reading the Sheriff's expression, he didn't need to ask, nor did he want to. Not wanting to bring up or relive past events, and needing to stay focused in the here-and-now he stated, "Sounds as if we may be cleaning house too, I reckon…" He then sat a moment pondering that very statement, and then asked, "Why target Miss Bryans' though?" then held up a palm. He knew why, so he instead amended his own question with, "Attempted murder…that there goes way beyond taking bribes. It's just out right bold. Not to mention stupid."

"Between you and me…I'd say that stupidity is a result of getting too big for his bitches—way too comfy and full of himself. I suspect he's done what he's done for so long and has gotten away with it all this time, that he probably thinks he's above the law and can do whatever he wants," the Sheriff concluded then nodded at the case file atop his desk. "Including, quite possibly vehicular homicide now. And if our DNA comes back to prove that frat-brat of his was the one indeed driving, then this is going to be huge—it's sure gonna open one big messy can-oh-worms for daddy to deal with. Which, I can imagine is something he would rather keep under wraps. Which, I suspect—and so do the Feds—is probably why somebody tried running Miss Bryans off the highway tonight."

"Which would explain the crank. She received a threat—a crank call, the other day, she said."

"She's aware?" the Sheriff asked, in regards to the depth of the issue.

"No, not yet. I don't think so anyway. And I didn't mention anything; figured we'd go over it with you, here. But, I gotta tell you, she's not dumb. She'd already figured out and had mentioned to me the other night that she thought there was something amiss with—"

"You know each other personally?" the Sheriff inquired, cutting him off.

Mark pursed his lips. Not certain how or why it mattered and now unsure which direction his boss was headed by asking, an unanticipated rush of heat washed over his face. "We've become…ah, acquainted, due to Holm's case," was all he offered.

"Good enough," the Sheriff replied. "Can't right see sticking Miss Bryans in some hotel room—Ask me, don't right like the idea myself anyhow...too dangerous. Rather she had a twenty-four-seven detail until all of this is cleared up, and with somebody that I can actually trust around here. Which it so happens is you. You okay with that?"

Mark stared at his boss for a split second. As he nodded in agreement heard himself answer, "Not a problem, sir." Much like the Sheriff, Mark would not have had it any other way…although he'd be a liar if he claimed he just agreed to do so solely out of professional duty alone. There was just something about that woman which drew him to her and it was something he just couldn't shake. And now that he was her appointed bodyguard, Mark couldn't help but to wonder how Miss Hannah Bryans would feel about such an arrangement herself.

Chapter 19

The sensation of a cold wet nose nudging about her fingers and palm indicated to Hannah that she might not be in the right place, the right house, let alone her own bed. Groggy, she lifted her head slightly and squinted to investigate that theory. Ears perked at attention, wide white stripe accentuated by one blue eye and one brown, a Border Collie stared back at her; panting around the tug-rope toy clamped securely within its teeth.

"Oh…hi, Casper," Hannah sighed. Rolling over she snuggled into the pillow. She closed her eyes allowing herself to momentarily drift back into slumber, and then sat straight up with startled awareness. On a surge of panic, she sprang off the bed then glanced backwards at the mattress just to see it was indeed vacant. While trying to adjust her eyes to the fingers of sunlight streaming through the gap in the curtain her gaze darted about picking out bits and pieces at random—a night stand, a nonfunctional digital clock atop of it; a matching dresser with a statue of horse mid-gallop. Confused, she looked at the dog. "You wouldn't happen to know anything about this, would you?"

The Border Collie cocked its head and then looking

guilty—of, well something—made a quick exit. Hannah followed, more than a little annoyed and now in search of an explanation. Pausing at the top of the stairs, she quickly looked down at herself relieved to see she was at least presentable to demand such an argument. Somewhat grateful to see the same tee-shirt and jeans she'd changed into last night she sighed and continued on her war-path.

Still being fully dressed was a plus on Mark's part, she thought, as she made her way past the bathroom and down the hall. Hitting the open living room the aroma of freshly brewed coffee, coupled with a potpourri of mouthwatering scents highlighted by the distinct hint of vanilla, welcomed her; teasing her nostrils and had her stomach growling in anticipation. She had to admit both annoyed as well as surprised her. It was another plus on his part—food, wonderful smelling food—she thought as she made a beeline toward the sound of utensils clanking against glassware.

"Just so you know, you'd better be adding bacon to whatever that wonderful smell is…that is, if you're indeed planning to bribe your way out of this with food," she announced, crossing her arms while leaning against the far counter. Casper sat at her side, dropping the tug-rope at her bare feet to sniff at the air himself and then looked up at her as if patiently waiting for her to take notice.

Mark smiled and glanced in their general direction. "Bacon it is then," he declared. Setting a wire whisk aside, he drowned a piece of bread within the concoction he'd just finished mixing and then added it to the pieces already starting to sizzle in the cast-iron skillet atop the stove. "I see Casper managed to wake you. Sorry. I was going to let you sleep in. How's your head—better?"

Hannah eyed him, suspicious, as he nonchalantly went about making breakfast, moving in between the stove the counter top and then the refrigerator—and doing so as if nothing at all was wrong with her standing there watching him. "I'll live."

"That's good. Does that happen often?"

"No not really—I mean, well sometimes…yes."

"Are they like that every time?"

"Not usually. Only gets that bad when I'm beyond stressed, and well when I forget to consume food on a regular basis in general," she admitted, and then snorted, "Apparently coffee and or cappuccino with the occasional handful of chocolate covered raisins isn't considered a staple…or even food group."

"Who knew," he gasped in mock disbelief, but then regarded her with an expression of which she would have much rather not identified with. After a second scrutinizing her, he commented, "Lucky for you, I'm familiar with all four of the food groups."

Reading authentic concern and a trace of awareness within that penetrating gaze of his, she became acutely conscious of the fact that his statement could have very well been: *Lucky for you I'm here, so let me take care of you.*

Slightly frazzled at the notion that unspoken message left, she stooped to Casper's level using the dog as a diversion to avoid eye contact. "I should be good for a few months. Unless of course something else catastrophic happens—" she laughed hoping to dispel her sudden bout of nervous self-conscious energy. "—I think it's an internal safety thing, really." Hannah stood, flipping a glance in his general direction just as his brow furrowed in question. "Sorta like my brain automatically induces a killer migraine whenever I happen to become overly stressed-out. That way, I'm too incapacitated to actually go postal on the innocent," she joked on a nervous laugh.

"Explains those uprooted flowers in your Zen garden," he chuckled, ducking inside the refrigerator to rummage about. Producing a package of bacon, he moved about the kitchen, retrieving another skillet and setting it on a burner. Turning it on, he then opened the package and began laying strips of bacon within the skillet itself.

However annoyed she was, she smiled at the fact that

he was actually going to bribe her with not only bacon but a home cooked breakfast—and one made from scratch by the looks of the items scattered about the counter top. She had to admit she was enjoying the attention, and the view. Dressed in faded Levi's and simple tee-shirt himself, Mark was clean-shaven and his damp hair stood in a rowdy spike. The hint of Irish Spring mingling with the fresh traces of male deodorant, suggested that he'd recently showered. Thinking about it, cued her to finger comb her hair and run her tongue across her teeth. She'd kill for a toothbrush and a shower right about now.

"So…I trust you slept well?" he inquired, while turning the bacon and pushing it around.

"Speaking of, why exactly was I sleeping in your bed?" Hannah asked, now wanting answers more than that toothbrush or shower.

She'd searched her brain, trying to recall the events which would've led her to be sleeping at this man's house in the first place, but so far had come up empty handed. The entire evening seemed hazy for some reason, as if she'd been on an all-night drunk.

"Because the hospital doesn't make French toast the way I do," he commented flipping the pieces over in the skillet. Task complete, he checked the bacon again and then smiling gave her his full attention. "I figured you'd be mad as a wet hen if I'd have let doctor Grainger admit you for observation. After seeing you had one of those injection pens, she realized it was a migraine setting in and not a concussion."

Hannah stared at him as the events of yesterday trickled through her memory. Working on the Holm's case; Kender's so-called friendly advice; staying late at the office to then flirting her way into the court house in order to search files after hours; someone trying to run her off the highway; escaping to Mark's house…to then almost passing out—whether or not she actually did she wasn't certain?—while filing a report at the station; a secretary helping her to the bathroom.

She made a face at that last recollection. "I didn't puke on anybody, did I?"

"Ah…I don't believe so, no."

"Well that's good. I seriously don't remember anything…matter of fact everything's pretty much lost in a fog," she admitted.

"Doc said that may happen. She gave you a shot of some heavy duty painkiller—think she called it Toradol. Said the combo—your headache stuff and that painkiller— would be more effective in the state you were in, but that it might knock you for a loop." He gave her a quick once over as if to make sure himself that she looked okay, before his gaze rested on hers. "And to answer your question, I figured you'd be more comfy in an actual bed, considering. So I tucked you in upstairs and then I crashed on the couch."

"You took me to the ER," Hannah stated, more in reflection than in question, as memories of the night's events filtered throughout her head.

"You gave us all a scare," he confessed. "And I had no other choice—and thank God I had, otherwise..." he paused as if expecting a snide remark or an argument, not receiving any he simply left it at that and then turned and poured a steamy cup of coffee offering it to her. "Cream or sugar?"

"No. And thanks." Accepting the mug, she took a test sip then took a longer one, savoring the bold richness of Columbian roast. Add that to the plus side also. "Um, I mean for last night…for, well for everything you've done. Sorry if I—well, I can be sort of pigheaded and a tad too independent at times."

That won her a grunt as well as a look.

Hannah laughed, "Okay. Most of the time."

She wandered toward the table as he finished making breakfast and sliding a chair out sat with her coffee to enjoy the view. Caught up in thinking she could get used to waking up to this every morning, she smiled as he began depositing plates of food onto the table. After a minute or two that fantasy ebbed once her gaze landed on the over-the-range microwave's digital clock. The time displayed was 8:53AM.

Realizing it was still a week-day, Hannah suddenly stood and exclaimed, "I need to go—or at least call the office and—"

"That's already been taken care of, so just relax."

Relax? She stared at him frustrated and even more puzzled. She was still waiting for an in-depth explanation. All he'd really offered her was coffee, scrumptious smelling French toast and her requested bribe of bacon with bits and pieces of random information. She wasn't letting him off that easy. "What do you mean, that's already been taken care of?"

"In light of the recent events…ah, you're otherwise indisposed."

"Excuse me?" Hannah crossed her arms now full of discord and attitude. "It's not up to you what I am—or for that matter, what I do. And I can't just *not* show up to work without a legitimate reason," she began.

"Is being dead a legitimate enough reason for you? Because the last time I checked, it's pretty hard to show up to work if you're dead," he cut, matching her snarky tone.

A jolt of shock spiked through her at his reply, causing her to step back. "How dare you—" she hissed temper already beyond flaring.

He shot her a heated look, barely holding on to his own irritation. "Somebody tried killing you last night, Hannah—or was that lost in the fog? You've been placed in protective custody. So stop being childish and just deal with it already."

"Oh…now I'm being childish? Well isn't that just ducky—and if I'm in this stupid so-called protective custody, then what am I even doing here!"

"Because…" he barked, then hesitating yanked out a

chair and sat. After a moment, he enlightened on a dangerously low and sour note, "Because I've been appointed the pleasure of keeping an eye on you."

Hannah glared at him, more at his vinegary air while making such a statement. She couldn't help wonder if he indeed felt that way; actually meant it...? "Really...well in that case, I don't want *you* as my personal bodyguard. Tell them to find somebody else."

"Take it up with the Feds, Hannah. I had nothing to do with it—I'm just following orders. So anything you say will pretty much be a moot point right now." Shelving her debate, he forked a slice of that yummy smelling toast and plopped it on his plate. "Trust me, I'm just as pleased about this as you are."

At that, her jaw dropped. Affronted, she sucked in an audible breath and gaped at him.

He was fine piece of work, this man. From one extreme to the other; if he wasn't wooing her with that mouth of his, then he sure seemed to have no problem using it to scold and or taunt her. Then again she wasn't helping matters. She attributed their constant power-play yo-yo to that steady riptide of sexual tension. An attraction they'd both indulged in, yet something of which they both seemed skittish of. Something she knew she should steer clear of herself, but whenever given the opportunity she sure as hell still dared to toy with—which, she figured explained their bouts of constant bickering. It was as if it was a damn game. If one was tugging, then the other one just had to be pulling. And maybe that's why she unconsciously remained standoffish? Because she knew he could pull harder. Bickering, at least, was way easier because snarky remarks and spouting off insults never broke hearts.

But, it was also exhausting. Dragging a hand through her hair, she sighed and now questioned if there could ever be a happy medium between them.

"Regardless of whether we like it or not, we're stuck

together for the time being. So might as well sit down, eat and play nice," he suggested without so much as a glance, tone quiet and even-keeled. "You're lucky you're here and not stashed away in some two-bit hotel with a Fed—likely, be eating a roll of powder donuts out of some vending machine and risk one of Bremer's henchmen finishing that job they started last night, if they happen to get wind of your whereabouts. And trust me, with the people we're dealing with, it could happen."

Landing hard in her chair she grappled with the idea he might be right. Maddened, she searched for a reason—any reason, to continue to argue; but wasn't certain what it was she should now argue about. He was on her side. And apparently he was now her bodyguard. He'd brought her here to his house for safe keeping, had tucked her in his bed—left her fully dressed even, and had slept on his own couch. In a way, she felt slightly insulted—considering. So, there it was. She was annoyed with him because he did not fit the mold. Because he was so unlike what she was used to dealing with? He had been a complete gentleman; had slept on the couch...instead of taking full advantage of the situation...and she just didn't know how to handle it; him.

Truth be told, she was not angry at him in the least. She was angry at herself for wishing he had...still wishing he would...and was now afraid of what she might do herself in order to provoke him enough into just kissing her and taking her mind off this entire ordeal she'd somehow found herself in.

Still fuming at the entire situation itself, Hannah stabbed a slice of French toast and dumped it on her plate to slather it with butter and syrup, then collected a segment of bacon and bit into it, chewing; still mulling over what she could possibly dispute. Testing the French toast, her insides melted and her toes curled in sheer pleasure. Damn. Her anxiety level skyrocketed to yet another altitude. Put another hash-mark on the plus side for Mark. The man could cook. His French toast was parallel to that carnal mouth of his…absolute heaven. She opted to not bring that tidbit to his attention, so they ate in complete silence with that undercurrent of restless unresolved energy still buzzing around them.

"So I'm dead?" she quietly probed, opting to be the one to break the stalemate. "I mean if that's really the only story the Feds could come up with, it's pretty lame."

Mark looked up at her, momentarily puzzled until it dawned on him what she was now talking about. He almost smiled. "No. You've taken a leave absence due to a migraine—have to recoup from it. If needed, you'll be able to work from your home office."

"Well that's a relief," she quipped. Still somewhat stewing, trying to now make sense of the events themselves and how she'd gotten stuck in the middle of…well of something that she apparently wasn't yet privy to, Hannah forced herself to remain calm and play nice as suggested. Snarky comments and bickering wasn't productive, and neither was trying to camouflage her own attraction to this man with constant rancor, so she inquired in a more pleasant and civil tone, "So why are the Feds suddenly involved anyway? And what on earth does any of this have to do with me?"

"You're fairly new around here. And that being so, we can at least assume Bremer doesn't have you on his private payroll."

"Well you're correct on that assumption."

Snatching a piece of bacon himself, Mark gestured with it in between bites as he debriefed her. "And it turns out you weren't so off base about the county attorney after all. Holm's case aside—and I'm only telling you this because you need to know—we've just learned that the FBI has been knee-deep in investigating Bremer for allegedly taking bribes. And yes before you say I told you so, is also under suspicion of extortion, tampering with evidence as well as altering court records. Nobody knows, but the Sheriff and I…and well now you. The Feds aren't ready to go public with any of this, themselves, just yet. There's too much at stake they said."

Reading his serious expression, Hannah nodded slowly while still digesting the brunt of the information. She realized he wasn't telling her just to confirm that she had been right all along. It went way beyond that. He was only disclosing such information to her for her own safety, and well mainly because she was now stuck right alongside him within this mess, until it all played out. "Understood."

"According to the Bureau, they're still collecting evidence in order to build a solid case."

"But shouldn't they have notified your department, from the get go? I mean isn't that norm?"

"The FBI does what it wants. If they had wanted us involved they would have involved us. But because Bremer has managed to gain eyes within the department itself, we were never involved or informed of the probe, let alone of their ongoing investigation—well, until now that is. Still have no clue who Bremer's eyes are or who they all belong to. If the feds know, they aren't sharing that info with us."

Hannah pondered that, then replied, "Won't Bremer and his cohorts realize something's up though, I mean, won't they realize there's feds roaming around town?"

"I sort of thought that myself." Mark took a swallow of coffee then set the mug aside. "Until, of course, the Sheriff and I were privileged to make the acquaintance of two of those special agents last night. Seems a handful of them have been here working undercover all along, some since the get go of their probe, others periodically planted to—"

"Seriously?" Hannah interrupted, now staring at him incredulous. "But…this is Hicksville USA—I mean, you'd think a bunch of feds roaming around would…well, they'd stick out like a sore thumb with their earbud walky-talkies and dark suits…well, wouldn't they?"

"This isn't the movies, Hannah. I reckon it'd be like any other normal citizen relocating. I'm a transplant. And so are you. You just moved here—what—three months ago? So do I or you stick out like sore thumbs? Hold up…" Hesitating, that sexy eyebrow shot skyward as he playfully eyed her then jokingly quizzed, "You're not a special agent are you?"

Hannah laughed with him; enjoying the diversion, leaning away as he leaned forward as if to actually check her ear for one of those ear-buds. "And what would you say if I told that I was?" she teased wearing what she thought was her best poker-face.

That won her a hearty laugh. "I wouldn't believe you."

Humming a defeated note, Hannah pouted and got up to retrieve the coffee pot, topping his mug off as well as her own before settling back in her chair. "And why not?" she then asked somewhat curious.

"Your face, last night…you should've seen it when I took my back-up out of the glove compartment," he chuckled.

Recalling more than just him pulling out his gun, Hannah blushed momentarily reliving that duo of simple yet tantalizing smooches that he'd knocked her socks off with. Unable to keep eye contact, she pushed what was left of her French toast around her plate and shrugged. "Yeah, well…guns, they sort of scare me with that whole bang your dead theory."

"As long as the business end is always pointed away from you, shouldn't be affected by that theory. I can teach you. Would be wise for you to know how to handle a firearm—at least a shotgun if nothing else."

Hannah stared at him, somewhat wary of accepting such an offer and not because of some unfounded fear she had of firearms. She was skittish of the man himself…well, not the man in particular, just what that carnal mouth of his could do to her. Those mischievous eyes and those awesome dimples were already doing a number on her right now. What was it about this man that had her head-over-heals? Sighing she smiled. Why fight it? Determined to play nice as he'd suggested, she hoped maybe they could find some type of happy medium.

"Gun-slinger and special agent were never on my what-do-you-want-to-be-when-you-grow-up   list....but,   okay maybe...we'll see."

"We can start with b-b-guns, if you want. Less scary," he suggested, then returned to the issue at hand. "Anyway, apparently a handful of agents have been working the case right underneath our damn noses, collecting their intel' as well as their evidence and never once saying a word to our office."

Although that part didn't really matter much to her, she chalked his subtle rancor up to some type of departmental territorial thing, then commented, "So, me investigating Holm's case and snooping in a way, sort of made me a target."

"Not made, *still makes* you."

Hannah swallowed hard at the idea; what she'd managed to get herself smack-dab in the middle of. And here she thought life in Hicksville USA would be boring. Ha! She shook her head at the thought.

"It also sent up red flags for Feds. That hair I found and the DNA sample of Holm's and the search warrant? Well, it had them scrambling once they caught wind of it. If the DNA comes back and proves Holm's innocent—"

"Wait...they're afraid Holm's case could blow their undercover probe?" Hannah interjected sounding almost insulted.

"Doesn't make sense, I know. But yeah...because they're federal, their investigation trumps ours. And they don't have to involve us—and they don't want us screwing them out of a few years' worth of hard-core undercover work. Don't agree with it, but I can't blame them. You'd know better than I do that one simple mess-up by a cop or agent, or anybody for that matter, could blow an entire case—possibly allow an otherwise guilty person to walk with the right attorney."

"Just because I'm a criminal defense attorney doesn't

mean I simply look for screw ups to get a client to walk free," Hannah said quietly somewhat insulted that he'd think that.

"Didn't mean you in particular…just in general. But we both know a clever and smart defense attorney will look for every angle. Regardless, the feds are afraid our case might screw their own up."

"But, if Holm is indeed found innocent, then Bremer's kid could possibly be brought up on vehicular manslaughter, which might expose daddy—Isn't that what it's all about—To expose him for the criminal he is and take him down? Give him the longest sentence?" Hannah stopped mid-sentence wheels turning as she tried calculating the various offences with their allotted penalties. Unable to do so without details, she simply left it at, "I mean, combined all the Fed's indictments along with accomplice to vehicular homicide as well as tampering with evidence, obstruction of justice and attempted murder…well, any logical person would think that *that* would pretty much seal the deal. They could put him away for…well for forever and then some."

"For forever and then some, huh?" he laughed. "That some form of technical lawyer lingo?"

Hannah smiled. "You know what I meant. For life…longer than life."

Chapter 20

"Since when does protective custody include slave labor?" Hannah asked stabbing the pitch-fork, she'd been given over an hour ago, into the ground.

"Since my ranch hand went AWOL," Mark joked with a smirk, "…and since you'd mentioned something about enjoying wielding manure shovels…reckon, I'd put you to work."

"Yeah well, I said wield a mean one…not enjoy," Hannah laughed. "This stall is done and so is this Filly," she announced, and then mumbled, "Think I'd rather learn how to shoot a gun…or better yet, ride a pony."

"Pick one."

"What?"

"Pick one. Riding a horse or shooting a gun?"

Hannah thought about it. "Horse," she opted. She figured it was the safer of the two.

"Okay…pick a horse and I'll show you how to ride," Mark suggested coming up beside her. "Or at least, how to stay on one," he chuckled giving her a playful nudge.

Repressing her own grin, Hannah eyed him. Not commenting on his remark, she scanned the paddock.

Turning toward the far pasture she searched for then spied the lone horse she'd seen only a couple of times before. He was beautiful and majestic. She nodded in the general direction of the pasture. "That one."

That won her a robust laugh. "Don't think so. No Limits is too green yet."

"You said pick any horse and now you're going to stand there and—" she began.

"I can barely stay on No Limits, myself," he explained, then chuckled. "Besides, I don't think there's enough superglue to keep you on him. And, I didn't say any...I said pick one, from over there...actually, that one right there would be a good choice for you."

"Oh so now you're picking my stud for me too?" she muttered while sauntering up to the metal gate of the paddock. Hannah glanced backward just in time to catch his knowing look and that sexy arch of his brow. Blushing, she felt her tummy flip-flop. Good Lord...she was bad. Risky was constantly toying with it; him. But one thing was for certain, she seriously enjoyed pushing his buttons, razzing and flirting with him.

"Ah...that's a mare. And her name is Xena," he told her. Approaching the gate, Mark made a clicking noise and held out his hand to the horse.

"Xena, huh? Princess warrior. Well that's fitting at least," she decided, looking the animal over, then told the horse, "I'm Hannah, princess. And as long you don't buck, bite or trample me...we should get along fine."

"She's older, so well mannered. Good horse for beginners to learn on."

"I'm not a *beginner*—beginner....after all, grew up around them. I know all sorts of stuff about them."

"Is that so?" Grinning, he tossed a vague gesture toward the barn. "Then, reckon, I don't have to show you what any of that stuff is, what to do, or how to put all that stuff—oh you know, like a saddle—on a horse."

"Oh, well...you mean *that* stuff." Hannah attempted to

repress the giggles as she now walked toward the barn with him. "Okay, have it your way. Beginner it is then."

Gathering what they needed she helped round up Hop-Scotch and Xena. After grooming them for riding, Mark showed her how to properly saddle a horse and then basically laughed at her as she stubbornly attempted to mount Xena herself; refusing his help. After two attempts she was successful and found herself sitting atop the animal, reins in hand and ready to go but with no clue on how to make the animal…well, start.

"Okay, I give up. Where's the gas pedal?" she joked.

"Squeeze with your thighs a bit—rock your bottom forward slightly, toward the horn…she'll know you mean business then and should start walking," he instructed.

"Oh…um, well…it's not working. Maybe this isn't such a good idea?"

"If you're nervous, Xena will be nervous. Just relax, Hannah. It's like riding a bike."

"Easy for you to say," Hannah remarked but then smiled in victory once she did as instructed yet again—this time calmer and with purpose—and the horse moved forward a few steps. "Um…okay, starting the thing up is mastered. Now, how do I steer it?"

Chuckling Mark rode up next her, on his own horse Hop-Scotch, in order to now show her. "Simply lay the reins across the left side of the neck—like this—to go to the right and across the right side of the neck—like this—to go left."

"Left goes right and right goes left…gee like that isn't confusing. You writing this all down, Xena?" Hannah tested each and was somewhat pleased with the results. Smiling, she looked up at Mark. "Okay, got it. Now what?"

"Follow me…ah, and try to stay on," he suggested on a chuckle as he trotted ahead of her.

"You hear that, Xena? He said you're supposed to follow him and make sure I stay on. So go…giddy up…scoot…shazam," she told the horse when it just stood there.

Huffing a breath, she glanced up to see Mark way ahead of her now. Squeezing her thighs repeatedly while now quickly rocking back and forth in the saddle, all in hopes of making the animal move, Hannah burst out laughing at the visual of what she must have looked like doing so; more so at the idea there should have been goofy circus music playing in the background. She then sucked in a startled breath when the horse decided to take off itself at a quick gate.

"Okay okay, princess…just not that fast. Crap, where's the brake pedal?" she mumbled to herself playing with the reins. Pulling back on them, she sighed as the horse slowed to a steady walk. "See…no reason to be nervous. Apparently *you* know exactly what you're doing…at least that makes one of us."

Hannah took a deep breath and released it, then sat up straighter and smiled; pretending to know exactly what she was doing while now riding past Mark. Bypassing him, she cut over her shoulder, "See, just like riding a bike. No biggy. Told you I wasn't a beginner."

"Uh-huh," he chuckled, while piloting Hop-Scotch to fall in step alongside them. They rode in silence for a brief few minutes. Mark nudged his own horse into a trot and, tossing a dimple riddled grin over his shoulder at her teased, "Nice bronco action you had going on back there, by the way. Looked like a real pro."

~ ~ ~

After towel drying her hair, Hannah tossed the plush bath towel aside to dig through her overnight bag, frowning at the items she'd hastily thrown inside of it the night before: A handful of various styled dress tops and two pair dark colored slacks for work; a pair of knee-high hose. In her rush she'd forgotten to pack underwear and a clean bra. But hey, she had four inch heeled dress shoes. And considering the circumstance—that being stuck here with Mark under protective custody—she wasn't in need of any of heels let alone the dress clothes she'd packed.

She wanted shorts and another tee-shirt…sneakers, maybe a tank-top. Sighing, she glanced at the jeans and tee-shirt she'd stripped out of before taking a shower. She didn't need to test sniff them to know they already reeked of horse from her spur of the moment riding lesson, and they were also still damp from sweat so more than likely stunk from helping Mark clean the stable and barn.

Picking up the tee-shirt, she frowned. Debating it, she then curled her nose at the idea all together. Hiking up the oversized robe Mark had loaned her, Hannah slipped her panties back off and tucked them inside the back pocket of her jeans. Snatching up her lacy bra, she tucked it in the opposite pocket. Satisfied, she tightened the sash of the robe, adjusted the neck and then grabbing the outfit headed downstairs.

"Mark? Can I borrow your washing machine?" she inquired gesturing with the wadded up clothes in her hands. "It seems all I packed are dress clothes for the office. So, um, these are my only other option…and they're kind of dirty from earlier and well from sleeping in them."

Fingers stilling above the pad of a small calculator, he glanced up from the papers that he'd been engrossed in since returning from their mid-morning riding lesson. Hannah couldn't ignore the boost it gave her seeing his gaze sweep down the length of her just to then trace slowly upward.

"Yeah sure." Standing, he abandoned the mess of bills scattered across the table and gestured for her to follow him through the kitchen to an alcove. One side of the nook housed built in shelves stocked with spices, various items and canned goods. The opposite side was a set of decorative louvered doors. Folding the doors open revealed a fancy top of the line washer and drier duo housed within the cubicle.

"Thanks," she said as he flipped open the lid to the

washer and held his hand out. As if she didn't know how to, or couldn't wash her own clothes. "I can get it…really. I know how wash my own clothes, Mark."

Hannah stared at him when he simply just stood there watching her, then huffing a breath turned and inconspicuously removed her bra and panties to try and toss them in the drum without him noticing them. She wasn't sure why, but did it just because. She then stuffed her jeans and tee-shirt inside the washer itself.

Glancing over the various knobs, she took her time reading each cycle to ensure she set it on the correct one. Catching her off guard, Mark reached around her and twisted a different knob, flipping the arrow to point to the small load setting. Further shocking her, he then shamelessly pulled his own tee-shirt up over his head and tossed it in with her clothes.

Drawing a silent breath, Hannah turned almost grateful he hadn't also stripped out of those snug fitting Levi's to add to the wash. She had to tell herself to continue breathing as she fought to not gawk at his midsection.

"Um, where do you keep the detergent?" she managed to ask, hoping to not sound too flustered at having him standing there half-naked now looking at her with those eyes of his.

The hint of a smile twitched that carnal mouth. Looking rather pleased by her reaction alone, he tossed a nod toward the cupboard built within the cubicle itself above the washer and dryer. He then brazenly stepped forward, almost pinning her to washer as he purposely leaned in while reaching up to retrieve the bottle of detergent for her.

"Mark."

"What?" he asked almost innocently while plopping a bottle of Gain detergent on the dryer.

The knowing arch of his eyebrow was a dead giveaway and cued her to the fact he was now the one flirting with her. Maddened, Hannah stared at him and willed herself to not to breath in his masculine scent as he unscrewed the cap and dumped a dollop of detergent inside the washer and flipped a switch turning it on. When he didn't move away, she gritted her teeth. The heady rush of desire was just too tempting for her to now try and deal with.

"You're not even going to measure it?" she cut, referring to his lack of using the measuring cup built into the cap; readily transferring the surge of unchecked desire into the more practical passion of sheer irritation. Doing so she hoped to ward…well, whatever this was he thought he was now doing, off.

"It's a pair of jeans, a pair of panties, one rather sexy bra and a couple of tee-shirts," he pointed out inching closer, closing the scant distance between them. What caught her off guard wasn't the mouth grazing hers, it was his low intimate whisper electrifying her senses as he teased against her lips, "You really need to control everything, don't you."

Heat prickled up her neck. Once his words registered, however, they just weren't as palatable as the mouth that was now enticing hers in a deep slow kiss. Side-stepping, she shoved at his chest and yanked the collar of the robe—that he'd somehow managed to part—back together.

"What? It's okay for you to tempt and tease…but I can't?" When she said nothing in response, he stepped back and continued, "So, I'm just supposed to ignore it— ignore you? Care to enlighten me on the rules of this little game of yours, Hannah?"

Hannah's jaw dropped. More so because she knew he was right. She had no problem flirting with and razzing him, testing his limits to see how far she could go herself without delivering. She had done so all morning; had enjoyed the rush; the results. Yet when the tables were turned, and he was the one taunting her, giving her exactly what she had been fishing for earlier, now she wasn't so sure how to handle it; him.

And he was right. If she wasn't in control, then she didn't want to play. This pull-tug-tug-pull game of theirs had been relatively safe, up until now. He'd turned the tables on her. She'd realized earlier that he was far more skilled at controlling his own reactions, was able to restrain himself under her antics. And more so than she was.

That same man, however, was right now standing before her, his hands on his hips with one leg cocked. Doing so not to hide his state of arousal but—she guessed—to dare her to now take notice of what she could do to him.

"Just because we happen to be stuck together does not mean we have to jump in the sack," she pointed out. "We're professionals. We should act accordingly—I, for one, cannot afford another mistake, like the other night in the gazebo."

His expression caused her to wince and want to mentally drop-kick herself; right after voicing that last half.

"Act accordingly?" He stood a moment incredulous, then looking wounded, before asking, "The gazebo was a mistake? Is that how you really feel?"

"I may be cop repellent, but I'm not munchkin proof," she enlightened. "And I for one...well, I seriously doubt you would want to be forced into something...well, out of a sense of duty, simply because of an oops-how'd-that-happen accident. It wouldn't be fair to you or me—well, and I simply do not need to add any more—let alone take care of..." Stopping she pulled her fingers through her damp hair. She was rambling and wasn't certain herself what it was she was now trying to explain or get across. "I don't expect somebody else to clean up the mess I've already managed to make of my life thus far," she then bluntly stated.

"Would that be so bad?" he questioned his voice dangerously intimate as he stepped closer. The awareness within his slate gray gaze pinned her to where she stood; the knowing within those eyes touched a chord of longing to stir to life from somewhere deep inside of her. "Letting somebody take care of you? Is that what you're scared of? Clearing up the confusion…scared of possibly letting somebody good into your life?"

When she didn't respond he traced a finger down the side of her cheek. Drawing her closer to the edge, he murmured, "I think you create all this havoc because you think if you do you'll keep people out. You're scared of a good thing, Hannah. That's what I think."

Desire spun and tightened like a spring, ready to snap. The powerful chemistry that constantly arced between them both thrilled, and excited her, yet also scared her to death. Tumbling into bed with this man—yet again, would be easy and was also the thrilling part…actually allowing him into her life, letting him possibly take care of her, conceivably losing herself completely as well as her heart while doing so, that is what frightened her.

"I'm not scared of anything, or anyone," she lied on a quavering whisper then went as far as to boldly state, "you, included."

"Really?" He inched forward, challenging her assertion, testing her resolve, daring her to push him away again; all while enticing her to let him in; with just his eyes and then his wonderful lips.

Her body automatically responded and, parting hers, she allowed his tongue to lead. Letting the tight grip she'd had on the bath robe lessen allowed his hands to explore, caress and tease.

"Upstairs," he suggested on hoarse murmur.

Releasing a moan and shaking her head no while jerking him closer, was a good enough reason for them both to stay put. Slipping the thick material off of her shoulders, the robe slid down her back to puddle around her feet. Anticipation swelled within, searing her with a flash of moist hot heat as he lifted her. A shiver spiked through her at the sensation of ice-cold metal kissing her bottom once he set her on the edge of the washing machine.

She concentrated on his mouth, the tender urgency of his own want and need as his fingers assisted hers in releasing the button-fly of his jeans. His mouth left hers just long enough to wrestle out of the denim and then returned, crushing over hers as she hooked her legs around his hips and tugged him to her. Snaking one arm around his neck, bracing her other palm on the cold metal, she rocked her hips with the desperate need to just feel him inside of her.

Obligingly he filled her, caught hold of her hips and set the pace; taking her beyond the threshold of mindless ecstasy before driving her over the brink of sheer madness until they were both left crying out and breathless.

"Should've waited for the spin cycle," Hannah breathed against his shoulder, then sighed, "Well, that at least took the edge off."

And it had, for the moment anyway. It was quick, hard and fast, just what she'd needed to release the pent up aggression and wanton desire which had built up within her. Regulating her breathing, she allowed Mark to assist her off the washing machine, and then sucked a startled breath when he caught the backs of her knees with one arm and hoisted her up against his chest with the other.

"What are you doing?" she quizzed wrapping her arms around his neck as he carried her through the house and up the stairwell to his bedroom.

"So, the gazebo was a mistake, huh? And now you're just looking for a quick fix?" he questioned, then laughed at her puzzled expression. "Sorry…nope, can't help you there, ma'am."

"Uh…huh?" Hannah made a face, squirming under his slate gray gaze after he deposited her on the bed. "I don't…um… Wait, why would you say that?" she then asked referring to his statement of not being able to help.

"Because," he grinned while dropping down beside her to gather her up within his arms. Rolling her underneath him, he gently pinned her hands above her head, eyes mischievous as he explained, "I'm just getting started—not even close to being finished with you yet."

Hannah squealed with delight as his lips explored, body arching into his mouth. Desire stirred to lash throughout her yet again under his calculated assault. Six years or not, the man defiantly still knew what he was doing. She told herself it would just be this...sex, a quick fix, a simple fling between them—two consenting adults. Nothing more; nothing less...she would not allow herself to fall for him. Or so she told herself.

Chapter 21

An annoying trill startled Hannah from a sound peaceful nap. Reaching over her, Mark silenced the noise—the phone, by answering it. Listening to him talk, she closed her eyes and smiled. When he untangled his limbs from hers, rolling over in the opposite direction, she buried her head in the plumpness of the pillow and pouted. She frowned then sighed feeling him shift to then exit the cozy cocoon they had created. She told herself to ignore the sudden absence; the pang of wanting, of waiting for him to return. She should never have let herself even get remotely used to having his limbs entangled with hers.

Pulling the sheets up around herself, she pouted when he did return. Hannah then propped herself on an elbow and watched Mark balance the cordless phone between his shoulder and ear as he rummaged through his dresser drawers collecting a pair of socks, underwear, jeans and a tee-shirt in order to get dressed as he spoke into the phone. Somewhat listening, she concluded it had to do with work.

Mark ended the call then finished dressing. Sitting on the edge of the bed he looked at her, somewhat pensive then explained, "That was Lynn—the sheriff?—ah, I need to go in for a bit. Will you be okay with me running into town?"

Hannah sat up. "I guess so. Why—what's going on? Anything I should be worried about?"

"Not really," he commented then admitted, "Crime lab is finishing up with your car but there are a few things they want to go over before releasing it. Sounds like shit is getting ready to seriously hit the fan." He glanced around the room as if distracted. "Feds are talking possibly bringing in Bremer, today, tonight, sometime within the very near future? Lynn wasn't certain himself? I don't feel right just leaving you out here—reckon, you could come with if you want…but, well, I just don't know how we'd explained it, really…you tagging along—and if anything happened to you at the station due to any of this going down—"

Hannah stared at him. In a round-about-way it almost sounded like he was trying to ditch her. Sighing she discarded the notion. After all, it didn't matter…or so she kept telling herself.

"Mark. I'll be fine. I'm a big girl. And besides, nobody knows I'm out here anyway…right?" She forced herself to smile, then pointed out, "Besides, if they're hauling in Bremer, then I don't need to be in protective custody anymore."

The actual idea stung a little right after she'd said it out loud. She wouldn't have an excuse to be stuck with him; no more reason to find herself in his bed.

"You have your cell phone right?"

Hannah yawned and nodded, trying to ignore the fact he didn't remark, or had reacted, on her recent comment. "Yeah. It's somewhere downstairs I think."

"Do you want me to load and leave one of my guns for you? Just in case?"

"Seriously? Um, no. I wouldn't know the first thing to do with it," she laughed. "I'll be fine. Really. Go."

He stood up, hesitant. "I'll lock the doors. Please stay

inside the house while I'm gone. I shouldn't be long—an hour, maybe two at the most. Okay?"

"Yeah sure. Stay inside, you'll lock the doors. Got it." She waited a second, then asked, "Hey, since you'll be in town, could you stop by the pharmacy at Wal-Mart and pick up my headache medicine? I used the last autopen and well if I need it, at least then I'll have it. Insurance should cover the cost."

Preoccupied, he nodded. "Yeah, sure." Turning, he paused and then headed out without another word.

Hannah sat dumbfounded, and then stared at nothing in particular; feeling the sting of tears, trying to ward off that familiar tug of rejection having had just witnessed him simply leave. No goodbye. No kiss. No hug. No nothing. Just a roll in the sack and then: hey, I got to run…

Ironic. The scenario she was used to usually went: hey thanks, I got to run back to my wife and family…or at least that's what it had been with Cole. In this case it was slightly different yet still felt the same. Funny…how something she'd become so accustomed and numb to, could now cut her to her very core.

Having no clue to how much time had elapsed while just sitting there pondering her messed up love life, Hannah sighed and shook her head. Pushing out of the bed, she wrapped the sheet around herself and wandered downstairs in search of her cell phone. She glanced outside one of the front windows.

The Silverado was gone, confirming Mark had indeed already left.

Spying her phone laying on the coffee table, she plucked it up on her way toward the kitchen. Taking the clean clothes out of the washer she tossed them in the dryer and turned it on. She then stood clutching the sheet together with one hand while scrolling through the various missed calls with the other; five from her office, one from Monique's personal cell, and an unidentified caller.

Punching buttons to check her voice mail, Hannah

scowled when it beeped and then completely shut-down due to not having charged the battery.

"Crap," she groaned.

She glanced around the alcove then the kitchen. She wasn't even sure if Mark's phone charger would be the correct mate to use with her phone if she even found it. Glancing at the floor, she stooped and scooped up the earlier discarded robe. Switching the bed sheet with the robe, she pulled it on and then tapped her dead phone against her palm, now scheming and then debating.

"Well...I never promised him I'd stay inside *this* house," she stated aloud. Leaning against the drier she made up her mind. Her plan was set. She'd just have to wait for her clothes to dry first before she could follow through with it.

◆ ◆ ◆

Hannah went to straight to the barn after she'd dressed. She remembered seeing a car parked inside of it while helping Mark do chores earlier. Smiling, she eyed it then tested the handle and squealed in victory when the door opened to her surprise. Climbing in behind the wheel she flipped the visor down, expectant, and then frowned.

"Figures. Keys...keys...where would I be if I were keys?" she breathed searching the dusty interior.

Coming up empty handed, she pouted then just sat a minute. She crawled back out of the vehicle and shut the door feeling a bit thwarted. Making her way back outside, Hannah sighed and squinted at the sun then folded her arms and just stood a moment; thinking. Huffing out a determined note she glanced about, eyes quickly searching the far pasture then resting on the paddock itself. She stood debating...*seriously, how hard could it be?*

"All-righty then...plan B it is."

Ducking back inside the barn, Hannah found and grabbed what she thought she'd need. Halter in hand, an apple in the other, she located and then enticed the horse named Xena—the same one she'd test drove earlier—with the apple. Talking quietly to it, she successfully placed and secured the halter on her first attempt. Thrilled, she quickly led the horse to the enclosure gate, managing to swing it open wide enough for both of them to exit then swung it shut so as not to let the other horses escape. Locking the gate, she then led the horse toward the barn, speaking softly to it while hoping she could also at least recall how to properly place and secure a saddle…because if she was indeed going to use a horse as her mode of transportation, she sure as hell wasn't going to do it bareback.

Chapter 22

Hannah managed to pilot Xena to her house; without being bucked, bitten or trampled. She was pretty impressed with herself. The actual trip had taken a little over a half an hour she guesstimated. She figured if she'd been skilled at horseback riding, the trip might have gone a bit faster.

She'd realized, after making it to the blacktop, that she couldn't stay on the highway itself. So she'd decided on taking the gravels in order to stay out of sight. Which in all truth were short cuts, so it should have made the trip that much faster. Then again, Xena's only speed was full walk and they'd kept that pace for the entire trip. After all, why risk breaking her neck trying to ride at full gallop for a phone charger, clean underwear and a few personal items?

Grateful just to be home, Hannah managed to dismount without falling off or landing on her butt. She led the horse to the back side of the garage in order to tie the reins securely to an old clothes line post. She then went in search of her gardening wagon. Filling the thing plum full with water, she pulled it to the back of the garage and parked it in front of the horse to offer it a cool drink of water before heading inside the house.

Once inside, Hannah ransacked the living room closest searching for a knapsack big enough to carry her things. On edge, every sound had her jumping and glancing out a window. She seriously half expected to see Mark pulling up in the drive.

Scolding herself, she went back to work. She'd decided that if Mark did show up then she would just use having to get her phone charger as a valid excuse. Which wasn't a lie exactly…she needed it, but nonetheless it wasn't the sole reason of why she'd decided upon going against his wishes and venturing out. And since she'd decided to do so, and had gone through the trouble of hijacking a horse to complete her mission, she figured since she was here she might as well gather up everything she thought she would need.

Locating the bag she wanted, Hannah raced upstairs and first grabbed a handful of clean underwear, another couple of pairs of jeans and some tops. Stuffing the items inside the bag, she snagged a pair sneakers and then paused. She would have loved to have taken a shower, but didn't have time. So instead she stripped off her already sweaty clothes and replaced them with a pair of cutoffs and a cotton tank-top then headed back downstairs to retrieve her laptop as well as her briefcase.

Movement caught her eye. The knock at the screen door a second later had her heart stopping and caused her to gasp.

Peeking through the kitchen, Hannah swore under her breath. Dropping the knapsack she nudged it behind one of the cardboard boxes for safe keeping. Then, edging her way into the kitchen, stared at Kender through the glass window of the door; slightly surprised and now nervous to see him standing on her porch looking in at her.

She couldn't recall locking the door and now eyed the ancient deadbolt itself.

"Hannah, I can see you. Are you going to answer the door?" he finally said.

"Uh...sure," Hannah mumbled. Forcing her feet to move she opened the door at last. Stepping back, she hugged herself then glanced around the kitchen in search of...well anything that she deemed would be worthy enough to use as a weapon.

"How are you feeling? Any better?" he probed, looking rather nervous himself, staying just within the doorway itself.

"Huh?"

He gestured with the small plant he held, causing Hannah to flinch. "Your head. They said you had a terrible migraine. Are you feeling any better now?"

"Oh um yeah...getting there," Hannah said watching his every move. Sizing him up, she couldn't imagine why he'd be here—unless of course her hunch about him had been right all along and was now about to prove true. The idea left a hollow pit in her gut.

"The office staff, they were worried about you. They all chipped in and well it isn't much but we got you this...oh, and a card."

Hannah took the plant, warily watching him as he now patted his breast pocket and then his pants pockets. "Must have left it in my car...?" he commented.

Having no clue why Kender would even drive out here to deliver a so-called get well plant and card, Hannah simply stared at him and said, "Oh..."

"So are you getting much done on the Holm case?" he asked, peering into the living room.

Hannah felt a stronger surge of panic and took another step back. "Oh...um," she then just stood there holding the plant. She faked a yawn to quell her edginess, now hoping to cover the awkward lull of silence she'd cued. She scanned the kitchen as if seeking a home for the plant. "Um no not really...Thanks, for the plant. Sorry. I've been sleeping most the day. Guess I'm still a little out of it," she lied, then kicked herself when she heard herself actually ask, "Would like some lemonade?"

"No, don't bother. I just wanted to stop by and check in on you. Make sure you were okay," Kender told her, then turning gestured toward his car outside. "I can just go get that card and—"

Gravel popping under rubber had both of them looking toward the lane leading up to her house. Hannah now hoped like hell it was Mark. The car was unfamiliar; the driver however wasn't. She breathed a silent breath of relief after the car parked and her secretary Monique pushed out of the vehicle itself to then waddle across the yard, in no hurry, toward the house.

"Well I can always just toss it in the mail," Kender said, now stepping outside on to the porch. Holding the screen door open for Monique, he nodded at her then told Hannah, "I'll let you two girls visit. Hope you get to feeling better." He then left without another word.

Hannah let the air swelling her lungs rush out, making the sound a horse would. She would have hugged her secretary if she wasn't still hugging the plant. "Oh my God, am I glad to see you!"

Monique laughed, her chunky caramel face screwed in question. "What on earth was that all about?"

Hannah shrugged and shook her head. She wanted to spill her guts, but knew she couldn't tell anybody what was going on. "No clue. He dropped this off. Said it was from the office staff?"

Monique eyed the plant, humming a note while looking rather suspicious herself. "Nobody said anything to me...?"

"Really, that's odd. Kender said the office staff got—" pausing, Hannah shuttered at the idea. Monique might have just saved her life. She'd thank her later.

"Maybe he's got the hots for you?" Monique teasingly suggested.

"Ewww, Kender? He gives me the creeps," Hannah admitted then sighed. "Let me go put this...ah, somewhere...?" She glanced around the cluttered counter top and then gestured toward the living room with the plant. "Be right back."

Monique laughed and waved a hand through the air, then called out after, "So...anything juicy you want to tell me?"

"About what?"

"Oh, I think you know."

"Seriously, I have no clue what you're talking about."

Monique clucked her tongue then waved a well-manicured fingernail at her. "You and certain deputy?"

"Oh…Deputy Bowman?" Hannah asked, then taking a calming breath she told herself to relax. "What about him?"

"Yes *him*. You haven't mentioned a single thing to me—at all. I think you're holding out on me, girlfriend."

"Nothing to tell," Hannah fibbed then laughed at the look Monique shot her as she leaned against the door frame folding her arms. Wanting to change the subject, needing to get the heck out of here and back to Mark's house, she nodded at the thermos Monique had tucked under her arm. "What's that you got there?"

"My great grandma'ma's special home-made chicken noodle soup. Sure to cure whatever ails you, girlfriend." Monique exclaimed and set the thermos on the counter. She then began opening cupboards at random, in search of a mug while jokingly teasing, "Girl, I can't believe you still haven't gotten this place up to snuff yet. Probably best you have nothing to tell—best not be having no man over here anyhow…might scare them off thinking you're some type of wallpaper-cardboard-box-paint-can hoarder."

"I've been called worse." Hannah frowned but laughed out loud with Monique, then sighed as she glanced over the untouched spools of wallpaper as well the boxes still in need of unpacking. "I'd be the president of the national procrastination guild, but I just haven't finished filling out the paperwork."

"It's all those late hours at the office, girlfriend. Should send you to workaholics anonymous," Monique scolded playfully. Locating a mug, she screwed off the cap to the thermos and poured a plentiful amount of soup into the mug. "Here you go. Now you sit down and drink up— that'll have you back on your feet and in the office in no time." Humming a note she waited a beat then again asked, "Why was Kender here?"

"Apparently he stopped by to give me a card and that get well plant." Hannah told her then glanced between the mug and Monique's mother-hen expression. "He forgot the card though. Thankfully you showed up. The man gives me the willies."

"Kender?" Monique snorted waving a hand through the air. "He's harmless, girlfriend."

Hannah rolled one shoulder playing it off. There just seemed to be something off. She just couldn't put her finger on it. Maybe it was her. Sneaking over to her own house, having had rode a horse here no less, had left her nerves a mess. She kept thinking Mark would any minute be driving up to find her then would probably bawl her out for taking off. And she hadn't expected anybody from her office to come out to visit her. First Kender and now Monique? The entire day just felt off. Luckily, Monique had shown up when she had. The thought of being alone with Kender, let alone uncertain why he'd even stopped by for a visit, caused a shiver to race up Hannah's spine.

"Hannah…you feeling okay? You look a bit pale. Here drink this. It'll help," Monique insisted.

Hannah glanced at the steamy mug of soup Monique held. She wasn't sick and didn't remotely even have a headache. But she couldn't very well say that to her secretary; she couldn't say anything of the sort…not yet. She'd have to wait until this whole thing blew over, before she could even thank Monique for showing up when she had. Lord knows what Kender might have done…or what he had intended to do.

"I'm fine. Just tired, I guess. You really didn't have to come out," Hannah told her. She eyed the mug Monique still held. She didn't want soup. It was ninety plus degrees outside; the last thing she wanted was to down a mug of steamy chicken noodle soup.

"It's the least I could do, girlfriend."

Sighing, Hannah smiled at her secretary, "Thanks." She took the mug and sat down at the cluttered kitchen table and then set the soup aside to let it cool off. She'd simply have to play along; sit a spell and chit-chat then somehow get rid of Monique as well. She could then finish gathering what she needed and get back to Mark's place before he got back himself. Now she just had to hurry Monique along without making it seem obvious, or rude.

"No problem. Always glad to help out a friend." Monique winked and again gestured for Hannah to drink up.

Hannah stared at the mug. If she didn't drink at least a little bit she may never get rid of Monique. With that thought, she finally gave in and brought the mug to her lips and took a test sip and then nodded in appreciation. It was the least she could do after Monique had driven out here to make sure she was okay. Thinking about it, Hannah made the mental note to make sure and get something nice for her secretary this Christmas.

"That's actually not bad," she then heard herself comment somewhat surprised, before taking a longer healthier drink of the broth. "Is this a secret family recipe, or can you jot it down before you go?"

"I'll make a copy for you, when I get to the office." Monique sat down herself and gestured at spools of wallpaper piled atop the table. "So when do you want me to come over and help wallpaper?"

"Once everything settles down, I guess," she replied then took another long sip and closed her eyes as she swallowed. Feeling somewhat lightheaded, Hannah glanced at the clock and then after a minute blew out a long slow breath. Sweat beaded across her forehead. "Is it hot? It's sort of hot in here...don't you think?"

"I feel fine. Must be the soup…"

Staring at the remaining broth, Hannah mumbled, "I…I don't feel so well…"

Smiling, Monique clucked her tongue and simply continued her mindless chitchat, "I'm free this weekend. We could knock it out, right quick, the two of us. Order up some of that Geno's pizza—Oh, and I can pick up some of that wine…oh what is the name of that one I liked so well? Oh yes, Guilty Pleasure…remember?"

Leaning forward, Hannah stared at her secretary as the woman's face fuzzed and blurred in a double image. Monique's words merged, dancing about the room to converge in a hollow time-warp just to re-expand and separate to normal sounds before darting off again leaving a strange echo within her head. Blinking, Hannah shook her head and then tried setting the mug down but failed, missing the table completely, dumping the remainder of the broth in her lap.

"Oh dear," Monique exclaimed standing up. "Let's get that cleaned up. Shall we?"

Hannah's head snapped up and squinting harder she tried to focus on just one of the three images now before her. "You…you…but…?" Clinging onto that last shred of focus, she struggled to form words but wasn't sure if she'd spoken them aloud or if they were merely trapped within thick gooey syrup which was beginning to smother her brain; rendering her capacity to function worthless.

"Oh there there, girlfriend." Monique gave her a quick pat on the shoulder and snorting hooked an arm around Hannah's, hauling her to her feet before she completely slid out of the chair. Propping her limp body against her more chunky frame, the woman began shuffling Hannah toward the door. "It's nothing personal, really. Just business, girlfriend."

Chapter 23

The sultry night air hit Hannah in the face as Monique shuffled her outside onto the porch. As Monique huffed and puffed, still gabbing about nothing in particular, Hannah forced herself to focus; screamed at herself inwardly to think through the thick dense fog which was now threatening to completely consume her. She had to do something, but her limbs felt heavy and numb. She could barely walk and Monique was yelling at her to now pick her feet up or risk being tossed down the porch steps.

Obeying, Hannah felt her captor pause mid-step and managed to half lift her own head at the pop of gravel under tires. A rush of relief surged through her, hope laced with a bout of courage welled to life at seeing a Sheriff's prowler pulling up to park a few feet from the porch. Shoving away from her captor she stumbled forward trying to yell, instead wincing as gravel bit into her skin as she landed full force on her hands and knees.

Despite it Hannah hustled, scrambling on all fours forcing herself to somehow move her limp limbs to propel her body toward the squad car, the deputy inside of it, while now pleading, "Help me….please help me."

The deputy jumped out. Hooking both of his meaty

paws under her armpits he hauled her upright. Hannah mumbled "tanks," then blinked hard to focus on his face, the vaguely familiar features, and then commanded herself to speak. "You to me help…please, she's…me…help," she gushed in a woozy tidal wave of gibberish and desperation.

"What on earth is going on here—?" his voice boomed in commanding question.

Hannah fell against his chest, her words mumbled and slurred. "She's trying to…trying to—"

"She's trying to escape—What's it look like, dumbass," Monique's jovial laugh bounced across the yard. "And it's about time—God, what took you so long?"

"*You* said she was at Bowman's place—? Christ, went there first. Send me out on some wild goose chase, then expect—"

"Stop your moaning and carry her the rest of the way. Good Lord, bet I threw my back out. For sure would've, if I'd have had to toss her scrawny little butt in the trunk myself. Good Lord, that girl is dead weight. Damn…will you look at that—little bitch made me break a nail. Be a sweety and just put her in the trunk while I go fetch the files and look for her laptop—"

"Change of plans…we gotta do this here and now."

The deputy's voice floated in the air above, now mingling with Monique's; their conversation looping and lacing around her head as Hannah felt her body slipping. Her head dropped back and then snapped forward as the deputy stood her up and then simply picked her up, tossing her half over his shoulder like some little kid being carried by their father potato-sack-fashion.

Joggled, she fought the sensation of hurling her guts and tried focusing on the ground as the deputy began walking. She needed to stay focused, had to try and remain with-it; somehow knew if she didn't fight whatever drug it was she'd been given, she was soon going to be unable to do much about any of this.

Watching her hands flop to-and-fro as the deputy clopped up the steps, Hannah suddenly commanded herself to control her arms. Managing to bring up one hand to her face, she jabbed a finger in her mouth and rammed it hard down her throat. Gagging, she did it again and was this time rewarded. Retching, she spewed the drug-laced soup she'd just consumed down the backside of the Deputy's tan duty pants and all over the backside of his boots.

"Dammit!"

Closing her eyes Hannah smiled hearing the deputy's disgust and applauded her own quick thinking as she drifted closer to the abyss of nothingness.

"What's wrong?" Monique quizzed, sounding more annoyed than concerned.

"Bitch just vomited all over my pants and shoes!"

"Oh for crying in the beer. Quit bellyaching and just get her inside. My God, Tippen, you act like you've never done this before."

"You're not the one who has to be on duty in a few hours. Now I smell like vomit. I'm gonna have to change out of these pants and clean my boots before I head in. How am I going to explain *this* to the wife? Quit fiddling with your nails and help me—could start by opening the door. We'll have to think of something and fast...and believable too so that..."

"Don't we always? My god, you are such a worrywart!"

"...and not screw-up this time—Like *somebody* who forgot to check the windshield."

Monique made a sound of disgust and smacked him upside the head. Hannah stirred at the commotion and moaned in protest as the deputy swore and side-stepped, jostling her around in the process.

Holding the door open, Monique followed him inside the house, chastising him the entire way, "Don't you be trying to blame that on me. You're the deputy—have twenty-four-seven access to that impound—I took care of the paperwork—as I recall *you* was supposed to double check the car, dumbass. If you had, then we wouldn't now be havin' to tidy up this mess up ourselves. Paul's pissed about this whole thing and now we godda—"

"Shut up and hand me that jug over there. I got an idea."

Hannah moaned as their voices rose and fell; as the sound of bickering wafted above her, the words themselves converging to swirl and tumble around her as if lost somewhere deep within a tunnel. Unable make any sense of anything being discussed, she simply focused on Monique's open-toed pumps as they came into her range of view before disappearing on the clap thud of heels echoing about the kitchen.

Startled awake, she clipped out a yelp at the sensation of falling then felt the deputy drop her hard into a chair. She slouched, unable to remain upright and slid almost falling off the chair onto her butt. A set of meaty paws grabbed her, hoisting her back up by the armpits. Hannah made a face, unable to do anything to stop those paws as they greedily affixed to her breasts and gave a test squeeze.

"Nice. Think they're fake?"

"No. She seems to be too nice of a girl to do fake, so I doubt it. Too bad she's nosy. I actually sort of liked her."

"You godda feel these—now I understand why Bowman was tapping that," he remarked snidely.

He leaned over her and sniffed at her hair and neck. Hannah inwardly flinched, silently whimpering as he pressed his slobbery mouth over hers; gagging her by jabbing his tongue in between her lips.

"Damn, for a criminal defense bitch, she taste good too—Hey, Monique, go outside and fiddle with your fingernails why don'cha. I gotta tap this sweet ass least once myself, before—"

"Stop it, you dumbass!" The words—to Hannah's relief and gratitude—were followed by the scuffle of heels and a loud smacking sound; causing the deputy to side-step and turn his full attention back to his bossy partner as she was now scolding him, "and keep your pants on—Nobody wants to see your tiny dick. Your luck they'd find your DNA somewhere…dumbass! Besides, we don't have time. Now grab that roll of Duck-tape over there and help me get her…"

Hannah sighed and allowed herself to float up-up-up and away; almost glad really, as their voices and bickering grew fainter and fainter the farther she wandered. Succumbing to the whatever drug it was—or at least what had managed to invade her system and take hold, before she'd vomited—Hannah drifted along the edge of the abyss until she capsized and free-fell into complete oblivion.

~ ~ ~

Mark punched speed-dial and sandwiched his cellphone between his shoulder and ear as he pulled out of the Wal-Mart parking lot. "Come on, Hannah…pick-up." Getting her outgoing message for the umpteenth time, he disconnected then scowled and slammed on the brakes as the traffic light ahead flipped from yellow to red. Taking advantage of the delay, he scrolled through his contacts and punched the correct one then waited for Tippen to answer. "Tippen—hey man, where you at?"

"Just south of nine. Heading in—Would've been there on time but had to make an emergency stop and then had to—"

"Yeah yeah," Mark interrupted not caring about the man's trivial matters at the moment. Seeing the light had turned green, he breathed a sigh of relief and punched it through the intersection, piloting his Silverado in and out of the slow moving traffic. He half wished he'd driven his prowler. He'd at least then might have been able to flip on the light-bar and go around the long line of traffic. "I need a favor—can you haul ass out to my place?"

"Ah…I'm sort of running late, I was supposed to cover for Bockner—but I haven't even stopped at the station to start my tour of duty yet," Tippen whined then hesitating asked, "Why, where are you?"

"In town, on my way to the station right now—I'll tell them you're running late. Look, Hannah's out at my place, but she isn't answering her phone—Just swing by on your way in and check on her…okay? Call me afterwards. I'll explain everything later—I gotta go."

~ ~ ~

"We're looking for a nineteen-eighty-seven Chevrolet Silverado half-ton truck. Lab confirmed the traces of paint collected off of the victim's vehicle is actually a basic automotive primer—light grey in color. Could be just a panel or it could be the whole truck is that color, we aren't certain."

"If it's basic primer that can be bought at any automotive store, how'd they come up with the make, model and year?" Mark asked, more so out of curiosity then of anything else.

The agent beamed at the question enthusiastically showcasing his expertise by explaining in depth, "Because the Silverado trim package not only included parking lamps on the front of the vehicle that had a unique rectangular shape, as well as nameplates with the Silverado logo…but also lip moldings, as well as tailgate and lower body side moldings—these were not found in any other trim package for the nineteen-eighty-seven Chevy half-ton. All external features included in the Custom Deluxe as well as the Scottsdale trim packages were also found in the Silverado package. These features included chrome bumpers and hubcaps, a silver-colored plastic insert for the grill, and silver-colored door handles and side-view mirrors…"

Mark grunted at the extent of information his inquiry had sparked and was now being provided. As the agent continued to rattle off even more specification bout the vehicle in question, he leaned toward the Sheriff and whispered, "They don't get out much, do they?"

"…lab confirms that a piece found, embedded within the victim's vehicle itself, is a piece from one of those rectangular shaped parking lamps—which, as I explained, is unique to that of a nineteen-eighty-seven Chevy Silverado half-ton truck," the agent summed up in conclusion.

Mark pursed his lips in utter amazement but, tamping down the desire to ask more questions, simply nodded. Although he was somewhat impressed with this agent's knowledge, he wasn't about to inquire on how they could figure all of that out from some tiny piece of evidence left behind. Not that he didn't want to know, in all truth forensic science interested him. The fact of the matter was they just didn't have time for yet another one of this agent's lengthy explanations. Drawing his full attention, his cell phone vibrated. Glancing at the caller ID listed James Tippen name was displayed.

"Excuse me. I have to take this," he explained holding up his phone. Ducking out into the hallway Mark answered simply with, "She okay?"

"Don't know. Stopped by like you asked, but she wasn't there…?"

"What do you mean *you don't know*?" Mark snapped, a sense of panic ripping through him

"Jeesh, Bowman—get a grip—Stopped by like you asked and she wasn't there. That's all I know."

Mark thanked him and hung up. Scrolling through his contacts, he then half jogged to the dispatcher's station. "Hey, can you get Brecker Haley and Merit on the horn for me? Thanks."

Punching a few buttons, the dispatcher then handed him the receiver and went about her own business of flipping through a Cosmo. Mark eyed the magazine and then the wall clock as he waited for somebody on the other end to pick up. Mid-afternoon the office should still be open.

"Brecker Haley and Merit. This is Monique. How may I

direct you?"

"Ah…" Mark hesitated not sure at first what to say or ask. It was long shot, but he hoped maybe Hannah had gone into the office despite the fact he'd told her to stay put. "Counselor Bryans, please."

"I'm sorry, she's taken a leave of absence. Is there something I can help you with—or would you care to leave a message?"

Mark sighed, annoyance now tagging along with that panic. "I know *that*—Monique, this Deputy Bowman…look, I've tried her cell but she isn't answering. I was hoping maybe—"

"Oh well isn't that funny," Monique gushed, cutting him off her business tone switching to bubbly and flirtatious. "Your ears must've been a ringing earlier, sweetheart, because I sure was talking about you."

Mark rolled his eyes and interrupted, "Have you, perchance, seen her—talked to her—at all, today?"

"Who, honey?"

"Counselor Bryans."

"Oh…no, no I haven't. Like I said, she's taken a leave of absence and won't be in—well I'm not sure when? Maybe not for a while. Oh, but you know what, wait just a minute. We took up a collection this morning to get her a little something. You know to help her feel better— although my first choice wouldn't have been a house plant…but Kender, that's what he ended up getting, oh and a cute little get well card. I think he said something about taking it to her house himself…something about needing to speak to her about the Holm case…? Hold on a sec, I'll buzz him…"

"Kender? Wait. Monique, did you say Kender?" Mark pinched the bridge of his nose, a stream of frustration jettisoning from his flared nostrils hearing music filter through the receiver. She'd placed him on hold. He glanced at the wall clock as he waited, scanned the thick bullet proof glass walls that separated the inner office from the lobby, while drumming his fingers across the counter.

"Well that's odd. Kender isn't answering—? He's either at the courthouse or must've taken the rest of the day off," Monique reported. "Would you like me to leave a message to have him call you? Or I could…"

Mark eyed the lobby's sliding glass door, which served as the porthole to the hallway adjoining the station to the courthouse, as it swooshed open and the man in question himself sauntered into the lobby. "Nope—that won't be necessary…" Without another word, he abandoned the receiver atop the dispatcher's counter as Monique's jovial voice continued to filter out; fist clenched, eyes now pinned on Kender.

The man didn't have a chance to even react—let alone, knew what hit him, after Mark burst through a door and clotheslined him in a fury of unadulterated rage, taking ahold of and then balling the lapels of his charcoal plaid Hickey Freeman suit within his fists and forcing him backwards. Ramming Kender into the lobby's Pepsi machine, their combined weight cracked the acrylic face as they crashed into it.

Mark gave the man another shove, pinning him while snarling, "Where's she at! What have you done with her? Where—is—she!"

"I…I—" Eyes wild, Kender cowered under the surprise attack and tried bringing up his hands, palms out fingers spread, as if to placate his aggressor. "I—Who?"

"Hannah Bryans—" Mark snarled through clenched enamel, now nose to nose with him, giving the man an extra incentive shove. "I swear to God if you hurt her I'll—"

Before he could explain in detail what exactly he would do, multiple sets of hands were pulling at his arms and shoulders attempting to drag him off of the man he still had pinned. Mark shrugged them off and stood his ground staring Kender down as a multitude of shouts and voices blended and rose above the buzzing rage coursing throughout him. A scuffle of more boots squealed and squeaked across the polished tile as a dozen or so feet came to a halt behind him—a handful of officers joining the deputies already at hand—all converging to congest the lobby, there either help or to just gawk.

"Bowman!" Sheriff Lynn Schmitt's voice boomed above the commotion, cueing Mark to release his hold on his still shocked and startled target. "My office—Now!"

"You better pray she's okay," Mark hissed in low threatening growl before retreating as ordered.

Chapter 24

Hannah came to, mind reeling in a clatter of crackling pops that retreated to a low snapping hiss—much like an out of tune radio being adjusted, hit and miss, belching bouts of white noise and static with only bits of coherent jargon. Blinking several times, she lifted her head slightly and shifted with the desperate need to roll off of her achy shoulder and elbow. She stopped all movement, sucking a sharp breath as raw burning pain raced down the entire length of her arm and bit in between her shoulder blades. She dropped her head and stilled, listening to the somewhat rhythmic crackling-pop-hiss that rose and fell in short burst.

Still somewhat out of it, she slowly scanned her environment. Scant fingers of sunlight snuck in through the breech of a piece of bent insulation which covered a jagged and crack pane in a farthest corner. Her eyes darted to the next porthole to find it too had been long ago sealed with spray foam and covered with thick blanket of pink fluff. Her eyes were drawn back to the meager patch of sunlight which somewhat illuminated a portion of the crumbling limestone wall.

Gathering her bearings, she took a moment and just

stared at the thin ribbons of smoke which continued to meander aimlessly, curling and looping lazily throughout the hazy atmosphere. She then studied the blackened outline of an ancient wooden shelving unit; an assortment of old ceramic jugs which still lined one of the shelves, long ago forgotten and covered with a layer of cobwebs and thick dust.

A surge of tears coupled with panic flooded her once she realized where she was; as she pieced together the events which had left her to be now lying bound on the floor in the old unused cellar of her grandmother's house—now her own house—out in the middle of the sticks.

Hannah closed her eyes and just breathed in and out, filling her nostrils with the staleness of the cellar air, damp limestone and earth, dust. A more pungent scent burned and nipped at her nostrils, which she didn't immediately recognize for certain but somehow equated with campfires and charred wood.

Clearing her mind, she mentally assessed her situation. Cold dampness numbed her cheek seeping up through the earth floor. Both of her arms were stretched backwards, pulled behind her tightly; something was binding her wrists. She wiggled her fingers just to realize her hands—at one point asleep and now coming back to full life with that pins-and-needles sensation—had been bound together with Duck-Tape behind her back. Her ankles had also been bound, but not as uncomfortably tight as her arms were. She could at least move her knees somewhat, shift her ankles a bit.

Dumbass…Monique's voice trickled through her thoughts, and the idea that Dumbass had been the one to bind her ankles cropped up in her head. Hannah choked on a half-hearted laugh. As if having the ability to move her knees or ankles even a little bit was going to be of any great help right now.

She laid there a moment contemplating, re-evaluating

her situation and then realized that charred smoky smell emanated from above and was the direct byproduct of the crackling-pop-hiss clatter. Panic skewered her gut once it registered.

"Oh my god, oh my god, oh my god," she ranted, fear-struck yet was also somewhat pissed to realize they'd set fire to her house; to all of her personal belongings.

Thinking fast, Hannah shifted, rocking back and forth on her side hoping to somehow roll onto her front. If she could at least get up onto her knees she might be able to…well, do something, although she wasn't sure of what. Determined, she ignored the pain biting at her arm as she continued to scoot and rock. Flipping her body over, she released a moan of agony as she attempted to balance herself on her knees, the round of her shoulder and her cheek. Now what? She thought. Doing so only for a split second then groaned, "No, no, no, no…" as gravity trumped her efforts and caused her body to collapse.

"Dammit!" she hurled out at the top of her lungs, angry at herself.

She took a moment to recoup. Lifting her head, Hannah then calculated the distance to the decrepit shelving unit. With a new plan set, she began shifting her knees—pulling and pushing against the strain of the Duck-tape. Up-down, up-down, up-down—as if trying to march in place while lying on her side. She laughed at thinking it was probably a waste of time; laughed at the image of herself doing so which came to mind, then squealed in delight and doubled her speed when she felt the Duck-tape give.

Hannah began moving her ankles, now working with the slack, pushing and pulling while coaching herself like some sadistic aerobics instructor, "Couple more times, come on, come on, couple more—don't give up! Don't you dare give up, come on…Yes, yes, yes—thank you Dumbass!" she exclaimed feeling the tape give way enough to almost wiggle a foot free.

A screeching crash above her squelched her small victory and startled Hannah enough into stilling to once again just listen in attempts to assess the situation above her. As the fingers of smoke expand and thickened, curling and licking their way downward toward the floor, a new surge of adrenaline was released and now fueled her as she pushed with her feet, scooting herself across the dirt floor on her side like an inch-worm strung out on speed.

Halting, Hannah rolled as far on to her back as her bound arms would allow her and began kicking her legs up and out; feet connecting with the wooden shelving unit causing a plume of dust and the long ago left items atop of it to teeter and pitch. On the third strike a ceramic jug toppled crashing to the floor with a solid hollow *thunk*.

Rolling back onto her side, Hannah stared at the thing, defeated, cynical. The jug had toppled, but it had not shattered as she had hoped. Scanning the shelving unit, she heaved a breath then went to work yet again, almost squealing when the decrepit shelving unit itself gave way and toppled, raining brown glass bottles, the ceramic jugs as well as its wooden planks across her and the floor. Brown glass shattered, scattering in a hundred jagged shards.

Energized with victory, Hannah scrambled, feeling about with the tips of her fingers until she located what felt to her as being a large enough piece; then went to work blind, awkwardly see-sawing and hacking away at the Duck-tape binding her wrists, and then removing the tape around her ankles. Free of her restraints, Hannah scrambled toward the mouth of the stairwell staying low on her hands and knees. She hastily assessed the steps leading up out of the cellar to the door, as a thick wall of choking black smoke belched out from around the door frame itself rolling its way down the steps toward her.

Backing away, she ignored the shards of glass nipping into her knees, digging into her palms as she crawled to the farthest wall. Aware that her only means of escape was impassable, now obstructed most likely by a wall of flames, she surveyed the cellar itself as the crackling-hiss-sizzle-pop of the fire roared on above her.

Hannah closed her eyes and commanded herself to think. She had to stay calm if she was going to get herself out of this. Glancing about the cellar, her eyes paused on the puffy glob of spray-foam insulation, the bent corner of pink fluff. She suddenly lurched forward, grabbing up a broken plank of wood from the destroyed shelving unit as she stood. Choking back a mouth and nose-full of smoke, she reached up and clawed at the blanket of pink fluffy insulation. Pulling it free, Hannah squinted against the rush of sunlight that streamed in through the clouded rectangular windowpane, illuminating the dense black smoke now pouring down the steps, filling the cellar, clogging the air and stealing vital oxygen from her.

Hannah held her breath and positioning the plank rammed it upward at the glass, shattering it; then after using the wood to clear away the jagged shards from the decrepit wooden frame itself, tossed it aside. Backing up, she then bolted forward leaping and throwing herself against the limestone wall. Latching on to the window frame, she whimpered and groaned; toes attempting to scale limestone, fingertips punctured by bits of splintered glass as she strained to somehow pull herself up in hopes of escaping through the small opening.

Gravity won. Falling backward, Hannah landed hard on her butt. Defeated, choking and coughing on the thick black smoke, tears sprouted. Not sure what to do, she simply screamed in frustration then picked up a ceramic jug and raising it above her head to hurl it out of spite and desperation—but then stopped short of actually throwing it.

Scrambling to her feet, Hannah choked and coughed trying not to breath, trying not to inhale the smoke as she set the jug on the floor below the window; then quickly gathered the rest setting them side by side forming square.

She then gathered up the old wooden plank shelves themselves and placed them atop the jugs creating a make-shift platform; hopefully one tall enough to give her the extra boost she'd need to pull herself up and out through the window.

Chapter 25

"Since you've taken it upon yourself to become unofficially acquainted…I'd like to now officially introduce you to Special Agent Kloppman," Lynn announced, and almost satirically, while popping the cap off of a brand new bottle of Tums and shaking a handful out just to stuff them in his mouth.

Pacing, Mark stopped to stare at his boss, incredulous, and then pushed a hand through his hair before pinching the bridge of his nose. He grunted at the thought, and then blowing out a long breath glanced at the man who was seated within Sheriff Lynn Schmit's office himself. The agent he'd just been introduced to; the same man that he'd just attacked and threatened.

"Special agent huh?" Mark croaked then tossed a nod at the man's rumpled suit. "Ah…real sorry about that."

"Risk of working undercover," the agent offered with a lopsided smile then informed Mark. "And to answer your recent question, Miss Bryans was at her house, safe and sound last time I saw her."

Mark landed in the other visitor chair. "At her house? When?"

'Few hours ago," he consulted his watch. "I took the opportunity to take a plant and get well card—that the office staff purchased for her—out to her place. Figured it would be the perfect guise, you know, in order to check up on her. Just wanted to make sure she was safe."

Whether the agent had intended it, or not, Mark felt the sting of accusation and negligence pierce his chest. "I shouldn't have left her alone," he commented. He glanced at the sheriff then returned his attention to the agent. "She'd told me you'd spoke to her, was trying to get her to drop the Holm case—felt somewhat threatened by what you said. So when Monique suggested that you—"

"Monique?"

"Yeah, I was speaking to her—well before...ah, before we met in the lobby," he put it mildly. "She told me that you might have gone out to deliver some get well plant—which is why I thought you—"

"Might have? Monique was there herself. Drove up just as I was leaving—?"

Cursing, Mark stood and within two strides was reaching for the door. Standing as well, the agent dug out a cell phone, flipped it open and began hastily relaying the information to whoever it was on the other end. The door itself pushed open before Mark could even take hold of the handle, causing him to side-step then back up as the sheriff's secretary pushed her way inside and in somewhat of a rush.

"Boss, we just got a call regarding a ten-seventy out on Elston Lane—Volunteer first responder saw smoke from the highway and called it in—Fire is being dispatched," she reported. After a quick breath she then explained, "Problem...Hoyet, Darling and Perkins are tied-up—out on highway sixty-seven—rounding up cattle to get them off the roadway. Darling said one cow was hit already; guess it's a real mess out there. Haven't heard from Tippen since he phoned that he'd be late. Should I call somebody in to cover...at least until things are under control?"

The sheriff stood, eyeing the huge map of the county spread across his office wall, then glanced questionably at his secretary. "Elston Lane? Isn't that the hedge-maze-Zen garden lady? Crazy old bat—"

"Yes, but sir…she passed away a while back," the secretary informed him.

"Oh…well, that's a shame—" Pausing, he surveyed the county map again. "If I recall, that house was abandoned—or was it was condemned?" The sheriff then pondered out loud before stating, "Either way, fire department should be able to handle that, don't you think?"

"No—no it wasn't," Mark corrected, shoving around the secretary to exit as a sense of panic coupled with dread twisted up through his gut. "Her granddaughter inherited it."

Pocketing his phone, the agent followed suit, hustling down the hall after Mark. Plowing through the exit, he chased him across the parking lot then caught up just as Mark swung open the door of his truck and slide behind the wheel.

"They're picking up Monique and bringing her in," the agent stated somewhat out of breath, now holding onto the driver side door so it could not be shut on him. "Want me to follow you out?" he asked just as multiple sirens erupted, the noise caterwauling throughout town; the main engine blasting its colossal horn demanding traffic yield and pull over way before the procession of strobe lights came into view themselves.

"Get in," Mark told him as he cranked the engine over and threw it in gear. Punching the accelerator before the agent's butt could warm the seat, he timed it just right; cutting across the parking lot at warp-speed then flew through the intersection to skid around the corner and join the line of fire and rescue vehicles already screaming down the roadway.

"You don't have one of those siren things?" the agent

asked, looking rather pale while fishing for the seatbelt and clipping it in place.

'No. Personal vehicle."

Nodding his head the agent made a sound of acceptance, then after noting the speedometer needle bouncing toward ninety, latched on to the 'oh crap' handle white knuckled while bracing his other hand against the dash as they weaved and bobbed while rocketing down the roadway. After a long moment he somewhat relaxed and then commented rather offhandedly, "You must love her a great deal."

Mark grunted, eyes trained on the open stretch of highway now before him. After a second or two, he glanced at the man in perplexed question. "What makes you say that?"

"Assaulting a Federal Agent aside," a soft chuckle eluded the man as he jerked his thumb backward and pointed out, "You just blew past that entire fleet of fire and rescue as if they were standing still."

~ ~ ~

Hannah groaned, gritting her teeth, straining to just pull herself up and out through the small opening. Coughing and sputtering, she felt herself drifting, slipping. And she'd almost given up but the distant echo of what she thought was sirens had given her a much needed boost.

With all her might, she pushed. Her head easily crowned the breech, and she momentarily paused to suck in much need oxygen gaining instead a lungful of piping-hot soot-filled air that wafted down from the blazing house above her. Soot and glowing ash rained down on top of her, which had her kicking and wiggling, arms trembling as she pushed. Raw, red-hot pain nipped and gnawed at her flesh, as she managed to hoist herself up enough to push her shoulders through the opening.

Wrenching one arm out, she cried out in agony as she freed the other. She then clawed at the ground, fingernails tilling dirt and uprooting grass while trying to tug the rest of her body free; her efforts rewarding her with a scant headway of only a painful couple of inches.

Her make-shift platform may have worked. But lack of oxygen and having inhaled so much of the thick black smoke was now beginning to take its toll. And she'd misjudged the actual size of rectangular window itself. Slightly on the a-hair-too-narrow side, she figured if the opening had not been edged with sharp glass fragments, it might have been relatively simple to squeeze through it.

Officially stuck and now beyond exhausted, Hannah felt her mind drifting. She just needed to rest a bit, she thought, as her eyelids sealed shut and she choked on a mournful half moan. The idea she was going to die, wedged within a cellar window frame, as her house burnt down on top of her was the last thought looping through her mind before she teetered then tumbled down the steep slope to blissful unconsciousness.

Snapping her back to semi-conscious, a set of strong hands affixed to her wrists and began tugging at her arms. The sudden action had her momentarily protesting. Lifting her head she was greeted the bluest eyes she'd ever seen. The mouth was moving but the words were disembodied, sucked up into the roar of white noise pulsating against her eardrums.

Laying her head back down, she drifted between semi-awareness and sweet oblivion as her body was hastily extracted and then quickly hauled across the earth. Coming to rest on a patch of soft cool grass, Hannah opened her eyes to those kind blue orbs now hovering above her. Voice too hoarse to speak, she instead silently thanked him with her eyes as an oxygen mask closed over her mouth and nose. Taking a deep breath she free-fell, floating back to the abyss of peaceful unconsciousness.

~ ~ ~

Mark slammed on the brakes. Coming to a rocking halt he cut the engine and sprang from his truck sprinting toward the house; feet faltering, heart sinking. Stopping short, his gaze transfixed with shock and horror as the roof of the porch collapsed. Engulfed in flames, the entire two-story structure creaked and shifted in an eerie symphony of hissing moans and cackling screeches as the fire raged out of control. Licking and jumping skyward, the flames crawled higher. As fire and rescue pulled in, an entire corner of the house submitted to the inferno; caving to spew a plume of hot ash and embers with a bellowing wheeze as it crashed.

Mark sprung forward, then was stopped short by the weight of the agent's hand on his shoulder. Not hearing a word the man said to him, he shrugged out of his grasp, shielding his own face against the scorching screen of heat wafting up from the blaze and backed away. Voices rose and fell around him as firefighters hustled, rolling out hoses working to link them and connect them to the main engine's onboard water supply…all of it executed in a rapid form of organized chaos.

Heart heavy, Mark moved back farther as a group of firefighters began trudging forward, aiming their hoses at what now looked more like a crumpled shell of gooey sicing melting off a glowing black wood frame. Working in groups, they began dousing the inferno from several angles, blasting the house with sheets of water.

Utterly lost, not sure what to do, Mark made his way aimlessly toward the cluster of rescue vehicles. Two firefighters, clad in their heavy protective gear, raced around him as if he wasn't even there.

"Do we know if anybody was inside the house?" one yelled in question through his facemask in order to be heard over the noise of main engine as he gathered up more equipment.

"That volunteer said he pulled a woman out. Paramedics should be here any minute," the other one shouted back in response.

A jolt of stunned disbelief toggled to a riptide of sheer relief and bolted straight through Mark. Turning toward the source of the muffled shouts, Mark grabbed onto one firefighter's thick protective sleeve, halting him and gaining himself a questionable look.

"Did you say a woman was pulled out?" he asked uncertain if he'd heard them correctly.

The man nodded while half shouting, "Yeah," through his face-mask.

"Where is she?"

The man tossed a nod in the general direction of the side yard and gazebo then, gathering the rest of his equipment, hustled back toward the burning inferno which used to be a house.

Chapter 26

Hannah stirred, awakened by a rather annoying squawk. Shifting positions, she grimaced at the achy throb of pain which seemed to radiate from every inch of her body and then pawed at her face, yanking the apparatus plugged into her nostrils free of her nose.

"Let's keep that on a while longer, okay?" a woman in a bright and colorful SpongeBob Square Pants scrub top suggested with a rather sympathetic smile while taking the device from out of her hands.

Hannah stilled and noted the woman's badge; the RN in bold black letters after the name implied she was both safe and alive. Compliant, she relaxed and inspected her surrounding as far as eye movement would allow as the woman leaned over her and adjusted the tubing before gently placing the prongs of the nasal cannula back inside her nostrils.

The room itself was dark, illuminated only by the wedge of light coming from the hallway and the diffused glow of various monitors and equipment. A large window partially concealed by vertical blinds, indicated that night had fallen some time ago; its blackness sporadically dotted by the soft glow of city lights. Sighing, she watched almost thankful as the nurse turned to the IV pole stationed next the bed and pushed a few buttons that silenced the annoying squawk.

"Where am I?" Hannah inquired. Her throat was sore; voice raspy and hoarse.

"Trinity Hospital. You're being treated for smoke inhalation," she explained, then said, "I'm Jen, your nurse—you were still pretty out of it at shift change, so we didn't get to officially meet when I came on."

Hannah stared at her a moment, groggy. Letting the information sink in she then quizzed, "How long do I have to stay?"

"Likely be discharged in the morning. Are you in any pain? You're due for another pain pill, if you want it...?"

"A little," Hannah reported inspecting the gauze bandages spanning her forearms. Not wanting to be drugged up yet again with painkillers she amended, "But I'll be fine for right now. What time is it?"

"Mmmm," the nurse consulted her wrist watch. "A little after midnight."

Hannah sighed and then winced when she shifted in hopes of sitting up. "I feel like a bus hit me."

The nurse made a sound of empathy. "You are one very lucky lady," she then commented.

Turning she consulted a roll-about laptop then requested her patient state her full name and birthdate while scanning Hannah's wristband with the wand attached to the setup. Reciting the required information, Hannah watched as the nurse scanned a large clear bag of fluid, before swapping it out with the almost empty one hanging from the pole before pushing buttons.

Hannah shifted and, after examining the clear tubing the nurse had stabbed into the bottom of the bag, inspected the tape affixing the IV that somebody had jabbed into the back of her hand. She studied it a moment longer and then the bandages, as blips of random memories surfaced trickling throughout her mind.

'Ommigosh, Xena! Is she okay?" she suddenly remembered and questioned aloud.

Completing her task, the nurse hit another button and then returned her full attention to her patient, a lopsided frown of genuine uncertainty displacing her soft kind features. "I'm sorry, I don't know anything about anybody named Xena...? But I can sure try and find out for you though...okay?"

'Xena is a horse. And is safe and sound—at home—where she belongs and should've stayed."

Hannah lifted her head with a jolt of surprise. Squinting toward the direction of the rich velvet twang, she made out the outline of a male standing in the shadows of the dimly lit room, leaning against the far wall. Arms folded across his chest, Mark stepped forward into the dim light. Hair in a rowdy spike above a brooding poker-face, he stared at her looking tough yet equally exhausted.

'Oh, um...hi," Hannah managed with a weak smile, hoping to somehow mollify the ambiguous tension which now seemed to permeate the room.

Mark was either extremely pissed off at her, or worried sick...she just wasn't certain herself of which yet, but figured it was probably the first of those two.

Neither of them spoke as the nurse finished up her assessment. Recording Hannah's vitals in the computer, she then pushed the roll-about across the room stashing it out of the way. Turning, she looked in between the two of them and then smiled and winked at Hannah.

'If you need anything, or if you decide you do want something for pain, just hit the call button," she told her before exiting and shutting the door behind her.

With the nurse now gone, Hannah felt somewhat uncomfortable as Mark stood another moment, silent, simply staring at her. Not that she feared him, she just rather not be scolded like some teenager who'd snuck out and had broken curfew. She just didn't feel like bickering with him. She wasn't in any way shape, form, or condition, to be thinking up valid excuses to why she'd gone to her house—let alone, why she had done so behind his back after he'd requested that she stay put for her own safety.

Closing her eyes, Hannah willed the stings of tears away as more memories hit recall in her mind. Maybe she should have accepted the pain medication? At least then she wouldn't have to lay here and remember being drugged by her own secretary, let alone waking up in the cellar bound with her house ablaze about to burn down around her.

Sighing at the idea she opened her eyes just as Mark was carefully perching himself on the side of her hospital bed. He stared at her another minute, expression tight and unreadable.

"I'm sorry," she at last offered, unable to stand it—the silence, the tension between them. The hot sting of tears sprout as she gushed, "I shouldn't have left—and before you say anything, let me just say: I have no good reason other than sheer stupidity on my part. I'm lucky I didn't break my neck riding that damn horse over to—"

Cutting her of mid-rant, Mark leaned forward gently cupping her chin. His lips grazing hers gained her full attention. "Jesus, I thought I'd lost you," he confessed in a rush of emotion against her lips.

Somewhat dumbfounded Hannah relaxed and simply enjoyed the sensation of his mouth on hers, became acutely aware of the intense emotions relayed within that single kiss. She then simply sighed once it ended and closed her eyes as he brushed a tear off her cheek with his knuckle before pressing his lips to her forehead.

Not sure what to say, she joked, "Yeah, well, I thought I lost me for a second there."

"I should have never left you alone," he told her straightening. "Keeping you safe was my responsibility. And now look at you."

"Oh no," she started and then told him, "You're not

taking responsibility for this. This was all my doing."

Watching the emotion scroll across his face, she realized he was serious—had honestly thought he'd lost her. Sitting up slightly she adjusted the head of the bed in order to sit all the way up.

'Mark, nobody is at fault...okay. Things happen—call it chance, fate, whatever...right? Everything happens for a reason. And besides, Monique—if it's anybody's fault, she's to blame. She's the one who drugged me." Pausing a moment to think about it, she then somewhat snorted, "And some guy she kept calling dumbass."

"Tippen," Mark supplied then enlightened, "Feds brought Monique in, as well as Bremer. Monique isn't talking. However Bremer is. Guess he's hoping to somehow lessen his own charges if he cooperates with the feds. Rolled like the yellow belly coward he is. Confessed to framing that Holm kid and he also supplied us with the names—Tippen...he was part of everything—all this time and I didn't even know." His features hardened, cast to stone by what Hannah guessed was due to the betrayal of a comrade. "...he's MIA—never showed up for duty. Feds have an APB out on him...he's the only one they haven't brought in yet."

Hannah nodded, then blowing out a long sigh, finally asked, "My house? Is it...well, is there anything left of it?"

Frowning he shook his head. "The fire completely destroyed it. Lucky you made it out alive."

"I only managed to make it half-way. Who pulled me the rest of the way out?" she asked as if it had just dawned on her that it hadn't been Mark himself.

"A volunteer first responder—saw smoke from the highway, so called it in and then investigated. He found you and pulled you to safety."

"Everything I own. It's all gone, isn't it," she stated quietly.

"Things can be replaced, Hannah. You however can't be. And if it's any consolation, you do have a few things still at my house…that's something to start with, at least."

"Yeah, a pair of heels and handful of dress clothes…that sure is something." Hannah leaned her head back on the pillow and closed her eyes. Wanting to change the subject she asked more so out of curiosity, "So what was Kender's part? Was he Bremer's right hand man?"

"Actually no," Mark laughed when she lifted her head and looked at him. "Shocked me as well. Ah, and sort of found that one out the hard way, myself. He's actually a special agent—"

"What? Special agent? No way…really? I would have never guessed *him* to be a special agent."

"Yup. Pretty insightful one too," he commented.

Hannah made a face, now studying his rather sheepish expression. Not sure what he was talking about, she narrowed her eyes slightly and asked him, "What do you mean, you found out the hard way? And insightful how?"

Drawing a deep breath he released it, slow and steady, and then studied her a second longer. "He seems to have this theory that I'm somehow head over heels in love with you," he then told her deadpan.

Hannah stilled, then met and held his slate gray stare. He wasn't joking; his face was serious. "Care to elaborate?" she at last questioned trying to sound calm, trying to regulate her now erratic heart-rate. She thought for sure the monitors would all start squawking and give her away. She glanced at them, grateful to see they had all been shut off.

Mark shrugged, a boyish grin now splitting his handsome features. "There was some discussion about playing leapfrog with fire and rescue at speeds of upward towards ninety-plus-something…but—" hesitating his expression softened, his lighthearted tone was now quiet almost reflective, "Apparently, he based this theory of his on the fact that I almost beat the tar out of him at the station, because I thought he'd hurt you—" he waited a second then admitted, "After thinking I'd lost you—no, even before thinking it…well, either way, reckon he just might be on to something."

Her eyes widened; her jaw dropped. Dumbfound she just stared at him. Hannah then did what she did best. Began to argue, "Well that's pretty spur of the moment, don't you think? I mean you do realize we just met—have only known each other for like, what?—a week, maybe, if that…? I just can't believe that anybody could—"

"Might be right so…but—" Reaching for her hand, he smiled as he laced his finger with hers; a perfect fit. "Why argue with fate?"

Hannah clamped her now agape mouth shut and just stared at him. Smiling, he stood and, turning, sat back down on the bed then worked his boots off. Playing with the side-rail he located the right control and lowered the head of the bed to a more pleasing level.

"What are you doing?" she giggled on a hush whisper, yet automatically scooted over making room once he gingerly slipped his arm behind her head and at the same time stretched his legs out to lay with her on the narrow hospital bed.

"Testing out a theory," he replied matter of fact then, brushing his knuckles down her cheek, hooked her chin and smiled once their eyes touched. That sexy eyebrow shot skyward. "Any objections, counselor?"

"Just one," Hannah sighed and then somewhat snorted at his expression. Eyes locking on his she managed to finally confess, "Mark, I've had my share of test-runs and trust me I need somebody who's sure, and one who's in it for the long-haul. I can't handle anything less right now."

"Good, 'cause I'm not looking for no eight second thrill ride." Gathering her up, mindful of her injuries, he gingerly drew her closer. Stroking her hair lazily, after a moment he then questioned, "Think you can handle me for forever and then some?"

Hannah smiled, feeling safe within his arms. She thought about her grandmother's house. The fire. What it all symbolized. She felt as if she had been cleansed and was now more than ready to start a fresh new life. And she could see herself doing that with Mark Bowman; right here, right now, together.

After a minute or two she propped herself up to look at him. "You do realize I'm a criminal defense attorney—cop repellent—right?"

"Lucky for you, I'm not a cop." Kissing her, he withdrew a scant inch to now study her somewhat puzzled expression then chuckled, "I'm a deputy sheriff. Huge difference. Now, are there any other objections, counselor?" In afterthought he held up a finger, halting her from answering. "Before you say anything, be warned...I can, and I am willing, to debate this all night, every night, for the rest of my life, and then some."

Hannah held his slate gray gaze. Taking in a deep breath, she parted her lips to speak but then hesitated when Mark waggled his finger cutting her off yet again.

"Besides, any argument you make now will be a moot point...because for the time being, you're stuck with me as I am your very own personal bodyguard, and this time that will be twenty-four-seven—until of course they find and haul in Tippen—" hesitating a seductive smile blossomed as he contemplated the idea of them being stuck together. Settling back he sighed. "To be honest, I'm hoping they never do find him."

"Well...since you put it that way." Hannah snorted then snuggled in against his chest. For once in her life she felt as if she was right where she belonged. And since she couldn't think of anything else to question or argue, she closed her eyes and sighed, "Just so you know, I expect that awesome French toast every morning for breakfast."

Shoulders boxing, a soft chuckle eluded his chest. "Reckon you'll be wanting bacon with that as well."

About The Author

Deena lives with her family in a small urban Iowa town along the beautiful Mississippi river.

Keep up to date with new releases, follow Deena Nehring on her official Facebook author page at www.facebook.com/PinkRibbonPress.

Proof

Made in the USA
Charleston, SC
23 May 2013